# INFINITE SACRIFICE

The First Book of the Infinite Series

**L.E. Waters**

Rock Castle Publishing

Copyright © 2011 by L.E. Waters

Cover Art by S. Frost Designs
Layout and typesetting by Guido Henkel

ISBN: 978-0-983911-11-1

Printed in U.S.A.

I dedicate this book to all of the characters in my life...

*thanks for the inspiration*

# Foreword

I researched the time periods portrayed in my books and pulled many of my ideas from historic events. When I involve historical people in my books, I try to portray them accurately but take fictional liberty with conversations, timelines, and mysteries—filling in the details absent from written record. The reader must remember that this is, first and foremost, historical fantasy fiction. I maintained a sense of magical realism throughout and hope the reader will take such leaps of imagination with me, assured that there is fundamental support underneath this novel but keeping an open mind to enjoy the story envisioned.

If there are any doubts as to the accuracy or plausibility of story lines, please visit my website, www.laurenwaters.net, where I dedicated a whole section to a bibliography and more detailed research behind this fictional piece just for those who might enjoy reading further about these cultures, events, and people.

In regards to the spiritual/religious aspect of this book, it is not meant to come across as non-fiction. This is how I perceived heaven to be in an artistic sense and hope there are readers out there who will consider it enough for the simple enjoyment of storytelling.

If at any time you should find yourself confused with so many intricate character histories, I have provided a helpful chart that tracks each character's traits and progression at the end of each life. It is there to use at any point during each life to enhance the reader's experience.

I would love to take this moment to thank you for reading this novel and if you could take a moment to review my book where you purchased it, I would be extremely appreciative. Reviews are essential to independent authors like me and even one or two comments can do wonders for my series' exposure.

# Prologue

Disharmonious, chopped sounds surround me as I fly through darkness. Lights flash far away in liquid black, as if I'm looking up from the ocean floor, the sun streaming through the distant surface. I speed nearer toward the light, which glares brilliantly with painless intensity. I absorb it through every pore. I crave getting closer to it, to penetrate farther, deeper—saturating me in a peace I never knew existed.

I find myself standing trail-edge in a forest, looking out across an expansive clearing with an island of wheat fields before me. The light is golden and glowing off the fields and a warm breeze causes the wheat and trees to roll like seaweed in strong current. I release the grip of my hand that Ellie was just clutching.

*Am I having another morphine dream? Did I slip into a coma? Where am I?*

A figure moves toward me, out of the pulsing light.

*Finn? I hope it's another dream about Finn.*

Instead, a simple old man dressed in a white tunic and loose pants strides forth, barefoot, and smiles as if we're good friends.

"Do I know you?" I ask, sure he's mistaken.

"I've known you all your lives." His sea-glass blue eyes gleam through happily squinted lids.

Nothing makes sense.

"Where's my family?" I say, turning away, searching for them. "I need to be with my family right now."

Stretching his arm up with surprising speed, he touches my shoulder; I calm, all anxiety forgotten. He takes my hand within his; warmth travels up my arm.

"Come with me." His measured words resonate.

The fields dissipate, and a vast ocean now rolls before us. Seagulls cry out, gliding on strong winds, and sandpipers scatter as the waves crash onto their sands. The old man gestures to pick one of the two wooden beach chairs facing the water.

"Where am I?"

He begins as I settle in the low chair, "My name is Zachariah. I am your spirit guide."

Pulling my hair from my face, I look over at him. "Am I dead?"

He simply nods but holds my eyes with a gentle look.

Strangely, I'm not panicking. The beach looks just like the beach where I spent my summers, with sea-green surf the shade of Finn's eyes as the waves crest with the sun behind it. I'm reminded of the first time I looked into them as he kept a tennis ball out of my reach—and how shimmering green—they stole my breath. As I dig my feet into the flour-like sand, it brings back memories of Finn and Ellie running with me on this same sand, playing games only children play. Yet we never stopped playing them, even after college. We drew looks from the passersby on the boardwalk as we wrestled, threw sand on each other, and ran into the surf with all our clothes on. I can hear Ellie's high-pitched lyrical laughter gliding on top of Finn's childish giggle, sailing to me in this chair where I sit without them now.

My hair blows across my eyes again, and I realize my short, brittle permanent is gone. My hair's long and silky around my shoulders. I glance down at my legs—the tan, strong legs I haven't seen for fifty years. I straighten up from the hunched position I'd grown so used to.

"I'm sixteen again!"

"Souls appear the age they felt their best."

My eyes dart to his aged form in silent question, and he grins. "This is how I feel most comfortable."

I look down at my hands—young hands! No spots, no veins, no shaking. Only smooth, peach, beautiful hands. Ah! I forgot how great this feels! No aches, no pains, only flexible strength and boundless energy. I want to run across the beach and do cartwheels!

As though he reads my mind, Zachariah gestures over to the sand. I bounce up and do ten perfect cartwheels in a row, the sand spiraling out from between my toes as I complete each one. I finish and point toward the water, and he nods with a smile. I take off, stepping over the small waves and jumping over the larger ones until I'm past the break. The waves surge and pull as I dive under the bubbled froth of white repeatedly. The womb-water calms, and I float over the now sleepy waves.

*When was the last time I swam?*

My ears are submerged as I stare into the cloud-filled sky.

*But where is everyone else?*

As soon as I think about leaving the water, I'm instantly back in the chair and dry to the touch. I turn to him with a puzzled look. Zachariah replies, palms up, "No towels in heaven."

I sigh and glance around for something more. "So is this it? Do I just sit here, swim all day, and do cartwheels with you?" His serious expression continues regardless of my attempt at making him laugh—maybe spirit guides don't laugh. "This can't be heaven. I thought I'd see those who passed before me. Where are my mom and dad? Why isn't Finn here?"

Things start to darken around me until Zachariah places his hand on my arm and everything illuminates.

After a long pause, he clears his quiet throat and divulges, "This is a *stage* in heaven."

I wait, hoping my silence will force him to elaborate.

He coughs again, as if his throat fought to stay closed, and states, "I brought you here to relax while you adjust. It's a difficult transition. My job is to keep you calm in order to bring you back to your full consciousness."

"Full consciousness?"

"While living, there are areas of the brain that remain off-limits. After you die, you're allowed full access. If I were to give you this access all at once it would be overwhelming and potentially dangerous."

"Why do I need to have full consciousness?"

"So you can remember your spiritual journey and all you've learned to go forward with your next phase."

"Like, have my life flash before me?"

His tight smile makes his eyes twinkle. "No, have your *lives* flash before you."

"Lives? I've lived before?"

*Just like that psychic had said.*

"Yes, a number of times before, Lazrina."

"My name is Maya," I say, suspicious he *did* mistake me.

He cracks a slight smile. "That was your last life's name, but your *soul's* name is Lazrina."

*The name that crazy psychic called me.*

I look around again. "Do you have to hypnotize me so I can access my full consciousness?"

"No need for that. When you are ready, I'll touch your arm and you'll gradually access different parts of your mind, absorbing it back and creating a cohesive whole. Then you can move on—move on to see your loved ones."

"Okay, I'm ready then." I close my eyes and put my arm out.

"No, you're not." He pushes my arm back toward me gently. "You need to understand a bit more before we do that. First, you need to understand you'll be seeing your lives like watching a video in your mind."

I try to imagine what that would be like. "Like I'm sitting in a theater watching it?"

"No, more like you're in a lucid dream. You'll open your eyes and you'll hear, see, smell, taste, and feel everything that happened to you before. Also like a dream, you won't be able to wake until the viewing is over."

This sounds like torture. "If I watch every moment, won't that take years to watch?"

"You're going to see your past lives as you remember them; there will be large gaps in time and missing information. You will only be watching moments of great importance. After you watch every life, you'll fully remember that life. It will become a part of you, which can be difficult and stressful to accept."

"Do I watch the life I've most recently left first?" A sick feeling in my stomach grows as I wonder if I'll witness it all over again; it was hard enough getting through it all the first time.

He shakes his head. "No, you must view each life from your first incarnation to your last."

"Can I choose not to go through with this?"

"You can. We can just sit here, but then you can't move on further to be reunited with the ones you want to be with right now."

It was like those mornings as a child when I'd wake up to the rare smell of pancakes, and when I rushed downstairs, all my siblings would be carrying syrupy plates to the sink—no one had thought to even wake me! Here they are again, somewhere farther in heaven, all together, without me, while I'm stalled in this whole process.

"All I want to do is see them. I've waited so long." Tears run down once I blink. "And now you're telling me that I may never see them again?"

"I have no doubt you will get through this. You always have, but I can wait until you feel you're ready to start. I'll try my best to prepare you and create a soothing atmosphere that will allow you to accept what you see. I can answer most questions you have and we can stop at any point until you are able to move on. Time is different here."

"What do you mean time is different here?" He couldn't gloss over that.

"Just like gravity is different on different planets, time is different here. It's not easy to compare to earth time. But you can relax and move at your own pace."

"Are you saying Ellie is already dead?"

"Yes, your sister's here."

The moments I've spent here with Zachariah must have been years on earth if Ellie had died. I feel terrible not being there for her, I wish I could've been there to welcome her but then again, Zachariah was the only one there for me.

"Is she going through this stage right now too?" I can just imagine her yelling at her spirit guide somewhere near here, even more frustrated at being delayed than I am.

He nods. "But all the others are waiting."

"All?"

"Everyone you've been waiting to see."

"Can I just see them first?" I scan the empty sand dunes blowing behind me.

"No, I'm sorry."

I close my eyes and bend into the lotus position in my chair. "Well, let's start, then, and get this over with."

He notices my assumed position. "Patience is definitely not one of your virtues. I think we should make a note of that for your next incarnation," he says, yet quickly adds, "That is, if you need another one, of course."

"You mean I might have to go back?" Panic flashes hot under my skin; I'd assumed once I reached heaven, I would get to stay. I can't go through it all again.

He places his hand on top of mine. "It's a very long journey, and it is possible you must live more lives."

"Does that mean everyone important to me might be done with their incarnating? Will I have to go back alone if I'm not done?"

He closes his eyes, and I witness the intense light flare from his hand clutching mine crawl up my arm and push out all worry from my tense body. I take a deep breath and relax again.

He withdraws his smooth hand. "Now, I have to tell you, once you start viewing, you can't stop until that life is done. Even if you are watching something difficult, I can only try to calm you, but it will still be unpleasant."

"Is that what you're doing when you touch me—some sort of mood control?"

His eyes twinkle. "One of my many talents."

I just want to get this over with. "Let's begin, then, before I change my mind."

"I must also warn you, we will be starting with your very first life. When a soul is in its early stages of evolution, it's raw. Everyone begins with much more negativity than positivity, but through difficulty and love, a soul steadily increases its vibration."

"Okay, you lost me. I think I need my full consciousness just to absorb this conversation." I squint. "Evolution... like Darwin?"

"We call it evolution here because it's the best way to explain the process. Similar to evolution, the soul is perpetually changing, and it takes many generations for evolution to occur. You have to look at many lives to see its progress."

He pauses and studies my expression to see if I absorbed that before continuing. "The speed of evolution can be different for different souls. Isolation of a population hastens this process, which is why so many souls reincarnate in the same groups."

"Groups?" I ask, but he keeps with his line of thought as if reading some sort of invisible manual.

"The greater the selective pressure is on a soul, the quicker the evolution. This is why many souls choose such tragic events but run the risk of suicide not being able to withstand the despair that ensues. Some cautious souls choose steadier lives at the risk of gradual change, while some may actually regress. Not all evolution serves a purpose. There is no formula for it."

"Have you been in any of my lives?" I don't think I absorbed half of what he said.

He looks away, gaze pensive on the waves. "I choose not to incarnate anymore." He draws one side of his closed mouth up and raises his eyebrows. "The evolution is slower, but I can still learn from you—vicariously, of course."

"Why do people even do this at all?"

"It is the only way we can become part of the light." He holds his slender hands up to the sky, where the light is shining down all around, unlike the sun I was used to—originating from one spot.

I hadn't even realized I was holding the arms of my chair so tight; I loosen my grip and wiggle my fingers to ease their tension.

Zachariah continues, "When you begin to reincarnate with some of the same people, there will be things you subconsciously recognize—certain identifying features they carry in every life."

"Which features?"

"To start, everyone's eyes stay identical. Always the same shape, size, and color. There's a profound effect when you look into someone's eyes that you have known for centuries." He taps a slender finger beside his jeweled eye.

"What else?"

"They're called beacons, and they exist to guide you to certain souls."

"I don't understand."

"In your first life, you will be brand-new, as are many of the key people in that life—hence all the chaos you will see. It's never a pretty picture when you get a lot of new souls together. In all the lives after, you will subconsciously recognize these marks. These beacons will either draw you in or repel you."

"What kind of marks?"

"The first traumatic death a soul experiences will stay with them. Where do you think you got that spot on your left hand from?"

"Oh, right! My mole!" I pull my hand in front of my face to see the mole I would never let the dermatologists remove.

"It gives a whole new understanding to the purpose of birthmarks, doesn't it?"

"This is from my very first death? What happened?"

"That you will have to see for yourself."

I stare at the spot, wondering how something as small as this dot could be a past life's downfall. "Are there any other markers?"

"People can adapt more markers with time, so you have to learn them as lives progress. Many personality traits and mannerisms survive into the next life. They build upon each other, and after many lives, you get some pretty interesting characters." He raises his eyebrows, probably referring to some of the characters I'd left back in my last life. "Certain tastes and interests follow you throughout each life, such as affinity for certain foods, clothing, places, music, and even certain objects—all creeping their way out of your subconscious."

I try to think of all my tastes and how I might guess what my first life will be.

"So if I have to go back again, I will at least have all my soul mates with me?"

He shakes his head, and I feel sick again.

*I don't want to imagine a life without Finn or Ellie.*

"The incarnate group will keep increasing for you. You might first start with only a few souls, but with each additional life, more people will come in and out of your group."

"Out of your group? Do some leave?"

"Not leave for good, but sometimes some lives don't incarnate together. It all depends on what the soul has to work on and if it fits with your goals."

*No guarantees to go back with the ones you loved the most.* "Okay, I think I've heard enough for now." I raise my hands in surrender. "Is there any way you can prepare me for what I'm about to see?"

He shakes his head. "No, I'm sorry. You have to see these lives as you experienced them to get the full effect of the memory."

I take a deep breath as though I'm plunging into the ocean's depths. "I'm ready to see my first life."

He leans closer to me, taking my arm, and peers deep into my eyes. "Yes, I think you are."

# First Life
# Dream Magician

# Chapter 1

Opening my eyes to darkness, I look up to see stars filling the whole stretch of moonless sky. Large stars twinkle and catch my eye, as small stars—white dust thrown across the black—make me squint to see them. I focus back to ground level, where I follow the rolling landscape of sand.

I stand fourth in a long line of robed young men, all identical and standing in silence before the Pyramid of Khufu with torches burning every few feet. Eight men pull a massive rock from the temple entrance, straining and grunting with the weight. Once the rock is moved halfway, two priests emerge with torches and nod their bald heads toward us as the first in line disappears; we all follow.

*I should have been first.*

The priests lead the way, chanting, accompanied by double clarinet musicians slowly blowing a snake-charmer melody as the cobra of our line follows obediently. The passageway is narrow, and the air is stale. The temperature is warmer inside the pyramid, a great relief since the thin robe helps little in the desert cold. The priests remove another door. Stepping up into a second corridor, I duck my head beneath the low ceiling. We come into a chamber where a statue of Amun and four other high priests stand. A priest takes the offerings the god Amun had feasted on and serves the first boy in line wine from a golden cup and white bread torn from the offering loaves. After he partakes, he is sent ahead to another chamber.

When it is finally my turn, the priest turns and asks, "You will loyally serve your gods and goddesses under Ra and the Pharaoh?"

I recite, "I will, or the Pharaoh take my life and Ra deny me afterlife."

I drink and eat to fulfill the initiation and step into an even lower-ceilinged passageway, where I wait until I'm waved in. Three groups are stationed in the queen's chamber. Two naked boys stand beside open fires in front of two groups. One tries to pull away from the priests who hold him, screaming as the surgeon makes a quick movement.

*Coward.*

I give no sign of hesitation as I remove my robe and march toward the third station. This is the mark of the priesthood and the highest act of purifying oneself. Each priest takes an arm, and the surgeon kneeling before me brushes the tip of my manhood with a tingling, brown liquid—the anesthetic. It weakens me to receive it.

The surgeon grasps a thin knife with a long handle, pulls my foreskin forward in one hand, and slices off the small piece of flesh with the other. I inhale sharply, registering the hot flash of pain. The surgeon throws the flesh into the fire, then places honey-soaked cotton with thyme around the wound, and covers it with a linen wrap. Turning to the priest wrapping a linen loin-cloth around my waist, I bow as they bow back.

I am one of the priesthood now.

# Chapter 2

Years later, my palm-wood-sandaled feet trot along the stone path through tall desert trees that provide much-needed relief from the dry heat of the land. I come to the end of my purification walk from my family dwelling outside the sacred city of Memphis. My thirty days of service is about to begin, and I'm eager to reclaim the position of my late father and his father before that. I already feel strength from my fast. I walk steadfast under the towering statues of Ra lining the walkway to the temple entrance. I'm beginning to feel alive again, every muscle tingling.

Above the door bears the sacred inscription: "The House of Life—The Learned Ones of Library Magic." Every time I pass under that engraving, pride consumes me. *I'm the high priest of such a temple.* The six guards at the entrance step aside and bow to me, allowing me access. I point for my lagging slave, Nun, to go to my sleeping chamber and prepare it for the evening. The interior of the temple drops twenty degrees, and my sweat cools instantly, causing a slight chill. Torches illuminate a path down the corridor as the smell of incense engulfs me.

Another guard opens the massive cypress door and bows on one knee while holding the heavy door open. Inside the high-ceilinged room stands an imposing statue of Serapis, God of Dreams, to which our temple is dedicated. All around the statue, offerings of fruit, nuts, beer, wine and fresh-killed lamb are piled up. Expensive oils and incense are burned in wide pots at the perimeter of the vast room, casting light on the papyrus plants, lotus, and palm trees painted to the top of the walls. I look to the flying birds and stars painted to the greatest height across the vaulted ceiling. A harpist plays soft music while beautiful virgins dance slowly. I walk to the altar and bow as a priestess wafts a cloud of incense and natron around me.

I head through the pyres to my right which lead me to the cleansing pool. I stand at the pool's steps, waiting with my arms out, as a stolist priest unties my cotton loincloth. Naked, I kneel down as another stolist lathers my head with scented lotion and shaves my hair to my scalp. I stand again as he shaves all of my body, hand-plucks my eyebrows and each eyelash.

As a viper feels after shedding its skin, I breathe deep and glide into the cool, pure water, then sink beneath. Breaching the surface and rubbing the water from my eyes, I catch my reflection in the golden mirrors lining the edge of the pool. Water runs down my brown skin, causing a glistening effect in the glowing dimness of the room. With all my hair gone, my features look chiseled, emphasizing my prominent nose and thick lips.

As I exit, the priests anoint my body in balanos oil and tie a clean white linen loincloth around my waist. I bow my head as one places the moonstone eye of Serapis around my neck and a gold arm cuff around my biceps. I turn to another who paints my eyes, brows, and lips black with kohl out of a lotus-shaped glass container. To finalize the cleansing, I rinse my mouth with salty natron water and spit into an alabaster flask. The priests bow to me as I walk back into the central room of the temple, again bow to Serapis, and continue to the dream-incubation chamber. I am to prepare the evening's special ceremony to find Nebu's—God Wife of Serapis—adopted Royal Daughter.

I walk into the large central chamber, where two lower priests are tending the giant fire pits on either side of my podium that holds my sacred books. I take my place at the altar, enclosed by the thick, stone columns, to review the last priest's journal entries. The tended fires blaze, illuminating the carvings of the dream gods carved on all four walls. Gods who are waiting for pharaohs, priests, scribes, wealthy merchants, and commoners to come to scry for cures, magical spells, hex removal, fertility, and prophesy. I hold their most vital hopes and dreams in my hands.

The two priests finish with the fires, refill incense oils, and then bow as they back out of the chamber; I wave them away.

Hearing sandals clicking down the corridor outside, I can tell it is Nebu's quick light feet as she comes to greet me. She is beautiful, as all of the wives of gods are expected to be. She wears her gold-and-lapis lazuli collar, gold headdress, and gold-painted long skirt wrapped around her hips. I bow before her, appreciating every inch of wasted splendor, since no earthly man can ever have her.

"Sokaris," she says with her hands out for me to grasp in greeting, "I hope your leave was restful?"

"I grew fat and bored as always, and I'm eager to dedicate myself again." I hold her hands and bow with her.

She begins to walk, silently commanding me to follow her down the corridor.

"It is time for me to pass down my position, but I do not want to choose poorly. I need to adopt an apprentice who will not merely fulfill my wifely duties but also please Serapis."

As we are approaching the main chamber, Edjo—Nebu's favored apprentice—comes limping down the corridor in tears. As

Edjo is normally a graceful and tranquil beauty, this is an abnormal event. Her tears cause her kohl to make black rivers down her fine-featured face, and her amber eyes look beseechingly to Nebu.

"Most High, I awoke this morning with a large and painful lesion above my knee." She points to a festering wound seeping clear fluid down her right leg. "It is a curse, I tell you! I dreamed of a jealous enemy last week!"

Nebu turns to me, and I nod in validation.

"I also have a rash that has spread all over my face and down the back of my neck."

We lean closer with a torch and see her skin is indeed raised and red.

Nebu shakes her head with disappointment. "I am sorry, Edjo, but these are all signs the gods do not find you fit for this position."

Edjo crumples to Nebu's feet.

"Once you are healed and purified, you are welcome to be one of my esteemed dancers," Nebu says as she pats her heaving back.

Edjo begins kissing her feet. "Please, Nebu, please see this for the treachery it is! I have been groomed for Serapis, raised to be his wife! I am Edjo, the daughter of Amun! This is my birthright! My family will be shamed!"

Nebu shakes her off her feet and starts moving down the hall to the other dancers.

Edjo shrieks from behind us, "I cannot bear this shame! I am going to drown myself in the Nile, and the one that has cursed me will be damned!"

Neither Nebu nor I give her a second look.

Nebu whispers under her breath, "Clearly not ordained."

The rhythmic drums and cymbals are heard from the corridor, and the chamber is filled with movement. Twenty royal dancers twist and turn to the beats, striving to stand out and impress Nebu. They can all turn the head of any man, but they dull like the dust stars next to the brightest and shining star. I stop hearing the music when I see her.

She watches her hands and the intricate movements they're making as her hips click with the beat. I don't know which part of her to watch first. She is the waves rolling from the center of the sea with no end and no beginning, an unrelenting ripple of her whole body. She starts with a large movement of her middle and lets it flow to an undulation out the tips of her hands and then back down to her toes. Her body reflects all of the flickers of the fire, making her cast a marbled glow. Her motions hypnotize me, and when I find the music has stopped—I want more.

I shake my head to break the spell and look to see if Nebu notices the trance she put me under, but she too is watching the girl. She claps her hands. "Satisfactory." Then, motioning to the harpist to begin playing, she commands, "Sing for Serapis."

When it's my dancing girl's turn to sing, she doesn't have perfect pitch, as did other girls, but she sings quietly and so sweetly. Her eyes! Her eyes are large, honey pools you can fall into and never climb out! She is the most intriguing and captivating woman I've ever seen. Something is different about her—something powerful—something mystifying. She moves, and my eyes follow; she speaks, and my ears tune out all other sound. I feel far away from her and want to be closer. I wish no one else were in the room.

Nebu interrupts my pain. "I see you agree with my choice."

I pretend to be only slightly interested. "There are many talented girls for you to pick from, but one does seem to have a magic air to her."

"Ah, you have noticed. Yes, that is a good way to put it." She smiles while gazing upon her. "I wonder, though, if she seems devout and disciplined enough?"

"That is hard to see in the arts. We will need to probe deeper and let our ancient knowledge guide us."

My heart races at the thought that I'll get to spend some time alone with her.

"Yes, we will have to trust the ancients—and you, Sokaris."

I leave to take my place in the dream-incubation chamber before Nebu sends her. I have to regain composure and steady myself for the important task ahead. I look up at my reflection in the brass incense burner, and I see her float in behind me. I turn, avoiding her eyes, and stare at my papyrus.

"Name?" I ask.

"Bastet, daughter of Ketuh." Her voice is melodious.

"Age?"

"Fifteen and a half years."

She's older than most royal daughters, but it is not unheard of for someone her age to be considered. Her blue glass ear studs catch my eye.

"Let me see your palm."

She outstretches a fragile, long-fingered hand and slowly turns it within my palm as she looks directly in my eyes. I feel a charge at her touch but continue my task. She has many great talents on her hand but carries three of the most ominous signs: a weak and broken lifeline that foretells a short life; she lacks the gift of willpower whorl on her thumb; and most intriguing to me, her mount of Venus is well padded, showing immense passion. Normally I wouldn't even let a candidate stay after this miserable reading, but I can't stand the thought of her leaving.

"Please follow me to your chamber for the night."

I lead her to the smaller chambers where dream incubation takes place. I motion her to enter the room first, pushing aside the urge to pull her to the bed with me.

She sits down on the side of the linen-draped bed and asks, "Who is looking upon me as I sleep?"

I freeze at her unabashed forwardness but thaw when she points to the carving on the headboard.

"That is the midget god, Bes: the Dream Protector." I motion her to come to the table beside me. When she nears, I can smell the remnants of scented wax in her braided wig releasing its sweet perfume. "Tonight you must pray to the god Serapis to send you a fortuitous dream, one that can tell us of your destiny with him. Please write his name on the papyrus."

She obeys with some skill, and I roll it up and place it in a lamp beside her bed.

I pray, "Will it be granted that Bastet, daughter of Ketuh, be Royal Daughter to Serapis? Reveal it to me; answer this little written prayer."

I light the papyrus to burn while she sleeps. She bows, and I leave her chamber to attempt to retire in the chamber next to hers. It is hours before my body relaxes enough to sleep, knowing she is so close.

*I'm getting back into bed and am fixing the scroll with my god's name when I feel something move by my leg under the sheet. I throw back the sheet to expose a writhing mass of snakes crawling and hissing on top of me. I scream as they all bite into me at once, igniting me in flames.*

I wake, thrashing and breathing hard.

*The same dream again and again!*

I write on my papyrus: GET SEHKET!

# Chapter 3

Bastet wakes in the morning and hands me her night vision to interpret. She walks away from me, her hips swaying in a beaded wrap as it plays a mesmerizing song. Regardless of what foretelling I hold in my hands, I know I'll create my own to keep her in my life. Yet I am curious and open her scroll to read:

*I was on the rooftop of the temple and walked to a well in the center. I looked into the deep hole and saw in the reflection Nebu, holding the scales, weighing my heart against a feather. I was frightened by a sound behind me. I turned to see a giant ostrich run by.*

I roll the scroll back up and burn it in the fire above the altar.

∞∞∞∞∞∞∞∞∞∞∞∞∞∞∞∞∞∞∞∞∞∞

Later that night, after the last purification of the day, Nebu inquires, "I am relieved to hear Bastet passed your palm reading, but I am anxious to hear of her dream."

"Yes, she has truly been a remarkable subject." I lie, "She displayed an amazing ability to connect with the spirit world."

Nebu raises her painted eyebrows in interest. "What have you interpreted?"

"There is no need for me to interpret since she had direct communication facilitated by Serapis."

She pulls back in surprise, never having had direct contact with him herself. I unroll the scroll and let her read:

*I was walking up to the statue of Serapis and saw my own dead form laid out as an offering. The statue of Serapis came alive, took his sacred offering of donkey meat, and put it in front of me. I came to life and ate the flesh.*

Nebu rolls the scroll back up and hands it to me. I don't need to tell her that those are the portents of long life, promotion, and divine acceptance.

"Serapis has spoken, then, and picked for us. I, his dutiful wife, will make sure his will is granted."

She humbly bows and walks off to notify her apprentices in the harem room.

∞∞∞∞∞∞∞∞∞∞∞∞∞∞∞∞∞∞∞∞∞∞∞

I've never wanted a woman more. My own wife, chosen by my father to secure our lands to the east of Memphis, thought to be attractive by most standards, is a wife for a man; Bastet is a wife for a god! In moments, I disregard all that is sacred to me, worshipping only Bastet.

That evening I retire to my own quarters provided beside the temple. I walk past the peasants putting their livestock safely away for the night, the farmers digging the grime from under their fingernails before supper, and the serenely empty crop fields. As I make my way down the row of simple sandstone dwellings, I watch the smoke lift from cooking fires on rooftops and blend into the darkening sky. Nun rushes to open the gate to the courtyard, and I wave away the plate of food offered as I head straight into my room.

Earlier that morning, I sent Nun on the half-day's walk back outside Memphis to fetch my tailless black cat, Sehket. All the wooden lamps were lit within, and I search the sparse room. My soul is finally at ease once Sehket's large, golden eyes stare up at me. I find Nun outside rubbing honey on blisters he acquired from his errand. I strike the small gong at the entranceway for him to serve me, and he limps inside carrying warm water from the fire. Nun washes, oils, and dries my feet, then retires to his woolen blanket beside the mud-baked firepot outside. Before getting into bed, I throw back the sheet and am relieved to find the bed empty. Sehket takes her usual place on my chest as I fall asleep to her loud purr, secure she'd protect me from the serpents that plague me.

*It's a glorious dawn, and I'm sitting in an orchard in the sun when something catches my eye. A flashing light surges out from an unfamiliar temple. Dark clouds start to gather, so I run to the temple for shelter. I enter and stand before a large statue of Edjo. The statue comes to life and hands me a deep cup. I drink from it, seeking refreshment, yet find it is warm beer, and I spit it out.*

I awake, nudge Sehket off of me, and drop to my knees by my bed. After such a nightmare, I recite the prayer: "Hail to thee, Isis my mother, thou good dream which art seen by night or by day. Driven forth are all evil filthy things which Seth, the son of Nut, has made. Even as Ra is vindicated against his enemies, so I am vindicated against my enemies."

The next afternoon, coming from my midday purification and heading to the dream chamber, I hear a faint noise within and pause outside the entranceway to listen. It is *her* voice. A voice I imprinted on days ago, chanting:

> "Hathor, Goddess of Love
> Make him think only of me.
> My lovely charms he can't resist.

My lover coax him to be.
The first part of my prayer fulfilled,
Hathor, you healed my strife,
Removed Edjo from Nebu's favor,
Secured me in line for wife.
The second, I prayed to pass.
He helped me in my quest.
Now that I am honored,
Hathor, fulfill the rest."

She whispers the last line a few times sharply, and I try to disappear into the dark corner beside the doorway as I hear her rush out. I hold my breath as she whips past me, too concerned with escape to look around. I hurry into the chamber to see a thin scroll ignited in one of my altar fire pits. Using the fire tender, I quickly sweep it from the fire onto the floor and blow it out. Once the embers dancing on the edges darken, I open up the charred paper to see my name intertwined with hers, bound with crimson blood—a conjured love spell. Bastet is more powerful than I gave her credit for, and I find her all the more seductive for it.

That night, as I arrive for the evening purification, Bastet stands at the edge of the glimmering cleansing pool bare, her skin glistening with oil. I try to take in her beauty, but the stolists disrupt my view, tying her dress around her waist. I stand beside her while she's painted with kohl. Disrobing in front of her, I notice she doesn't turn away.

Fully immersed in the pool, I bring only my eyes out of the water, and I see she's still watching me. I disappear beneath the surface once again, and my heart sinks when I reemerge as she's walking away. Right before she rounds the corner, she extends her arm out, curling her finger for me to follow. Rising from the pool and ripping the loincloth from the stolist's extended hands, I hurry to catch her, slipping as I secure the linen around my waist. She's waiting, leaning back in the shadows, shimmering. I grab her in the corridor outside the dream chamber, pin her to the wall, and kiss her.

She pulls her lips away after too short a moment but stays within my embrace.

"You must tell Nebu you need to come for dream incubation. I will make sure we are alone by having my slave watch the door. We will have no interruption. No one will ever know of our bliss."

"There are consequences that can come from such bliss, consequences that the Royal Daughter is not allowed."

I look into her darkened eyes. "There are trusted potions for such things."

She hesitates as I kiss down her neck. "But will we never get into the afterlife if we continue further?"

"Don't we priests feast from the gods' morning offerings after they have taken their spiritual fill? How is this not different?"

She kisses me back in passionate agreement and hurries back to Nebu. I turn to go into the incubation room, and Khons, the house scribe, is standing there leaning on the altar where his son left him. His failing body, so riddled with stiffness, renders him utterly dependent on his son's assistance.

"Khons, you got here so fast." I check to see the distance between where he's standing and where I exchanged with Bastet.

He laughs. "I do not think I get anywhere fast anymore."

I'm relieved at how jovial he is, assured he hadn't overheard. In his advanced years, he must be somewhat deaf by now.

"That may be so, but your wisdom is priceless to the House of Life. What new fascinating topic are you writing about today?"

"Oh, you would not believe the magic that surrounds us, Sokaris! Each day I wake up in pain and wonder why I want to trudge through another day, and by every night, I am mystified and charged by all the charms that encircle us." He swirls his hands above his head to illustrate before continuing. "Today I met with a man from Thebes who swears he is a master of rain charms. He showed me the very documents from the King's Library of Periods of Drought. He performed his enchantments, and sure enough, it rained! Amazing, what an amazing world." His sagging brown eyes glisten with excitement.

I smile. "What answers do you seek tonight?"

"I suddenly need some clarification on a topic I am trying to understand better." He sighs.

"By all means, let me assist you to your chamber." I help him to the bed and lay him down on the linen sheets. After lighting his lamp for him, I ask him again if he needs anything, and he shakes his head. I walk out on the rooftop terrace before retiring in the dream chamber. The sky is burning red on the horizon.

∞∞∞∞∞∞∞∞∞∞∞∞∞∞∞∞∞∞∞∞∞∞

Bastet and I are feasting at a table displaying an assortment of fruits, breads, and meats. I turn and see she has both her hands full of a large melon. She gorges on it; the juices drip down her perfect face.

I awake and shake Nun's scrawny form to his feet. "I expect you to come inside the temple to assist me tonight."

"*Inside* the temple, Master? Slaves are forbidden."

"Yes, I am aware of that, which is why you will need to purify yourself at the public bath and enter through the workshop entrance. You will wear this."

I throw him my fine linen loincloth. He holds it gingerly, since slaves are not allowed clothes, let alone linen.

"What if someone catches me? I could be killed for an offense such as this?"

"Do not question me! You must obey my wishes. If you do not obey me, I will cast out those who depend on you!"

I knew that threatening to throw out his useless, ailing mother would put an end to his misbehaving.

He looks down. "I beg forgiveness, Master. Please tell me where to meet you."

∞∞∞∞∞∞∞∞∞∞∞∞∞∞∞∞∞∞

On my way into the temple, I see a slight movement on the rooftop. There, swallowed by the darkness, stands an astronomer-priest, squinting to the starlit sky, solving some perplexing mystery of the cosmos. I walk into the grand library, where I bow to Khons, busy writing at his desk.

"Sokaris." He replaces his reed into his ink flask and asks, "How can I assist you?"

"I did not mean to interrupt you." I bow.

"Oh no, I was simply writing a draft on the periodic returns of the two heavenly bodies, the moon and the sun." He stretches and straightens his gnarled legs. "What are you in search of?"

"I request the use of the library. I am in search of fertility concerns and rituals."

He looks up, squinting as he searches his personal archives within his mind, then beckons me to follow. I slowly walk behind his hunched form earned from many years of slumping over a desk, writing volume upon volume. We walk into the cavernous adjoining room, where shelves filled with books reach to an extreme height and tables are stacked with giant rolls of pure leather.

He makes his way through the shelves, holding onto them for support. "This library is shrouded in great secrecy, as it holds many sacred rituals, writings, and secrets of the inner sanctum of religion itself. These secrets could harm the Pharaoh, the priests, and all of Egypt." He pauses and opens his arms around him, drawing attention to the never-ending sea of books. "This is for all of posterity!"

He smiles proudly, narrows one eye, and points to an area reached only by ladder. Once I climb to the designated area, I scan the bindings of books painted with golden symbols.

*The Book of Driving Away Lions, Repulsing Crocodiles, and Repelling Reptiles; The Protection of the Hour, Protection of the Body, Spells for Repelling the Evil Eye; The Book of Capture; Knowing all the Se-*

*crets of the Laboratory; The Book of Smiting Demons; Book of Medicinal Cures for Fertility and Contraceptive Purpose.*

I open it up while still on the ladder and find a contraceptive charm of mixing honey with natron. I replace the book and climb down, bowing to Khons in thanks. He watches me, deep in thought, as I leave.

I'm stirring up the sticky mixture when Nun enters, crouching.

"Did anyone notice you?"

Dripping with sweat, he pants, "I was stopped by two guards at the passageway between the workshop and the temple. I told them I was your apprentice, and they asked why I was coming through the workshop entrance. I told them I was confused. After a moment they let me pass."

"Oh yes, I forgot they had guards at that door," I say, barely listening.

Noticing this, Nun says flatly, "What do you need assistance with, Master?"

"I need you to guard the entrance to this room. Play this flute to warn me if anyone should approach."

He eyes me questioningly, wondering why I would need the door watched, when in walks Bastet, glowing.

Nun takes one look at her, and dread sweeps across his face. "You are provoking the gods! We will all be judged for this!"

I give him a seething look and spit, "On the streets!"

Nun exhales, reaches for the flute, and goes back into the corridor. Bastet stands there smiling, not allowing the ominous comments from Nun to faze her.

"Dance for me. Not Serapis but me," I say as I lean back on my altar to observe.

Her body starts moving, and I can hear the imagined beat. She spins, and her eyes follow me. After a few minutes, I can't resist any longer and remove my loincloth. I coat myself in the contraceptive, then pick her small frame up easily and shove my sacred Omina on the floor. I place my new religion on the altar, where I read every passage and have all my prayers answered.

# Chapter 4

Bastet and I meet four more times before my month-long rotation is complete. Whenever the dream chamber is empty and Bastet can get away from Nebu's watchful eye, we meet under Nun's surveillance. I hate leaving the temple to walk back home. Leaving the fertile black lands to travel to the edges of the sterile red lands of my fathers. Reaching the threshold of the white-walled fortress that surrounds the city, I force myself to step onto the sparkling limestone pathway that leads up to the lush country villas. The thought of not seeing her again for three months is painful. I touch my wife only in times of extreme desperation, and even then, I think of her: she who consumes me.

Twenty-one days into my prison sentence, I seek solitude in the shadows of the date and fig trees in my estate's garden. As I watch the ducks dive among the lotus flowers, a message comes from the temple. It bears Nebu's writing,

*Sokaris, come at once.*

I call for Nun to pack up my things and order him to hurry. Running most of the way in the midday heat, I arrive at the temple by dusk. Frustrated at the time it takes to be shaved and cleansed, I rush into Nebu's harem room and become frantic when I see Bastet is not beside her.

"What is wrong? Why have you sent for me?"

Nebu, surprised by my haste and paranoia, says, "Calm yourself, Sokaris. This is not a matter over which you should be so alarmed."

She snaps for a servant to bring me a cushion. I force myself to relax enough to bend into a sitting position.

I ask, "Where is Bastet? She is usually at your side."

She picks up a gold hand mirror to check how tightly her servants curled her wig. After testing the bounce of the curls that line her forehead and running her thin fingers down the long braids that hide beneath the curls, she nods in acceptance. "Bastet is why I summoned you. She has failed us greatly."

"What do you mean?"

She points for the ebony-and-gold cosmetic box to be brought to her. "She has been deceiving us and Serapis."

My blood thickens, and she has the nerve to fix her kohl as I wait.

"She is with child, Sokaris."

"With child? That is impossible!" I can't sit.

Not realizing how I meant that exclamation, she says, "Obviously, she has spit in the face of all that is sacred and has lain with a man. A man within this very temple, since she is not permitted outside these walls."

"How are you sure?"

"I am obligated to test my Royal Daughter's urine monthly."

Thinking of the barley-and-wheat test I ask, "The grains grew?"

"Yes, and I tested her twice to be sure."

"Where is she now?" I begin to pace.

"I notified the Pharaoh's magistrate, Overseer of the Six Great Mansions, and the guards have taken her away. Her trial is tomorrow."

*What am I to do?*

"Sokaris, we must find the man responsible for this." She puts the brush away and snaps the lid shut.

I shake my head, feigning thoughtfulness. "I will go to incubate at once to see what I can scry."

I rush to the dream chamber, rip the sheets back, and fall asleep to try to save her.

*Bastet is on a great ship, alone, acting as steersman. She looks worried and is crying, "Sokaris! Sokaris!"*

*I shout, "I will save you!" as I pull my arm up and prick myself deep with a thorn.*

*Instantly, Nun is up on the deck steering the massive ship, and I tell Bastet, "Jump to me!"*

*She steps backward to gain speed and leaps to me on the riverbank. We both watch as Nun and the ship sail away downstream.*

I wake and kiss Bes, carved above my head, and say, "Thank you! Thank you!"

I scribble down an entry and backdate it forty-two days. I leave the temple and clap to wake up Nun, sleeping on the stone walkway after waiting for me all night. Under a red sky in the east, I run to the mansion where Bastet is being judged.

○○○○○○○○○○○○○○○○○○○○○○○○○○

I rush past the alabaster sphinx guarding the road that leads to the Pharaoh's palace. The burnt landscape slowly turns green as I near the mouth of the Nile, where the imposing jaws of the courthouse looms. The mansion stands sternly against the happy backdrop of the banks of the Nile, where peasant women beat their laundry against rocks, servants fill clay vessels carrying them away on their heads, and children splash and play games as their mothers watch for crocodiles. Thick columns of three heights guard the entrance as statues of justice judge all who enter. The most important people in Memphis are there: the Pharaoh's vizier, the high priests, scribes, and many of the lower priests. It's unusual to have an event such as this occur within temple walls. I sit with others from the House of Life on the benches provided under the covered section of the roofless court. Khons attends with his son, Aapep, and I nod to him in respect.

The vizier presiding speaks from his great chair in the center under a canopy held by slaves. "We are all witness to a most disrespectful and defiling crime. This is an offense not only against all those honoring the gods but a crime against Serapis himself!"

The priests all nod in agreement.

"Bring her in." He motions to the guards, grey eyes flashing.

Bastet looks so small between the two towering guards. She looks like such a child now—a faint shadow of the woman who glowed before me in my dream chamber. Her powerful force that has compelled my allegiance and charmed my worship has deserted her, and she now stands before the court, shaking. She's forced to stand before the vizier in direct sun.

"Bastet, daughter of Ketuh, is it true you are carrying a child in your womb?"

"Yes, High One."

The audience is a mass of bald heads all shaking in disgust.

"Nebu, reigning wife of Serapis of The House of Life temple, has testified you took an oath of celibacy as her initiated Royal Daughter."

"Yes, oh High One."

"Is this child the spawn of man?"

"Yes, High One."

"Who is the man who has disrespected Serapis and has caused the gods to seek earthly judgment upon him?"

*What will I do if she says my name!*

I clench my fists.

"I cannot say. Have mercy on me, High One." She begins to cry and covers her face with her delicate hands.

Now the audience breaks out in murmurs as some get up in anger to leave. I feel a wave of relief that I might be able to escape this disgrace and still help her.

"If you will not answer, we will have no choice but to sentence you to death by spear. You will be granted mercy for your unborn child's soul, and your punishment will be carried out upon its birth."

Bastet merely shakes her head and bows. The vizier nods for the guards to take her back to her prison.

I stand up and state with head bowed, "I humbly offer my testimony up to the Pharaoh."

Bastet looks worried, obviously fearful that I'll confess. She opens her mouth to speak, but I bring a bent finger up to my lips subtly in message. She quiets and smiles with her eyes as the guards take her away.

"Certainly, priest, you may speak."

"I have information that I cannot withhold that may shed light on this daughter's corruption."

"Continue."

"About forty days past, my slave, Nun, from house of Sokaris, requested a dream be interpreted by me. As that is my priestly profession, I obliged, as any benevolent master would. He dreamt of grabbing the wooden staff out of Serapis's hand and taking it for himself. I interpreted this to mean my slave coveted something of Serapis's. He continued on, saying he took the staff and sailed downstream with it, a strong portent of violence, as even laymen know. I told my slave a different interpretation for fear of feeding his desires, but I worried that an event such as this would take place as his dream foretold. I have it documented in the scry book if the court so wishes proof."

The vizier nods respectfully and commands a guard to hasten to the temple to fetch the journal.

"On more than five occasions, I have had my priestly linen loincloths taken from my dwellings when only Nun had access to them. Of course, I flogged him for it, but he confessed nothing. I have since dreamt that Serapis himself has come to me, seeking vengeance for my slave's violent and forceful actions upon his Royal Daughter. After hearing today how she has been disgraced, I know who is undoubtedly to blame."

"Where is this slave, Nun, from the house of Sokaris?"

"He is right outside this court."

"Seize him! Sokaris, take the guards to collect him and bring him to me!"

As I walk out with the guards behind me, I comfort myself.

*He's a slave, of little use to the world. I'm a learned and destined priest in the esteemed House of Life. The gods would surely rather have my homage and service than this lowly slave. Bastet committed no wrong. We simply made a mistake and Nun would help us rectify it: a sacrifice for our repentance.*

In the commotion, the crowds step aside as the armed court guards march behind me. I see Nun sitting cross-legged by the side of the building. He stirs and rises to bow as if we'll pass him. When we stop before him, he looks up, shocked.

"There is the accused." I stare down into his green eyes.

They seize his thin, frail frame and drag him into the court screaming.

"Silence the prisoner!" the vizier demands.

One of the guards grabs a wool rag and stuffs it into the slave's mouth.

"Are you Nun, slave of the house of Sokaris?"

Nun tries to spit the cloth out to answer.

The vizier shouts, "Nod or shake!"

Nun quickly nods with his eyes wide in fear.

"Have you entered the Temple of Serapis, even though it is forbidden by the Pharaoh?"

He again tries to spit the cloth out.

The vizier screams, "Nod or shake, slave!"

The vizier's slaves fan him furiously to cool his reddened face.

Nun pauses here, hangs his shoulders, and looks around at me, eyes narrowed.

"Do you understand the question?" the vizier shouts.

Nun turns back and nods.

"Answer, then! Have you entered the Temple of Serapis, even though it is forbidden by the Pharaoh?" he shouts louder as though Nun is deaf.

Nun looks again at me, this time defeated, and nods his head. The court is buzzing.

The vizier then asks, after the noise dies down a bit, "Have you wronged Serapis, committing a crime against him, violating his Royal Daughter?"

Nun seems torn by this statement, and I smile inside, knowing that the wording is auspicious. He shrinks further in defeat and nods. The room explodes with noise.

"Silence, or I will have the court closed!" The vizier turns to his guards. "Bring out the girl!"

As soon as Bastet looks around, she takes in Nun standing there in front of the courts. I hope she understands, but she appears confused. I hold my breath and pray she will know what to do.

"Bastet, do you know this man?"

"Yes." She looks perplexed until the vizier speaks again.

"Is this the man who violated you?"

She meets my eyes, comprehending, and then looks back at the vizier, her eyes full of tears.

She cries out, "Yes! That is the man who forced himself on me in the temple of Serapis!"

I exhale with pride at her drive for life.

"Why did you not tell a priest or your mother, Nebu, that this violation occurred?"

She thinks fast and cries to great effect, "I knew the violation would bring shame upon my family and my position at the temple would be disgraced. He threatened the lives of my family if I did not obey his demands!"

Everyone in the court is quiet in disgust, leering at Nun while he juts his chin out in simmering anger.

"Is this true?" he shouts at Nun.

Nun doesn't even reply with eye contact, simply stares at the floor.

The vizier picks his teeth, then speaks. "I have no choice but to sentence you, Nun, slave of the house of Sokaris, to death by spear. You will be executed tomorrow in the public courtyard at dawn, before our morning rituals, to amend the betrayal you committed upon the gods.

"Bastet, you are free to return to your family and have your child. Your shame, even though it was not willed by you, makes you unfit for temple duties."

She bows her head in acceptance.

The vizier finishes, "It would serve you and the soul of your child well to make an offering of forgiveness to Serapis tomorrow, after the execution of your violator."

She agrees again and bows in thanks. The guards take Nun away and set Bastet free.

# Chapter 5

I wish to run to her but know I can't. I give her a quick wink across the room when no one is looking and leave. I pass Khons's crippled form assisted by Aapep.

"Justice always prevails," I say to Khons.

Khons looks up oddly and says, "Has it really, Sokaris?" as he limps past.

I hesitate mid-bow, unsure of what he means, but nothing can get in the way of what has happened. The gods have smiled down on us! As the sun fades, I walk home through the cluttered city, past all the peasant houses, stacked upon each other wherever they find space to build, to my temporary dwelling, all the while trying to figure out a way to see Bastet again. In Nun's absence, the fires and lamps are not lit that night, but in the darkness what unnerves me most is not having Sehket's presence. Tomorrow, I'll send another slave from my residence to bring her.

Hoping to see Bastet before she returns to her father's house, I need to stay in the city. I calculate how long I'll have to wait before I can take her as my second wife. I smile, thinking of the large dowry her father will give in light of her great disgrace. How auspicious this all came to be! I pull my sheets back ritualistically and accept that I will have to go to sleep with dirty feet that night.

*Khons's hunched and twisted form walks in front of the courthouse. As he watches me coming, he lifts up a deep goblet of dark red wine and spills it down his throat. Then the heavens rain down upon only me, soaking me through to the skin, while leaving Khons perfectly dry. In anger, I lunge at Khons with a spear but upon inspecting his body, see a dead ox. I refill Khons's spilt goblet with its blood and drink.*

Even though the sun hasn't risen enough to shed light, I reach for my satchel and dart out of bed in the direction of the Temple Library. I slink into the scribes' study, and the deaf old man doesn't even stir at my entrance. I creep up behind him while he affixes his seal to the letter he's just completed.

I say right behind his head, "What has you working so early, Khons?"

He jumps and drops the wax he's holding above the candle and gasps.

"Oh, so sorry to frighten you. You must have been deep in thought."

I walk around to the side of the desk so I can see his face, but he continues to look down. Trembling, he tucks the letter into his robe's deep pocket.

"Oh, you are shaking. Have you not had your breakfast yet?" I notice the untouched tray of breads, figs, and wine on the three-legged low table beside his desk. "You have not touched a morsel." I click my tongue twice. "We must not spoil this offering."

I turn back to see Khons, quaking as he grips his desk for support, and I motion him to sit on a cushion at the table.

He shakes his head and says, "I am waiting for Aapep to come and assist me into the city."

"Well, that is perfect. Have a seat, and we can put something in our bellies while you wait."

He glances toward the door, searching for some way out. I smile, knowing he can't make his way down the corridor without assistance. Hesitant, he hobbles over, protecting the pocket.

"What business do you have in the city this early?"

He coughs a few times, clearly trying to gain time to think. "I requested permission to record the execution of your slave this morning. I think it will be important to document it."

*How clever he thinks he is.*

I stare at his face—so odd with its many tiny spots—a thing of rarity among people of dark skin.

"Oh yes, yes. Good idea. You are so wise, Khons."

I touch his hand, and he recoils slightly. I draw back, place goblets in front of us, and fill them, the scarlet liquid spinning for a moment as Khons watches the door.

"Ah, thank you, truly a feast. Khons, can you fetch me that knife on your desk to cut the bread?"

As he turns his back to get the sharp knife, I spill the contents of a small flask into his goblet.

He returns and says, "I will do the honor of cutting, thank you."

I smile. He thinks I might harm him with the knife. He slices the wide flatbread, wraps the knife in linen, and tucks it away in the satchel worn at his side. I can hardly contain my laughter—he thinks he avoided a threat! Khons picks up his goblet with a tremorring, spotted hand and drinks thirstily. He replaces it and is mid-chew on a large piece of bread when he begins to choke.

He spits his bread at me and gasps out, "You murderer! You have Nun's blood on your hands and now mine!"

He reaches up, holding his neck, gagging as frothy blood dribbles out of the corners of his mouth.

He drops to the floor and gurgles, "May Ra eat your heart!" One last rattle and his eyes go blank as his breathing ceases. In haste, I wipe his mouth, pick up his bony body, and place it at his desk. Putting the inked reed in his hand, I leave it propped on an empty piece of paper. Aapep will soon be here and surmise he died alone. I drink my wine and spill the poisoned wine into a linen cloth, wiping out any remnants. As I am leaving, I realize I forgot the most important thing! I reach into his robe and remove the vital scroll.

*Foolish Khons.*

∞∞∞∞∞∞∞∞∞∞∞∞∞∞∞∞∞∞∞∞∞

Once home, I take the letter out in the safety of my dwelling and read his perfect writing:

*Most Esteemed Vizier,*

*I write to you with heavy guilt and shame that I did not have the courage or pure heart to speak out in court yesterday. I had a difficult time deciding if the life of a slave was equal to the life of a skilled and trusted priest. It took a night of soul-searching and much lamenting to realize that my heart would not be light on Anubis's scales if an innocent slave were put to death, wrongly accused. I was present in the dream chamber awaiting my incubation when I overheard two lovers talking of a secret and forbidden meeting.*

*The male, who I can identify as Sokaris, Dream Magician of the House of Life, reassured the female, the Royal Daughter, that all would be well with his slave watching out for them. I have to confess, at risk of punishment on my own part, that I thought little of this lustful crime. I respect Sokaris, feel he is a valuable member to the House of Life, and thought so little of the offense taken so seriously by the righteous temple priests. I only felt a crime occurred*

*when this slave, Nun, was unjustly accused and scheduled to die
this new morning. Please spare the slave's life and have mercy on
these young lovers' sin.*

*Khons, son of Thutmose*

I burn the letter in the fire and think of how well I averted
disaster as the papyrus curls in movements that remind me of
Bastet. She should be at the temple now, getting ready to watch
Nun's execution. I have to speak to her.

∞∞∞∞∞∞∞∞∞∞∞∞∞∞∞∞∞∞∞∞∞∞∞

The sun is rising, and the land is golden with its renewed energy. People are all gathering at the temple square, as children
stand on stonewalls trying to see over tall figures. I search the
crowd for Bastet, but even a diamond can't be found in such dull
chaos. The drumming begins, and the people part for the procession of guards. In the middle of the guards walks Nun, his hands
tied in front of him. As he passes, I can see the brand of my family—a falcon, seared into his flesh with its wings spread. Sokaris,
the falcon god I am named after. They lead him to the execution
altar and lay him out on the tablet.

A lector priest starts reading him holy rites, preparing him for
his death. I grow bored watching and scan the crowd, searching
for my star. In the background, the drums start to roll and
abruptly cease with the quick cracking sound of the spear going
into Nun's head. He twitches for a few moments, and the crowd
cheers. With all the movement of the crowd, there's no way to
find her. I decide I'll have better luck if I go back to the temple to
meet her, but I'm distracted by a loud and piercing woman's
scream. The sea of people surges toward the sound.

I too go to see what happened, and my heart beats cold as I
look over the steep temple stairs to see my diamond lying in a
puddle of blood at the bottom. I rush to her and turn her around

in my arms, but she slumps lifeless in my embrace. I pull back to see her once-flawless features ruined by a deep gash in the middle of her forehead, from which thick blood paints her whole face. I hold her for a few moments more until she is gone. There is a murmur throughout the crowd that she was pushed.

A commoner shouts above the masses, "It was a man. Came up right behind her and shoved her down the steps. He ran back through the crowd."

The temple guards rush to break up the hovering crowd, and when they see Bastet, they call for the temple priests. Knowing it will not bode well to be found crying over her, I place her body on the ground and wipe away my tears. I head to pray the rest of the day for her soul in the temple, ending the terrible day in the comfort of my dream chamber.

*I get back into bed and fix the scroll with my god's name on it, when I call for Sehket. She doesn't come like she usually does, so I call again. Instead, Nun comes walking in, chuckling, and hurls Sehket's lifeless body next to my bed. I feel something move by my leg under the sheet. I throw back the sheet to expose a writhing mass of vipers, all crawling and hissing on top of me. I scream as they bite into my flesh and my body bursts into flame.*

I recite the prayer to undo misfortunes predicted in inauspicious dreams but still feel unsettled and uneasy. I need to be sure Nun is, in fact, dead. I can't understand why I would dream of him killing me if he is gone in this life.

I find the lector priest who presided over the execution and ask, "Where did they dispose of the slave's body?

"One of the priests had the slave sent for funeral rites."

"Funeral rites?" I scoff.

He shrugs and returns to what he was doing before my interruption.

The City of the Dead looms lonely near Pepy Meryre's pyramid. A wall of rectangles rises from the ground to a singular apex in the center with a dark gaping mouth beckoning me within. I enter and follow the long corridor that leads to a large pool. In the marbled glow of torches reflecting on water, I see the shine of jewel-embellished scales just under the water. The enormous sacred crocodile guarding the House of the Dead watches me pass the pool, and I bow to him in respect and fear. I enter the first ceremonial room I come across, where I see Nun's body lying on the table beneath three funeral priests.

One ancient digs in Nun's mouth with his finger and says, "The force of the spear through the slave's mouth was so great it thrust his front teeth apart."

As the other two bend forward to examine him, my attention diverts to Aapep sitting at the scribe's desk, recording the funeral rite in place of his father.

"Aapep, why are you here?"

He glances up with his flashing black eyes. "You are fully aware that my father is dead."

"Oh no, I did not know. I am very sorry to hear of his death."

Aapep looks away, back to Nun's body.

*Does he suspect me?*

I wonder how much Khons told him about his early morning errand.

"Why are you here, Sokaris? You do not own slaves after death," Aapep says even-toned.

"I went to claim his body and found he had already been moved to have funeral rites. That is not standard for executions."

"I had him moved. My family is paying for proper funeral rites." He sets his gaze on mine.

"Why would you do so?"

"The gods will not rest until injustices are righted," he says with his cold eyes squinted.

*I now know who pushed Bastet.*

# Chapter 6

I back out of the room and return to my dwelling to plan how I will avenge her. The new slave I sent for is here. He kneels, and I name him Aten. I tell him to fetch some hot water to clean my feet so that I can retire and enter my dwelling. I look for Sehket and find no cat in my room. I yell for Aten, who hurries in, bowing.

"When I sent for you, I instructed you to bring my favored cat Sehket. Where is she?"

He wrings his hands and sputters, "I gathered the black tailless cat you asked for and put her in this basket with linen tied around the top. I was walking by the temple square at the time of Nun's execution, and when the crowd broke out in cheers, the cat went wild. The basket fell out of my arms, and the cat ran away. I could not get her back."

I strike the slave with my open hand and proceed to beat upon his bent-over form.

The slave falls to his knees, covering his head as I yell, "Get out of my sight!"

He scurries outside but stoops to pick up his blanket. I throw the empty basket at him, hitting him in the back of his head as he runs away, leaving the moth-eaten blanket behind.

"UGHHH!" I scream out, falling to my knees, drawing the attention of slaves on rooftops within range of my cry.

*How did my life fall to ruin like this? How could so much change in two days' time?*

"Bastet, Bastet, Bastet." I lament like a woman.

Pulling myself back up, I retreat to the solitude of my room. I slump down on my bed in despair but jump up realizing I haven't checked the bed yet. I pull the sheets back to see nothing there. Breathing a sigh of relief, I fall on the bed and extinguish the candle by my side.

Moments later, in the moonlight, I see a peculiar movement but it flits away into the shadows.

Sitting up with my hands braced at my side, I call out into the darkness, "Aten, is that you?"

When mere silence echoes back, I wish I had not sent my slave and only protector away. The air is thick with an unseen presence. I still my breathing to listen for evidence of an intruder.

*What is that? Is it coming nearer?*

My eyes dart into the dark corners where the moonlight can't reach. I wait. Nothing comes.

I release my held breath and lie back down, scoffing loudly at my delusions.

Something lunges toward me. I scream out as it stabs deep into my left hand. I pull my hand in tight, trying to hold off the pain. Expecting to feel where the reptile had punctured me, instead I feel something stuck in the flesh of my hand. I yank it out and hold it to the moonlight. A sharpened quill glistens in the blue light, still dripping clear fluid. I lick the liquid, which instantly burns, numbing my tongue.

*Poison.*

I pray I removed it in time. The shadow moves across the walls and disappears out the door. I look down and see the wound is ominously turning black. A searing, burning fire creeps up my arm. I feel the poison flow into my heart, and after several painful spasms, my heart slows.

In my last few moments, struggling to breathe, I try to piece together how this all could have happened without any warning from Serapis.

*How could I have been so blind? Aapep's namesake—the moon snake god!*

Something bounds through the window beside my bed and I call out, "Aapep? Come back... to watch... me die?"

I brace for his final blow but instead feel the familiar pull on the linens as she leaps on top of me, and I hear her comforting purr. Sehket quickly settles in, her paws tucked on my chest, and warms my cooling heart as I close my eyes.

| Beacons | Life 1 Eygpt |
|---|---|
| Mole on left hand--Prophetic dreams | Sokaris |
| Scar on forehead--Large, honey-brown eyes--Magic | Bastet |
| Space between teeth--Green sparkling eyes | Nun |
| Mole by wide-set--Dark eyes | Nebu |
| Freckles--Brown eyes | Khons |
| Birthmark above knee-Amber eyes | Edjo |
| Two moles on jaw--Black eyes | Apep |
| Picks teeth--Steel-grey eyes | Vizier |
| Golden eyes--Animal | Sehket-Cat |

# Second Life
# Spartan Education

# Chapter 1

The sea air dampens my long hair as I ride Proauga through my father's countryside. A sunny crisp day in glorious Sparta and it was torture waiting until my lessons were done and my mother finally let me go outside. The sweat from my black filly's back soaks into my tunic as I ride bareback. I'm one with her as she gallops over the hills, knowing the way to my favorite spot. She slows as soon as she reaches the cliffs. I dismount and lay in the silken grass, looking over the turquoise Gytheio harbor, watching all the little white sails flashing and cracking in the wind as fisherman gather up their heavy nets. I can smell the sea from all the way up here.

A thunderstorm rattles the earth, causing me to roll onto my knees in search of lightning, but the sky is blue and free from clouds. Then everything shakes. Proauga's golden eyes widen as she shrills a frantic whinny and speeds into the thick brush. I fight the momentum of the earth's shaking and retreat from the cliff toward the trees. An estate crumbles in the distance, its majestic columns falling over like felled trees. The roof and walls collapse forward onto fountains and statues in the garden. The helot slaves go running in every direction, screaming for their lives. The cliffs give way, and the ground I'd just been standing on crashes to the shores below.

We had earthquakes before, but nothing compared to this. Five minutes pass until the quaking stops. As soon as I can get Proauga to come to me, I mount, desperate for home.

I pray to Hestia as Proauga flies through the never-ending olive groves, my fists white in her dark mane. Approaching, I see our helots deep in rubble, lifting away stones. I know in that instant my life has changed. I rush to where I'd left my mother sitting with her weaving and start digging there first. I remove the stone covering her feet and yell for the helots to come lift off the rest of the debris on top of her. I turn away once I see her crushed into something unfamiliar, recognizable only by the mole beside her eye. One of the helots removes his tunic and places it over her, attempting to erase the memory from our minds.

"Father!" I cry as I strain to move more stones, then shout at the slaves, "Why aren't you all digging faster!"

Two other bodies are found before we find my father's. One is our helot, Delia, the household slave who cared for me for all of my sixteen years. The other is her daughter, Kharis, who had been raised with me. Father is found last, under the collapsed timbers in the barn. All who meant home to me were wiped away in a single moment. My house is in ruin, with only one wall still standing.

I watch from a safer distance on the hillside as our helots carry my parents to the supply wagon and cover them with the linen my mother wove that morning. I split a long piece of grass in two as I remember neither would be allowed a marked grave, which were reserved only for battlefield deaths and women who died in childbirth. They will be buried somewhere I can never find them. A tear breaks free from my burning eye as flames ignite in the cleared field beside the house. As the hungry cremation flames reach to the sky, I realize Delia and Kharis should be so lucky.

*Where am I to go?*

I can think of only one other place. Leaving everything behind, I ride in haste to see how my uncle's estate has fared. From far away, his situation looks bleak. Like all the other estates I pass, everything is reduced to dust. However, as I ride closer, I hear the booming voice of my uncle, Nereus, yelling at his helots. Relieved to see him well, I embrace him.

"Alcina, you've survived! And how so my brother?"

"Everyone's dead." My voice breaks. "Mother, Father, Kharis, and Delia."

"Oh Poseidon! What have you done?" he says to the sky. "Alcina, you'll stay with me for now. We'll have to forget all we've lost and regain our strength to build a shelter before nightfall."

We work alongside the helots all day, building back up the walls to one room. We use the sails from Nereus's sailboat to provide a roof for us that night. Three of his household helots sleep with us on straw, while the others go home to their village outside Sparta. The next day, only some of his helots return.

"A rebellion's broken out in Sparta," one helot informs Nereus.

"I knew this day would come and may Zeus strike them dead for taking advantage of this disaster!" Nereus says through his teeth. "Where's the other half of my helots?"

Another helot says, "They've taken up with the rebellion."

"I hope the hoplites kill them all," he says, tight-lipped.

He marches into the shelter and returns in his armor with sword and shield in hand. After a moment of contemplation, he turns to me. "I have to go into the city to make sure this is under control. Keep a close eye on these helots." Handing me his large army knife, he adds, "If you use it, use it well."

He straddles his horse and rides down toward the city.

I slip the knife under the leather straps of my sandals and sit under a tree to get a little shade. A girl about my age catches my eye; she has the same misplaced look as me. I walk over to her by the gardens. "My name is Alcina."

She glances up and away but replies, "Ophira."

We're quiet for a few moments. I notice she's quite pretty—for a helot. By her fair skin, I deduce she spends most of her time in the house weaving or doing chores. Even though we are girls of similar age, I could pick her up and carry her. Her frame is short and slight due to the deprivation in which most non-Spartan girls are raised; nutritious food is saved for the males of those households. She averts eye contact and plays with the medallion around her neck as I look her up and down.

She has large, honey-brown eyes, and the only flaw on her well-formed face is a small scar on her forehead. As she notices the knife tied to my calf, she pulls her skin cloak up over her head, shrinking away from me. Many helots fear Spartans and try to avoid them, but I'm so lonely I'm not going to let her get away.

"Do you belong to my uncle's household?"

She looks down and says, "I came here to talk to your uncle."

"I've been left in control while he's away. You can speak to me."

She seems hesitant. "My husband, father, and mother were all killed in the revolt. It's not safe in the city. Seeing that your uncle has lost some of his helots, I'm hoping to be reassigned out here in the country."

Surprised she's already married, I wonder if I've misjudged her age but then remember Spartans marry much later.

"What housework can you do?"

"I can do anything: cook, clean, care for children, fetch water, weave."

"I've lost my parents in the earthquake, and my house needs to be rebuilt. Once it's standing, I'll need household help, since some of our helots perished."

She brightens at this. "There's no man in the household?"

I know her concern; household helot women have other uses as well.

"Not now," I say, and she breathes easy. "It would be nice to have company." I smile, and she cracks a weak smile back.

By nightfall, Ophira and I dig access to the supply house, from which we scrounge up jugs of wine, bags of maza, dried fruit, and salted fish. In the distance, Nereus screams at his horse. Nereus isn't good with horses. He prefers the water, even the roughest sea, over the most beautiful day on land.

"No! Back home! Back home!" he fumes while pulling hopelessly at the reins.

I sprint to help him walk his horse back up.

"Ah, many thanks, Alcina," he says as he wipes the sweat from his brow. "I think Zale is much improved, though; I didn't have any problems on the way there."

Showing his age, he's breathing heavily now and stands back mid-step to catch his breath. Old age is a rarity in Sparta, since most men don't live long enough to retire from military service. He still needs another moment to catch his breath, and he reaches up to push his greying hair to the side, flashing a long scar running down his forearm.

"Nereus, how did you get that scar?"

Always willing to retell a tale, he needs no encouragement. Rolling up his tunic sleeve slowly, in large cuffs, he exposes the scar that extends to his biceps.

"I've only reached this great age by making one very wise choice." He never begins with the answer to your question but starts at the beginning of his whole tale. "While Spartans are strongest on foot and earth, I'm a fish in Poseidon's shining seas. One day, in a great coastal battle, I was commanded to bring my ship to shore and reinforce the footmen. I should have known my place was the sea, but I rushed out like all young men do. I was Heracles himself! As soon as my foot touched soil, I was instantly sliced from shoulder to wrist by a Persian sword." He traces the thick white line and then looks out to the sea. "I never left Poseidon again, no matter the command. I stayed behind to watch the ships and let others die onshore."

"So that is why you spend so little time onshore now, Uncle?"

He laughs. "If I never had to step foot on land again and could live off the seas indefinitely, you would never see me again." He lights up with one eye closed and one eye widened and says, "The trick is to know all of Greece's rocks, shallow spots, and harbors like the insides of your eyelids. Once you do that, there's nothing to fear." He pulls back like he entrusted me with the secret of life.

Finally up the hill, I ask, "Has the rebellion been extinguished?"

"The hoplites managed to contain the helot rebels in the region of Mount Ithome, in Messenia, but they lacked the strength to defeat them and their vast numbers. We appealed to our allies for help; hopefully, they'll assist us."

I worry about what would happen if the slaves finally revolt and gain power.

"Did I ever tell you about the time..." He begins his tales again, and I decide it's a good time to gallop Zale back to her makeshift stables.

When Nereus realizes he's cut off and sees the ease with which I control Zale, he calls up between his hands around his mouth, "Hubris, I tell you, hubris!"

His laughter carries through the crumbled hills.

# Chapter 2

Nereus allows Ophira to live with us. It's amusing, watching him tell her story after story, since she can't tell him to stop. I'll find Nereus following around after her, busy with chores, filling her head with tales. It's hard to leave once my family's helots and freed skilled workers finish rebuilding my house, since we'd found a little happiness in our pulled-together family. Nevertheless, I need to be there daily to keep the helots busy. I'd been trained by my mother to run the farm, and I'm now going to have to take over earlier than I ever thought.

Nereus lays his hands heavily on Ophira's and my head. "Come back whenever you need company."

I would have felt sorry for him to be left, but Nereus is never distressed at being alone. He takes off daily to go fishing in his little boat and can find a way to talk with anyone who crosses his path. Nereus drives his chariot back to my farm, since Ophira can't ride, and I follow behind on Proauga.

Ophira takes one look at the rebuilt estate, with its columned terrace looking out on the gardens, livestock, and the barley fields below, and asks, "This all belongs to you?"

"My father was an accomplished hoplite. Sparta gave him great rewards for his bravery."

"They will allow a girl to run this alone?"

"Women run *Sparta* while men are away, fighting for more land to occupy and protecting the state. In two years, I'll most likely be married and will run *two* households. I've been taught everything I need to know."

She looks wary of my promise, coming from a world where even their men aren't given their own households to run.

"Where do we begin?" She squints up at the imposing size of the house.

"You'll make dinner for us tonight." I clap at two helots leaning on a fence. "You boys!" I offer up Proauga's reins. "Feed and water my horse, then set her out on the east pasture."

∞∞∞∞∞∞∞∞∞∞∞∞∞∞∞∞∞∞∞∞∞∞

A year drifts by, Ophira and I are content in our little world and my mother would've been proud.

Ophira asks one day while we're preparing dinner, "Why didn't your parents have more children?"

"They did. My mother gave birth to two other sons."

I strain the wheat grains and dump them onto the stone to pound into gruel for bread.

She looks confused but keeps adding wood to the fire below the three-legged clay oven.

I explain before she figures out how to inquire. "Both times, my mother was forced to bathe the babies in pure red wine to test their constitutions, but the strong fumes only sickened the children and sent them into convulsions. My father brought each one to the Lesche for the elders to inspect. Both times my father came home empty-handed."

She stands up quickly. "What did they do with them?"

"The infants were left to die in a chasm at the foot of Mount Taygetos." I see her appalled look. "It was the sadness of both of my parents. My mother could never go near there. We would ride twice the distance to avoid the area on our way into the city. Not having a son in a Spartan household is an embarrassment. My mother didn't want to go through the experience ever again, so there were no others." Wanting to leave the thought behind, I ask, "Tell me of your family."

She goes back to chopping cabbage for relish as the water begins to boil. "They had to live in a state-granted house in Laconia which had two other families living in it. Each family occupied two small rooms. My mother had a half-Spartan/half-helot—"

"A mothax," I interrupt.

She flinches at the sound of the word, but continues, "—a son, who was sent away to the Citizens' Army, and we never saw him again. I was forced to marry a man at fifteen who was twenty years older. We had to live with my parents."

"Did you care about your husband?" Judging by the "forced" comment I gather she did not.

"He had these disgusting big toes." She starts laughing with her knife pointed up in the air. "I would look down and see these two, hairy, oversized toes, and it would make me sick." She laughs so hard she has to look up. I laugh along with her.

"Do you miss your family?"

I drizzle the honey over the kneaded loaves, making golden glistening swirls.

She glances up. "I miss my mother, but I'm happier than I've ever been in my whole life. I can't believe I'm this happy."

That night I make her practice running with me since the next day is the annual Festival of Naked Youths. We take our clothes off and sprint around the fields. Ever faster than Ophira, it is so much fun to hear her complain as she falls farther behind me. After racing, Ophira and I dance up on the cliffs to the rhythmic sounds of the ocean. This is something she does better than me, though. I sit back and watch her move, never needing music. I imagine steady, mysterious hip-drum beats, meandering abdominal harps, accented with the cymbaled climax of her delicate hands and expressive eyes. Even though she is a helot, she could've turned many suitors' heads at the race tomorrow. It's a shame I can't bring her. Nereus is also forbidden, since Sparta punishes those who never married by not letting them attend any state events. I'll have to brave it alone, but I'm sure I will win.

# Chapter 3

I strip my short, belted tunic off and rub oil all over until I shine along with all the other young men and women. We've been competing with each other since we were small: wrestling, throwing javelins, tossing discuses, and racing. Sparta believes that to make stronger men, you have to make the women who give birth to them stronger, and I'm glad for it. Once all the girls are oiled, we parade around and flirt with the boys we most admire. This is the time we can catch their attention and coax them into considering us for marriage. Many of the young men have been allowed a pass from their military school, Agoge, to compete.

Even though I'm not light-haired, as most men cherish, I have the ideal female shape. I'm tall, almost as tall as a man, with long, thick legs that curve in taut muscle. My back and middle are powerful, with broad shoulders and strong arms.

I am the racehorse of women.

It's my turn to wrestle, and I'm in the highest heat. I've already won the discus, javelin, and all three short-distance races. Although those were only against females, wrestling is much more challenging since I can compete with the boys.

I pin the first two boys quickly by staying low and keeping my feet moving. I know I'm going to have trouble when Leander enters the ring. He's taller, has fully developed chest muscles, and biceps much larger than mine. If I'm going to win, I'll have to use my leg strength and not let him pick me up. We get into our wrestling stances, and my eyes focus on the two large moles he has on his jaw.

The match begins, and we collide low. He tries to get under to throw me, but I fight to get under him. He catches me in a number of holds, yet I always manage to squirm free. The match goes on like this until it is announced he wins. Disappointed, I throw my tunic back on, gather all my laurel wreaths, and walk out before the feasting begins.

I feel a tap on my shoulder, and I'm surprised to see Leander standing there.

"Are you leaving?" he asks.

"Yes."

"Before the feast begins?"

"I have to get home," I say over my shoulder as I walk away.

He follows behind me and calls out, "Is it true you have no parents?"

I stop. "What is it of your concern?"

"I've some business to discuss with the head of your household."

"They died in the earthquake," I answer. "I have to go."

I turn and nudge through the current of citizens on their way in for the feast.

Unfazed, he catches up to me. "Then you run your own household?'

"Leave me be, I must get home." I begin to make some headway, but he pulls me back toward him, within the swirling mass of the crowd.

"I'm interested in marriage, and I'd normally ask your father or brother, but you have none."

Leander's one of the strongest young men, and at twenty, he's only days away from initiation into the revered full-citizen hoplite army.

"You can ask me," I say, pulling my chin up in the air, pretending not to be surprised.

"Will you meet me in secret to wed?"

"Which day?" Chin still high.

"Meet me in your barn on the new moon."

"I might be there."

I walk away and head home thinking of how his black eyes sparkled like polished onyx, yet something strangely unsettling gnawed down deep.

∞∞∞∞∞∞∞∞∞∞∞∞∞∞∞∞∞∞∞∞∞

Seven days later, under the first night of the new moon, acting as my bridesmaid, Ophira shaves my head.

She holds the shears up to my hair and asks, "Explain to me why I'm doing this horrible thing to you?"

"It's tradition to display how I've changed my maiden hair to the shorter hair of a married woman."

She snips the first lock of hair and starts laughing. "I can't do this!"

She tries to shove the shears back in my hand.

"It'll grow back." I shove them back. "Now do as I say!"

After she's done, she holds up a mirror, and I truly look like a man. We both hold our sides in laughter. Ophira can't even look at me after without laughing.

"Get yourself together and fetch the rest of the things I need," I say, still laughing.

She helps me get on the ceremonial red soldier's cloak and sandals.

On our way down to the barn in the dark, Ophira says, "This is the strangest wedding I have ever witnessed." A rooster flaps in from behind the hen house, late to roost, causing Ophira to erupt in a high-pitched hoot and grab on to me.

"No moon aids Leander, but it certainly doesn't make it easier for us."

She breaks out in laughter again looking at me, but now I'm in no mood to laugh. It seems so real now.

She stops laughing and breaks the tension. "Why is this a secret?"

"It's called a bride capture, and it's done in secret because the man steals away from his mess group in the night to meet his bride in a hidden place. They share a moment, and then he returns before anyone notices his absence. The marriage can't be made public until she's pregnant, since it would be easier to go their separate ways if one is unable to conceive."

"This is all very strange. You don't see this?" She squints with her palms up to me.

"I think it's exciting and mysterious, and if I don't like him, I'm not stuck with him for life."

"Make sure you check his toes, then."

We both laugh so hard we stumble down the hill. In jet dark, we hold each other's hands to find our way.

"Don't you find it a little odd how you're made to look like *a boy* for him?"

"It's done to ward off bad spirits that might get jealous of our youthful passion," I say, but pause and quickly add, "or soldiers might like boys."

Our laughter carries off through the valley and I put a finger to my lips before entering the large barn. Ophira gathers up a straw bed and lays me down. I whisper her good-bye. She leaves swiftly, unsure when he'll appear. It's strange to be out here in total darkness. I hear some field mice running past me as I hold my breath. I wonder then, if I should have confirmed I'd definitely be here. Maybe he thought I wasn't serious and I'd be sitting here all night in the dark. Or maybe he's waiting in one of the smaller out-buildings. Something moves in the corner; someone has been there waiting this whole time. He steps toward me, and his tall form looms above me.

Leander reaches down, releases my thick belt effortlessly in the dark, and pulls me out of my robe. I feel weightless in his strong arms and welcome his warmth with the night air so cold. He places me back down in the straw and presses himself against me. He puts his hands up to feel my shaved head. No stranger to what it feels like to have a man so close when undressed, I'm unprepared how different it is in the dark, alone.

He rolls off to my side, panting. "We'll meet again in two new moons."

"Two moons?"

"It's the earliest I can sneak away. If I'm caught leaving, I'll be punished."

"But everyone knows men leave their messes for such secret meetings."

"It's a test for the soldiers to practice stealth and I can't be caught. This is the most I can sneak away."

"All right, then, we'll meet again in two new moons."

With that, he puts back on his cloak and leaves without sound. I, on the other hand, bump into every tool and bucket left out by the helots and receive a good bruise to my shin in the process. When I return, Ophira's waiting up by the fire. I tell her all the details, which lasts all of two minutes.

She giggles, saying, "That was about what it was like for me, except mine was soaked in wine."

∞∞∞∞∞∞∞∞∞∞∞∞∞∞∞∞∞∞∞∞∞∞∞

I watch the next moon come and go, wait all month, and when the full moon appears, I'm never happier for it to disappear. Ophira gives me an exaggerated wink before I run down to the barn. Dressed again in only my cloak, I sit on the straw, searching every dark corner.

Something moves to my left, and when I hear two helots talking, I shout, "Everyone out of the barn! It is nightfall, you're not permitted here!"

He will not come if anyone is near. I wait twenty more minutes and have to kick curious mice away. Finally, I hear the barn door close quietly, and I became so excited I forget to breathe. He walks over to the hay, puts his hand down checking to see if I'm there, and is startled when he finds me.

He steps back and whispers, "Alcina?"

"I'm here."

He casts off his robe, pulls off mine, and takes me immediately. When it's done, he lays next to me. I'm hoping he'll stay a moment so I can talk to him.

I wait for him to speak, but he only reaches around for his robe.

Hoping to stay him, I spurt out, "You've given me a child."

He sits up in surprise. "So soon? After only one meeting?"

"I am sure."

He looks slightly suspicious for a moment but then tilts his head to one side. "Good."

He gives me a light belly pat and gets his cloak to go.

I stop him when I see the faint light coming in through the door. "We don't need to meet in secret any longer. When will I see you again?"

"I will come when I can."

The barn door slams.

∞∞∞∞∞∞∞∞∞∞∞∞∞∞∞∞∞∞∞∞

Happily, the Artemis Ortheia Festival comes during the wait, and I'm hoping to see Leander there. I ride Proauga down to the Evrotas river valley, nestled deep within the cleavage of Mt. Taygetos and Mt. Parnon. The snow on the highest summits stands out oddly among the rest of the warm greenery. I leave Proauga to graze in lush grasses and make my way toward the crowded theater to find a seat among the stone benches. Alone, I find a seat in front of the many steps that lead up to the Goddess of the Hunt's altar. Winged Artemis stands frozen in stone, her arms outstretched and grasping a bird in either hand. She looks down upon the bloodstained steps where many years ago human sacrifices were made, but now Sparta's found another way to satiate her bloodlust as well as entertain the people.

Beside the altar, young men dance naked as choruses of girls sing war songs to flutes, lyres, and cymbals. Women hurry to place wheels of cheese in various positions on the steps. I hear a commotion to the west and can't help but smile when I see a troop of young men run down the valley driven by their leaders on chariots. Leander's leading the sandal-less pack of bare-chested men. The residing priestess chooses her favorite male dancer and bequeaths him a prize sickle as Leander and the others are allowed to drink from the river before the rite begins. I can't help but cross my fingers for him to do well. The leaders leave their chariots and take out their whips tied to their kilts. Each powerful man chooses his position among the steps carefully as the doomed lot gathers in racing position at the foot of the steps. The priestess brings her hands up in front of Artemis and claps them together to start the competition.

The men dart to reach the cheeses closest to them as the whips crack hard against every back. Some men recoil to grab the sting of ripped flesh as others, like Leander, ignore the pain to reach a wheel of cheese. Leander's whipped again as he descends the steps to lay down his offering of cheese but only grimaces and spins to his left to climb ten more steps to another wheel. Other men are not faring so well; at least two are badly bleeding from wounds that tore around their backs to slice their necks or chests. They stand hesitant at the steps, trying to pick an opportune time to attempt another try, but the leaders are watching them out of the corners of their eyes as they whip the stronger boys piling up their cheeses.

One of the weaker men makes a move to go behind, but the leader spins around with a crack so loud it sounds like thunder over our heads. The man screams in agony and falls upon the steps. A splatter of blood sprays the crowd when the whip is brought back. The leader spits in his direction, waiting for him to try to get up once again. Leander makes his way to the top step to the last wheel under the priestess's foot and receives two whips on either side of him before making it back to his pile. With all the cheese snatched, the priestess brings her hands together again, but not before the fallen man receives one last punishing sting. Pride wells up within me as Leander is chosen as the winner and allowed to present the cheeses to his goddess. The rowdy crowd cheers, and I try to make my way toward him in the chaotic crowd as the men wash their blood off in the river.

"Leander!" I cry, and I catch a quick glimpse from him as he climbs back out on the banks. He looks away, though, and assembles behind his leader who ties up his whip and lashes his chariot forward. The red tiger-striped backs of men disappear over the mountain as they leave their fallen disgrace back upon the steps; no one dares to help him. It will be a miracle if he makes it back to his men that night.

# Chapter 4

It's amazing what you cling to when you're given very little. Those moments in the barn and later in the darkness of our bedroom, I made a love story. I made his rare appearance, quick movements, and few words into a fantasy, yet every time was like the first. Since I'm pregnant, we're officially married, but we will not move in together until he turns thirty, when he'll be given a household by the military. The bigger my stomach grows, the less he wants to meet me, and after four meetings, he tells me to send notice when the baby arrives.

My mother had prepared me for this life. Spartan men belong to the state. They're sent away to school at seven, suffer agoge until twenty, live with their military group until thirty, and from thirty to sixty, they're at the beck and call of the military. If something comes up and the army needs reinforcements, they're forced to join until the campaign is over. However, I'm just as content to be in control and with Ophira.

At about nine months, I have a terrible dream:

*I hold a large melon, the size of a horse head. I drop it, and it splatters into many pieces. A huge pig comes at once to eat the melon, and I try to shoo the pig away. I'm protecting two seeds, but the pig pushes me over, eats the smaller seed, and then jumps off the cliff I'm standing on. I watch as it plummets down into the dark chasm squealing like a baby.*

I wake up crying and think for an instant I wet the bed. I feel my stomach tightening, and I call for Ophira.

She comes running. "I'll go get Leander."

But I yell to her as she opens the door to my bedroom. "No Ophira! Stay here!"

"He told me to fetch him at once." She stands there confused.

"I don't want them throwing my baby off a cliff!" I scream out, trying to breathe between pains that are worsening.

She closes the door, understanding. "We're going to get in trouble Alcina! Sparta's the only one who gets to decide who's fit or not."

I try to sit up. "I'll say I was outside in the fields, and the baby came so fast."

Ophira helps me get through hours of labor. She tells me to get on the floor and kneel while she supports me. Kneeling feels much better than the pressure my belly put on me. When I feel the urge to push, I push, not able to stop as I feel myself tear open. I can only scream as Ophira catches my squirming baby boy. She cleans him and lifts him up for me to see. Strong and so loud, he's every Spartan woman's dream. I know he'll pass the Spartan test for sure. I feel foolish now, realizing my dream was nonsense.

I start getting contractions again, and Ophira instructs, "Push the afterbirth," but she soon screams, "Another son!"

We're crying from the shock, and I use all the strength I have left to push off the bed to see the surprise in her hands.

My heart sinks.

He must be half the size of the firstborn. His color is poor, and he isn't making any noise, even after Ophira spanks him—no cry, only struggling fish-like gulps of air. We don't speak for a long time, and the air carries the metallic smell of blood. I stare on as Ophira cleans and bundles up each one. She puts the first-born baby in my arms; I name him Arcen. She drapes her cloak around her shoulders, cradles the second baby, and she comes over to get him.

I hold on to Arcen and say, "There must be something we can do?"

She speaks through her tears. "There's nothing we can do; it is your Spartan law!"

"Wait a moment, I have to think."

She hesitates but looks like she lost all hope.

I gasp and say, "Spartan mothers cannot raise a weak boy, but they care nothing of weak helot children!"

It takes one minute to register, and then her eyes widen in shock at the idea.

"You want *me* to be his mother?"

I nod with tears of joy.

"No, I don't even have a man. No one will believe this!" she says backing up as if she can walk away from this.

"Leander has not seen you in months. No one knows about you or if you have a husband away fighting. I bet no one will even ask."

I move back toward her and pull the blanket down to show the weak one's little face. She looks down at the fragile, pale baby who studies her face through its narrow swollen slits.

"Look at this child! How can you hand him over to be thrown against rocks! Rocks, Ophira!"

Her eyebrows pinch together under her scar. "How will I even feed this child?"

"I'll send for a wet nurse for Arcen, and I'll nurse this one in secret."

She looks again at him, smiles, and says through happy tears, "I will call you Theodon, god-given."

Ophira puts her cloak back on and readies to take Arcen to Leander. I give Arcen a parting kiss, knowing I'll see him again. Ophira fishes out her medallion and lifts it over her head and free of her long wavy hair.

She places it over Theodon's tiny head, and as she tucks it into his blanket, she whispers, "For protection and strength."

As they leave, I gaze out to the sun setting in a red sky and sit to nurse Theodon. When I look down at his tiny face, I know I already love him.

∞∞∞∞∞∞∞∞∞∞∞∞∞∞∞∞∞∞∞

Leander returns that night glowing and proclaims, "I held my son up for all to see, and the Lesche all said there has never been a stronger baby seen!"

My heart wells with pride. Leander has never talked this much for so long. Everything is blooming.

Leander hears another baby crying, and he looks at me, perplexed.

"That is Ophira's son. She gave birth a few weeks ago."

He cocks his head to the side. "Is she married?"

"Yes, her husband has been away fighting in the Citizens' Army for months."

I note to be sure to tell him of his death in battle soon.

"Well, I'm sure he is not anything like the son we have!" He holds Arcen up in the air, hardly supporting his rolling head. "Strong one!"

Leander goes back to his men, and a specialized helot comes to nurse Arcen. She takes over his care entirely. I miss much sleep sneaking in and out of Ophira's room nursing Theodon. Even though I'm tired, these moments of closeness in the dark with him are such peaceful moments; moments I lose with Arcen. Every respectable Spartan mother gets a wet nurse, but I can see there is something about nursing that attaches a baby so. I can tell Ophira resents how he seems to want me whenever she picks him up.

One day Ophira comes to me and says, "I think we should start giving Theodon brothed maza now."

"He is too young for food yet," I snap, a little too quickly.

"Alcina, do you want him to grow up and think of you as his mother? Because that's what will happen!"

I don't say anything.

"You need him to think of me as his mother, or we'll both get killed for this."

The words hang in the air for a stale moment until I hear its honesty. "I understand. We will start feeding him maza."

∞∞∞∞∞∞∞∞∞∞∞∞∞∞∞∞∞∞∞∞

The boys are in the field playing with the scattering grey-hounds, and I go call them in for dinner. A frail boy with freckles darts by.

I grab him by the arm and tickle him. "Come in for dinner. Where's Theodon?"

He points behind a tree and leaves to go clean up inside. I smile, seeing part of a sandal behind the tree trunk.

I tiptoe off to the tree and jump out. "Whaaaaa!"

Theodon screams and runs across the field with me in pursuit, his copper-colored hair shining and bouncing in the light. He's shirtless with a wrap around his waist, and even though he's only seven, he has the muscles of a ten-year-old. I finally catch him and roll on the ground with him. He throws his head back and giggles, showing the small space between his teeth I love so much. We sit down to sausages and hard-boiled eggs, our small family of four. Leander will come in for a few nights at a time, but this is the way we all liked it best. Today is a little sad, though, since it's our last day before sending Arcen away to agoge and I secretly hope it'll make him stronger. He seemed to wither as Theodon flourishes. Theodon wins every race, every match, and every game. Arcen doesn't excel at anything. I hope the severe conditions of agoge will give him the motivation to thrive. Maybe the heavy competition and relentless drills will give him strength. Maybe the deprivation of needs and starvation will make him hungry to steal and fight. I'm sure he has it in him to be strong. The worst thing a son can do is fail agoge or to be accused of cowardliness.

In the morning, I pack his bag with the scanty things they let him bring. Arcen sits on his straw mattress, fiddling with a piece of straw he plucked out, tears hitting his hands.

Pulling his chin in the air, I demand, "Spartan men do not cry!"

He begins a high-pitched whine and cries, "But I'm scared. I don't want to go."

I slap his face hard. "You're no longer a boy! Today you're a man, and you've had your last cry! Cry again and you'll be flogged for it!"

I grab his arm up and yank him through the house. Theodon's standing with Ophira outside the front door.

I take him by the shoulders and look into his wounded eyes. "You must listen to your commanders and be strong. Show no weakness. Make me and your father proud."

Arcen delicately reaches up for the bag, still sniveling, and drops it to his side as he walks off into the city alone. He tries to look brave by walking fast but ends up looking more pathetic with all the rocks he trips on. He looks back once when he reaches the apex of the hill and I can tell he's crying again. My shoulders drop and I turn to see beautiful Theodon standing there, watching his best friend go off to the place he so wishes he could go too.

∞∞∞∞∞∞∞∞∞∞∞∞∞∞∞∞∞∞∞∞∞∞∞

I become Theodon's best friend while Ophira is busy doing housework. Theodon follows me all over the farm watching me manage the helots. When all my work is done, he's standing there, holding our bows and arrows, ready to go boar hunting. He catches his first boar at nine. Everything he tries, he masters. Even though it's not customary to school your helots, I teach him all the reading and writing a Spartan citizen should know. I never expect him to work like a helot, and I can tell the others don't accept him for it.

One night, home after a long sea voyage, Nereus comes to visit for a dinner of black broth. I go out to greet him as he's pulling Zale with all his weight toward the stables. I throw an apple in the stables and the horse drags Nereus with him in pursuit. Theodon loves to hear his embellished stories of the perils of sea travel. Nereus will get louder and louder while the story climaxes, reaching the point where you can't even understand what he's saying as he rolls his head back and forth, his mouth wide open, laughing as he yells the best part.

However, you can see Theodon's green eyes glimmer. He yearns for one day when he might have such journeys beyond this farm. He laughs the hardest, though, when one of Nereus's inverted burps erupts mid-sentence, and he simply continues like nothing happened. Theodon will giggle until he can barely breathe. All throughout his stories, Nereus keeps dipping his bread in the blood broth but pushes his bowl with the back of his hand in front of Theodon. "My teeth just can't handle the pork any longer."

Theodon grabs the bowl eagerly as I bring a tray of dessert figs and a new jug of wine. Theodon takes a fistful of dried figs before Ophira decides it is time for him to go to bed, and I get a pang of jealousy, since she gets to tuck him in.

Nereus distracts me. "What I really came here for was to tell you unpleasant news about Arcen."

My heart drops; somehow I suspect what he's going to say. I open the seal on the terracotta jug and refill Nereus's kylix.

After I pour, he turns the jug to read the stamp, raises his eyebrows, and says, "Cretan wine?" Then he swallows happily before continuing. "I was in the city last night and spoke with one of the commanders of the agoge—a good friend of mine. When I asked about how my grandnephew was faring he turned to me and shook his head. He said he was the most picked on and ridiculed boy in the group. He causes the other boys to receive more punishment for his weaknesses, and they torture him for it. They deprive him of food, hoping he'll go and steal, but he's quickly wasting away. He's not going to make it if he doesn't get stronger."

A great shame comes over me. "What can I do, Uncle?"

He shrugs. "Too bad he's not like Ophira's boy. What a specimen! Shame he's a helot, though. What a waste," he says as he wipes his hands with barley bread and feeds it to the dogs.

# Chapter 5

Leander's army is sent to Thebes. I'm relieved not having to give him the news of Arcen, although he has probably heard through the army by now. I cringe to think what he'll do about it. The best parts of my day are spent with Theodon and Ophira. One unusually beautiful day, when the intensely blue sky is scattered with fat clouds by a warm caressing wind, we take our dinner down to the cliffs. Theodon and I decide to run down to the beach and go swimming. He shuffles his feet down the steep rock steps that lead to the sand.

I begin to run down after him but turn to a stalled Ophira. "Come on!"

She shakes her head. "I'm not running down these stairs; I'm too old for this."

"We're the same age you ninny." I run down a few more to show her how easy it is, but she shakes her head sternly.

She yells, "We don't all still look like you Alcina. If you had long hair, I swear nothing's changed since the day I met you." She chooses to walk down the safer path. "I'm going this way. I don't know why, but I feel like something is going to come and push me down those steps."

I scoff at her paranoia and try to catch up with Theodon, already halfway down.

We dive in after peeling our tunics off, leaving them to fall wherever on the scant, pebbled shore behind us. As we play in the crystal, waveless water, Theodon comes up behind me and pushes down on my shoulders, shoving me under. I have to throw him off to come up for air. We laugh and laugh with our heads bobbing in the deep, rolling tide. Then we scale back up the cliff, soaking wet, and Ophira starts dancing, pulling us up to join her. The three of us dance around the countryside together, delirious in our tiny world.

We straggle back into the house, laughing, and decide the night wouldn't be complete without a late-night dessert before retiring. As Ophira fetches some figs and cheeses, I bring out some wine. I lean over Theodon to fill his cup.

Theodon starts tapping his thumb on the table. "I wanted to talk to you, Mother."

Ophira turns, even though I want to, and she answers, "Yes, what is it?"

"I'm sixteen now, and Arcen's in agoge while I've nothing. I'm not working or living with the other helots, yet I'm one of them. I'm either going to join the Citizens' Army—"

I wince at the thought of the army Sparta uses as their shield in return for promised citizenship.

"—or live with the helots down in Laconia."

"You're not happy here with me and Alcina?"

He looks at me quickly as I sit down across the table from him. "I need to be around helots my own age."

This strikes fear in both Ophira's and my heart. He is our world. We don't need anyone else.

As soon as he leaves for bed, Ophira looks at me with shoulders shrugged. "He's growing up, and with that comes his independence. He can't stay with us forever on this farm. We're going to have to find some safe place for him."

∞∞∞∞∞∞∞∞∞∞∞∞∞∞∞∞∞∞∞∞∞∞

Sparta's armies are away so long that an elected magistrate of Sparta drives up to the house. Ophira and Theodon come running at the sight of the stately chariot. My thoughts jump first to Leander falling in battle, but then they heighten into the more likely fear of Arcen killed in agoge.

The ephor says at the sight of me, "Be calm, Mother, we have news sent by the kings." He holds his hands out to me. "Your husband and son are fine. This has to do with you and Sparta."

As soon as he walks into the house, he sniffs the air and with a thick grin asks, "Is that fresh bread I smell?"

With only a nod, Ophira fetches the ephor some bread, and we all sit down at my table in silence as he quickly stuffs in the bread, still steaming.

He finally explains, "Sparta's men have been away at war for years, and normally, our men come back at breaks to provide Sparta with children." He picks at one of his teeth and draws back to see what he found, obviously disinterested from continuous retelling. "But now there's no time for breaks. We're at war on every front, and the future of Sparta rests in our mothers' hands."

We wait for him to continue.

"Dire times are cause for dire actions, and the kings have instructed our Spartan women to go forth and procreate. Even half a Spartan is better than no Spartan at all. Our mothers must choose wisely. Pick the strongest, healthiest helot you can find."

He then eyes Theodon's powerful physique with his steel-grey eyes. "Any mother who does not procreate within the next six months will be fined heavily. By order of the kings." He bows his head to me, and on his way out, says to Theodon, "You're aware that the Citizens' Army takes full helots, aren't you?"

Theodon nods.

"And you know it is the only way you can win your freedom? No one else can grant you that, since you *belong* to Sparta." The ephor eyes me. "You fight in the army and you win full freedom and citizenship."

He turns and walks away, glancing back at Theodon's perfect form one more time.

Ophira and I look at each other and laugh. Later on, during our walk from the barn, Ophira points down to the helots working below and says, "How about that one?"

Then she grabs my arm and points to another one. "What about him? Ahhh," she cries out, "that's a nice one there scratching his backside!"

She giggles away as the swarthy helot digs his hand halfway into his pants, too far away to hear our peals of laughter. We fall over each other in fits. Theodon doesn't think it's so funny, and he walks back into the house without waiting for us.

∞∞∞∞∞∞∞∞∞∞∞∞∞∞∞∞∞∞∞∞∞∞

*I'm standing on my cliff, when the ground tremors just like it had so many years ago. I run for cover and watch as an old wind-beaten cypress splits in two. After the shaking ceases, a young child with strawberry-blonde hair emerges out of the torn trunk. She laughs like a nymph and claps her hand as I pick her up and spin her in the sea air.*

Waking up in the grey haze before the sun shows, I miss the child of my dream and wonder if this was the result of the ephor's visit. I realize I do have to take the order seriously, though, since they'll fine us heavily and Leander would want me to comply. I go out for an early walk alone to try to see if any of my helots are in satisfactory condition as the sun begins to retrieve the night's dew. I fold my arms up under my chin and lean against the fence overlooking the work fields, when Theodon comes up next to me. The barley is blowing in the wind coming off the sea, carrying with it smells of the newly fertilized field. A piece of my hair blows across my eyes, and he reaches up, sticks it behind my ear, and looks back down with a smile.

He clears his throat. "The helots who work for you are a worthless bunch, all of them drunkards. They drink unmixed wine as soon as they get home and drink until they stagger back here in the morning. Not a one fit for you, if that's what you're up here thinking."

I realize he's right. There isn't one with good qualities.

He looks out onto the fields instead of at me, with his hand nervously perched on the edge of his lips. "I know I'm young"— putting his arm down, he directs his beautiful, shining green eyes at me—"but I don't look helot at all."

I turn away immediately, not at all expecting him to say what he did.

"Look at me. Look at me, Alcina." He grabs both of my shoulders and forces me to look at him. "No one knows you better than me."

I look down, not knowing how I can turn him away.

"I don't want to be with anyone else."

"Theodon, this can *never* happen."

I put my hand up, wanting to avoid this embarrassment, but he pulls it down; an unfamiliar fire flashes in his eyes.

"I know that's not possible, but at least give me this. Instead of some useless stranger! I will stay if you will grant this. I would stay here forever."

*How could this happen? What can I say?*

He exhales purposely and tenses his jaw as he states, "I know you care about me too."

I pull away from him, but he steps toward me. "Why else would you take all this special interest in me? All of the other helots see how different you treat me. How you have never made me lift a finger on this farm."

He takes another step closer, and I can feel his breath on my neck.

He whispers, "I can see that you love me when you look in my eyes."

*How can this be happening!*

He tries to catch my eyes, but I avert them now. I can't think of anything to say that will make this all go away. He reaches down to hug me like he has so many times before, but now it feels under a different intent. I push him away and run out to my cliffs, hoping he won't follow me, hoping I'll think of something that will make this all disappear.

That night I come back home after he's asleep, and Ophira's waiting up for me.

She asks, "What happened?"

I explain what occurred, and she holds her hand to her mouth the whole time in horror at the predicament. Something horribly twisted, yet she understands completely.

She says, "We need to send him away at once to start his own life."

We both nod and cry.

# Chapter 6

The next day, I call for a boy to bring me Proauga. Even though she's my oldest horse, she's still hardy and fast enough. I ride her like I did so many times when I was young, over my cliffs and down to Nereus's by the harbor.

He hears me gallop up and is leaning in his doorway. "Oh, to what do I owe this honor?"

I hop off and tie her reins to a small tree by the house. "I need to look at your helots."

He smiles immediately. "I've heard of the order." He purses up his lips as though he's up to something. "You're more than welcome to my helots, although I don't think any of them are as fine as Theodon there."

I cringe.

"He's not so young. That should not sway you. He can do the job at seventeen." He looks up to the sky. "Oh, to be seventeen again."

"No, Theodon is entirely out of the question. I'm practically his mother," I say, wishing I can take practically out so he will stop this conversation.

"I see, all right, fine, then. My helots are your helots."

With a smile, he sweeps his hand across the field to show me all of them working below.

"Is there one or two that stand out?" Squinting, I try to discern them from our distance.

He looks down. "Well, if I was, say, interested in men"—he looks back up, straight in my eyes—"which I'm most certainly not, I would have to say there is one fine helot who's going to be joining up next month with the Citizens' Army. Very Spartan-like."

"Which one is he?" I say with my hand over my eyes to block the glare.

Nereus points to a tall man with broad shoulders as he heaves a bale of hay onto a cart. He is nice-looking and does have a pleasing shape.

"How's his temperament?"

"A good worker and never causes any trouble."

"Do you mind sending him up to the farm tonight, so I can talk to him and see if he would agree?"

Nereus smiles wickedly, and I know this is too much fun for him. "I'll do what I can."

Part of me is nervous he'll wreck the whole thing, but it's my only option. I get back on Proauga and ride back home. I pass right by Theodon on his horse, and I stop, hoping he'll talk to me, but he keeps riding with his gaze fixed in front of him.

I tell Ophira all about the helot, and she laughs. "Maybe I can do my part for Sparta too!"

She does a provocative little dance right as the helot rides his horse up. I make a face at her, and she almost drops the chicken she just cooked. Shooing her back into the kitchen, I go out to meet him. I thought he was tall in the fields, but now I see he's towering.

"What's your name?" I ask.

"Demetrius," he says with a nervous little bow of his head as he removes his dog-skin cap, releasing waves of dark brown hair.

This is a mistake. How is somebody supposed to make something like this happen? I decide to give up on the idea and simply get through dinner.

"My name is Alcina."

I gesture for him to come inside and notice he has to duck under the low doorways. Once he is seated at the table, I offer him a bowl of olives to start, and he removes a few with his well-washed hands. After I pour him some wine, he starts feeling more comfortable and looks up, exposing his beautiful, grey-blue eyes.

Ophira tries to make conversation lighthearted after she's set down the chicken, goat cheese, and vegetables and asks, "Does Nereus bless you with all his stories of sailing the high seas?"

He relaxes at this. "He follows all of us around, and it has gotten so that we came up with a rooster call"—he demonstrates with gumption—"and we all run and hide." We all laugh, and he keeps going, "And whenever we see he has someone trapped, another will pretend to need the captive's help to release him, though it backfires since Nereus usually volunteers too." As if suddenly remembering I'm not a helot, he swiftly says, "But he treats us very well."

Ophira switches the subject as she gets up to serve us both. "Do you live with family?"

I tense at the question. If he speaks of a wife and children, I'll have to say goodnight to him there.

He shakes his head. "I stay with friends." He looks up from his plate. "I've nothing to worry about when I leave for the army."

"Why are you going to take your chances on Sparta's front-line?" I ask.

He connects with my eyes. "There is nothing better to die for than the freedom of your future children."

With this answer, Ophira gives me a subtle nod of approval, and I say, "That is a good reason."

Ophira and I both think of Theodon.

Just then, Theodon walks in and looks Demetrius up and down across the table. Demetrius seems confused, as if he's wondering if I'm testing a couple of helots out for the job.

"Demetrius this is Theodon. Theodon this is—" I try.

"A helot. I get it."

Ophira gives him a full plate. He looks down and starts shoving the food in his mouth as fast as he can so he can leave the table.

"Theodon is Ophira's son," I say as I place a bowl of grilled chestnuts and pomegranates before Demetrius.

Demetrius looks relieved and takes a piece of pomegranate to his mouth. He asks Theodon, "Are you joining up also?"

Theodon glances up with a dead stare at Demetrius. "For the Citizens' Army or for her?"

After an uncomfortable pause, a confused Demetrius clarifies, "The army."

Theodon glares at me. "I probably will."

"Do you live in Laconia?" Demetrius asks, his lips turning crimson from the rubied seeds.

Theodon shoots back quickly, "Do you work for Nereus?"

Demetrius nods, probably wondering why he's asking, and Theodon drops his fork, grabs a handful of chestnuts right in front of Demetrius, and leaves the table.

Silence clouds the room.

"I should go now." Demetrius stands with his hat in hands. "Alcina, can I talk with you outside?"

We walk outside. The stars are out in glorious numbers. I hold my arms, unprepared for the early fall chill.

He stands in front of me. "Nereus told me about what you need, and I'd be glad to help."

I'm surprised he's so forward. He seemed so quiet at the table.

"I need to think about it a little more, but thank you for offering your... service."

He nods, replaces his hat, and mounts Zale—handling her much better than Nereus could. He gallops away, and I wonder if I'll actually see him again.

∞∞∞∞∞∞∞∞∞∞∞∞∞∞∞∞∞∞∞∞∞

The next morning, I wake to Ophira screaming for me. I run outside to see Theodon throwing all sorts of things into our cart with his horse attached. He glares at me and continues to stack things.

"He's leaving! He's leaving for Laconia!" Ophira cries hysterically. She looks at me like I can do something, then turns to yell at Theodon, "You can't go out there by yourself. The fall is when they have krypteia! Spartan soldiers kill helots without repercussion! They always attack the strongest helots!"

"Well, Demetrius seems to be much more preferred by Spartans, so I'm safely inferior," Theodon directs at me.

"Alcina! Tell him he can't take your things! Tell him he can't take your cart!" Ophira desperately pleads.

Theodon pauses, testing me if I'll assert this power for the first time in his life.

"I won't tell him not to take the cart, Ophira." She covers her face in her hands as I continue, "But Theodon, don't you think it would be better to go after the fall when the ceremony is over?"

"Stop telling me what to do! I'm a grown man. I'm not your lapdog. I can take care of myself, and I'll be fine. I will be more than fine!"

I hold Ophira back and say, "If it's your wish to go, then please take everything you need from the stock house." Ophira continues to cry. "Make sure you bring the hunting knife and spears to protect yourself."

"As if you care."

He walks over to Ophira and takes away the hands covering her face.

He wipes her tears with his sleeve and whispers, "Do not worry. I have everything I'll need. I will be fine. I love you."

Ophira reaches to pull off her medallion, but Theodon shakes his head. "I don't need it anymore, you keep it."

He kisses her forehead, and she finds her hands again to fill with tears. We lock eyes, and neither of us speaks. The words I have for so long kept from him are dancing on my tongue. He leans forward to kiss my cheek but changes direction at the last moment to leave a quick kiss on my lips. He turns and steps up on the cart and tells the horse to go.

As he rolls out, he shouts back, "I will be back after I'm settled."

Ophira crumples to her knees.

# Chapter 7

A few days later, due to the sadness and emptiness in the house, I realize I must have another child. If Leander had been home years ago, I could've had another son by now, one who would've filled my time and made me proud. I send word through a helot to Demetrius to meet me at the top of the cliff that night. I ride Proauga out and watch the sun go down. Darkness falls all around me; I lie down on a wide, woolen blanket and wait.

I hear gravel footsteps, and I realize he must not have ridden. By the time I stand, he's right behind me. I freeze, and without a word, he begins to touch my hair. I'm relieved I won't have to suffer through the beginning awkwardness. He starts touching the back of my neck with his hand, brushes aside my hair, and kisses my neck. He continues to explore carefully, then lays me down on the blanket. I'm in heaven under the stars.

I tell Ophira all about the night as she's weaving in the bright light of the morning sun. She says, "Maybe I should head down to Nereus's farm and see what he has there for me!"

I grin. "It just might be worth your while."

"When are you going to see him again?"

"As soon as I possibly can."

Laughter rings again through our empty house.

Over the next three weeks, I meet Demetrius every night. His last night, I fight back useless tears since I know he's leaving and I will never see him again. Spartans are never supposed to have such silly attachments anyway.

Lying next to me under the thick, woolen blanket under cool, fall stars, he reaches out to pluck one of the last hardy wildflowers left in the fading field. "These wildflowers are so beautiful and appear so fragile, but see how well they survive the frosts and keep coming up with the sunshine." He tucks it into my hair with a steady, warm hand.

I brush a weak tear away quickly as he pulls his coarse tunic over his head before he turns back to me.

In his most cheerful voice, he tries, "Look on the bright side—if you aren't with child, you'll get to hand-pick another fine helot."

I hit his arm, angry he would joke about such things.

He stands up and brushes himself off. "It was the happiest three weeks I've ever had." He kisses my forehead. "Either I'll die happy or I'll come back to claim you."

He removes the worn dog-skin hat and crowns my head with it, then, with a sad smile and glistening eyes, he turns and walks out of my life.

∞∞∞∞∞∞∞∞∞∞∞∞∞∞∞∞∞∞∞∞∞

Three weeks later, I'm getting sick, ecstatic I'm going to have a child. The sadness of Theodon and Demetrius disappears to be replaced by new hopeful thoughts. Theodon comes back at this time and gives a weak, "Congratulations" when Ophira tells him of my news. It's great to have him back, but he's different—unhappy and distant. Before he leaves, he tells us he won't be coming back for months, since it's a dangerous time to travel with krypteia coming. Ophira hugs him, and he leaves on his horse.

Two weeks later, Nereus is banging on our door. We run out to see Arcen, bloodied and bruised in the back of Nereus's cart.

Nereus steps off the cart and wipes his brow. "That old friend of mine in agoge brought him to me. Said he found him by the road like this and thought we should take care of him before the agoge boys got to him." Nereus gives me a serious look. "For him to lose like this is a disgrace punishable by death or exile."

"Please thank your friend for me."

Ophira and I carry him in while Nereus ties up the horse. Ophira gathers everything we'll need to try to fix him and lays him down on his old mattress. He's gotten so much taller since the last time we'd seen him, but his growth has stretched his already frail flesh thinner. We do what we can and go to bed. It takes two days before he can speak to us.

As we're feeding him chicken broth, he tells us what happened. "I was sent out for krypteia with nothing but my cloak. I had to steal everything I needed or find it in the wilderness. I was alone, with no one else to help me."

I turn my eyes away as he breaks down in sniveling tears.

Ophira hands him a piece of cloth to wipe his nose, and he continues, "I couldn't come back until I killed a helot. I knew I had to prove myself, knew I could finally make them respect me. That's when I saw him—this big, strong helot walking down the road alone at night. I grabbed a stick, snuck up, and clubbed him on the back of the head. He fell, and I hurried to strangle him before others could come to help him. As I was choking him, I saw it was Theodon."

Ophira's hands fly to her mouth and stomach.

A wave of fear sweeps through me, and I grab him by his scrawny shoulders. "What did you do, Arcen! Tell me what you did!"

He winces in pain and cries out, "Of course I stopped! But he went mad, started punching and hitting me like I'd known it was him! I didn't even get a chance to explain to him!"

Ophira starts crying as I put my hands to my head. "Was he hurt?" I ask.

"Oh, you would care about him first! I'm your son, but whom are you concerned with? The helot boy!"

Ophira flees the room as I stand above him and say in a low tone, "You're lucky you're so badly damaged, son, because if you were not, I would beat you until you realized how disrespectful you are."

I walk out, and neither of us checks on him the rest of the day.

Nereus returns a week later at night and says he has to sneak Arcen back into Laconia as agoge reassembles. I go in to fetch Arcen, who still lies in his bed.

"I'm not going back," he says, arms crossed.

I expect this. "You're going back."

"I can't go back. You don't even know the hell I've been through since you sent me away. They starve you. Freeze you. Beat you and have all the other boys beat you! I'm not like them. I'm not good at this!"

I grab his cloak and whip it at him. "Arcen, you're a Spartan. There is no choice for a Spartan! You can't learn a trade or be a philosopher. It is not allowed in Sparta. There is nothing else!" I stand right in front of him. "Stand up, go back, and finish agoge. Once you get into the army, it'll be much easier. They're hard on you to make you stronger. You're almost through. You must finish!"

He grasps his cloak and bunches it up in idle hands. "If I go back without killing a helot, they will not pass me."

"Nonsense. Go back, tell them you fought, and you don't know if the slave was killed since two helots came to his defense and took him away."

A smile breaks across his face like it just might work. I feel so disgusted he's mine.

"Now come. Nereus will take you back under the cover of darkness, and please, whatever you do, stay away from Theodon! Don't fight anyone! Focus on feeding yourself."

I stick a whole loaf of bread under his arm. I kiss him, and he's gone.

# Chapter 8

It's months before we hear from anyone again. Nereus stops by one evening and with a big smile. "You will be happy to know Arcen graduated agoge today."

Ophira lets out a little scream, hugs me, and I sicken at the thought I should be so relieved my son didn't run back home.

Nereus continues, "They wasted no time in sending them out as reinforcements to Leander's army."

Thinking of Leander seeing Arcen in action makes me wring my hands. Regardless, we had a celebratory feast that night with wine, listened to Nereus's stories, and enjoyed every word and peal of laughter. I start in labor on a summer day. I ask Ophira to help me outside and up to the cliff since I had my heart set on the baby being born up there among Demetrius's wildflowers. This time we don't worry if we shall call anyone because Leander is away and this baby won't be examined since it's a mothax. I labor more quickly this time, and when it's time to push, I look out over the cliffs and hope this baby will be blessed. Ophira holds her up for me to see; she's thick and strong. She has a full head of strawberry-blonde hair, pomegranate-red lips, and a peculiar mark above her right knee, but it only endears her to me more. I name her Kali and having her to take care of fills our days. She makes every day wonderful. She walks early and is running before her birthday comes around again. Theodon comes a few times to see her and is slow in giving her attention at first, but soon realizes she's irresistible. Theodon visits one day, especially to spend time with her, and is here when we see a few carts and horses coming up our road.

I scream inside.

Leander, dressed in full armor, is on his way back. Legs hang off the back of his cart. I rush down the hill to them so fast it's hard to stop. There is Arcen, lying upon his embossed shield, dead. I start crying; Ophira catches up and holds me.

Leander gets off and nods to me. "Don't waste your tears. He died a coward."

With that, he rolls Arcen over to show five broken arrows in his back.

*He was shot while running away.*

"Oh no, oh no, oh no."

This is great shame to a family. Leander and I will be disgraced and Kali might not even be able to marry now. There's nothing so vile as a coward in Sparta; a leper's more welcome at a ceremony. To be the mother of a coward is like death. Ophira pulls me up the hill and I can see Leander up ahead hesitating at Theodon.

He shouts down to me, grabbing Theodon's thick shoulder. "You see this! This is what a real son looks like! This is something a man like me should have! I would've been better off breeding with this helot!" He points despairingly toward Ophira.

I can't take it anymore and burst out, "No need for that! Theodon *is* yours! He's both of ours! He was born Arcen's twin! He came from my womb! I nursed him for a year!"

Leander looks shocked at first and then amused. "Is this true, Ophira, or is she losing her mind?"

Ophira lets go of me in anger, turns to me, and says, "Of course she's losing her mind. What else will jealousy and a cowardly dead son do?"

I look at Theodon, who seems so utterly confused. Ophira goes up to him and whispers something in his ear, rubs his shoulder, and takes him to his horse. I can't believe Ophira took this from me. Leander walks up to Kali, who is tottering around sweetly, mindless of what's occurring in front of her.

He shouts, "And once this mothax turns ten, we're sending her away!"

His angry voice now scares her, and she comes running to me. I hold her tight as I cry in her hair and watch Arcen's dead body lie still.

∞∞∞∞∞∞∞∞∞∞∞∞∞∞∞∞∞∞∞∞∞∞∞

Other than commands and nods, Ophira and I stop talking. Though she still works for me, it's amazing how little we have to communicate. I understand why she had to deny my confession for both our sakes, but we still cannot repair the disconnect I caused. I find out through Nereus that Theodon has finally joined the Citizens' Army. Nereus says he's already winning great acclaim and respect. All Ophira and I have is Kali, and we enjoy her separately. She's torn between us, but it becomes normal for her. Leander leaves for war again as soon as Arcen is buried: not in a hero's grave, but a regular civilian's grave, given his cowardice.

A few months later, Nereus is found dead in his sleep by one of his household helots. We place him in his boat and send him adrift with his sails flying—to finally float indefinitely. I keep the knife he gave me on me daily, still wrapped in my sandal straps in memory of him. His household is passed down to me, his only surviving relative. I now am in charge of three households, an almost unheard of feat.

We watch Kali grow, and her looks start to change. Her nose becomes slightly eagle-shaped, and her lips lose their deep color. Her hair is wispy, and her shape is long and lanky. I'd hoped her beauty would attract a man who would overlook her mixed breeding, but now I see her fading. Every week, I get in my cart and force Kali to come with me to the oracle of Helen where we pray for Helen to bestow her beauty on her. Each time, we make our way to the temple on the mountaintop, past the statues lining the steep path, and climb the stairs to the columned circle. The air is hard to breathe so high up; I nearly faint when I bow before the oracle. I hold Kali's hand as we recite our prayer, and when she drinks from the temple spring, I notice Ophira has given Kali her powerful medallion to wear. We do this for a year, and sure enough, she blossoms once again. Her muscle tone builds up to give her curves where there were none; her hair turns a bright strawberry-blonde, flowing thickly over her shoulders, and her eyes flash unusual amber.

She's not allowed to go to the festivals, being a mothax, but every time I go into the city, I bring her with me to be seen. I see how all of the men and women notice her. I watch from the house as Ophira teaches her to dance in the fields below. Kali's almost as graceful as she is; they look like two sirens flittering between the bushes and trees. I worry every day that passes is one day closer to her being sent away. I pray to Hades to take Leander's life. I think if he never comes back, no one will know she is still with me. Leander survives, to my regret. He comes home again up the dirt road on his warhorse. He aged, though, much older than my forty-five years. War took a toll on him, and he's walking stiffer and slower for it.

He comes into the house without even acknowledging me, throws down his feathered helmet, and declares, "I have decided to wife-share with Nicholas. She has produced four fine sons, all fine specimens, all excelling in agoge even though they're still young. He's agreed to share her as long as I promise my household to the future child, and I'm agreeing to this."

I was expecting this one day and am ready for it. "If you are asking me for my permission, you can have it, but there is a price."

He looks curious but wary. "What price?"

"Kali can stay, and when it comes time, I get to decide who I leave *my* households to." He nods in agreement, but I continue, "You will also live in your house until you're dead, and then you can give it to whomever you want."

Even though it's beneficial for a woman to own three households, it's important only if you have someone to give them to. Kali's all I have left, and she can own a household only through marriage. He picks up his helmet, walks out to his horse, and rides out on my dirt road for the last time. Neither of us even cared enough to say good-bye. I feel free from the worry of Leander sending Kali away. Ophira seems to understand what happened after Leander never comes back, even though she knows the army has returned. She seems a little happier too.

It catches us off guard when the ephor returns with a horse, cart, and six soldiers.

I ask, "What brings you here?"

"We have come to collect the mothax," the ephor calls out.

"There is no mothax in our house."

"It's written here and signed by your mark that you birthed a child of Spartan-helot descent. Is this not your mark?"

"Yes it is, but that child perished."

He must have heard this before upon collecting, since he retorts, "We have searched the records before we were sent here."

Unfortunately, Kali runs up to us at this time.

"I presume this is the child." He reads his orders. "Female, age ten."

"This is my helot's child," I say, hoping Ophira will play along again.

"Is that true?" he asks Ophira.

Ophira does not hesitate. "She's my child."

"Every helot born has to be recorded as state property."

"She has a record." Ophira's at least buying us time. He looks suspicious but knows he has to have proof before removing her.

"I'll be back if I find no ten-year-old, female, full helot bound to this residence."

"Ephor!" I call out, "Where are you sending the mothakes?"

He smiles suspiciously. "The kings have been generous enough to grant them their own colony of Tarentum. They'll be able to live amongst their own kind. It's what is best for them."

Kali jumps into Ophira's arms when he leaves, and Ophira says, "We'll never let them take you."

Ophira looks at me and, for the first time in a long while, speaks to me directly. "How much time do we have?"

"I don't know, a week?"

Ophira gives Kali a push. "We need to talk. Go play."

Kali, looking thrilled we're talking to each other, runs off.

"Alcina, we could send her to live amongst the helots."

I consider this. "But the only helot we trust is in the Citizens' Army. Can she be left at ten to fend for herself?"

"I could always take her and get another home to work in."

"That means you'd have to bring her with you, and they would want her full helot papers, which we don't have."

Ophira shakes her head. "She is too young to marry."

"We might have no choice."

We both sit down in frustrated silence.

∞∞∞∞∞∞∞∞∞∞∞∞∞∞∞∞∞∞∞∞∞∞

A week later, the ephor's back, looking greatly displeased. We've prepared her for this day and where she'll be going. She must have been scared, but she didn't want us to feel guilty.

She even says in her cheerful voice, "This will be good for me. I can't wait to be with people my own age."

We pack her bags, hug her, and I tell her, "You will come back. This is your home, and we'll send for you as soon as we can." I take out the dog-skin cap I'd been saving and place it on her small head. "This was your father's."

That causes a lone tear to stream down her cheek, but she sucks back any others. "I'll be fine. I love you, Mother." She gives me another hug and turns. "I love you, Ophira."

Ophira's a mess of tears. Kali gets onto the cart stoically, waves to us with a gleaming smile, grasping her bag. When she disappears down the hill, I turn to Ophira, and we cry in each other's arms.

# Chapter 9

Months later, one of my more loyal helots comes yelling, "An enemy's invading Sparta!"

Ophira rushes with me over the mountains and into the city to hear more on the situation. The same steel-eyed ephor who took Kali away is standing in the middle of the square. Women, children, and old men are gathered, desperate for news. The rest of the normally crowded city streets are deserted—the calm before the storm.

"This is an emergency," the ephor shouts to the worried crowd. The marble statue of King Leonidas looms above. "The majority of our army is engaged in Crete. Pyrrhus has taken this vulnerable time to attack. It'll take days for reinforcements to get here. The only defense we have is the Citizens' Army and agoge. We have merely slaves, young men, and boys to rely on now." The crowd surges, but the ephor screams louder, "Sparta's sending all of its women and children to refuge in Crete."

Furious uproar rolls over the crowd.

A woman among us stands up and shouts, "Don't let them take us away! So we survive? We'll have nothing to come back to!"

Everyone cheers and rallies behind her.

I call out, "Spartan women! If we send our sons off to die for Sparta, then we must stay and die for Sparta too!"

Ophira stands up with me in the pulsing crowd, fists hammering toward the sky in unyielding patriotism.

The ephor gets up to speak again. "Our brave women of Sparta, we should have known you would not be taken from your city! Let us all stand together and fight!"

We watch the Citizens' Army march into the center square in their thinner, simpler armor. Theodon walks beside important leaders in the front. He nods slightly in our direction but stands stoically at the arm of his commander.

His leader speaks. "Women of Sparta, we commend you for your allegiance. The enemy is fast approaching with numbers tripling the forces we have at our disposal. With no fortifications we need to dig deep trenches immediately, all around the city entrances to keep their elephants at bay."

"Elephants?" Ophira looks at me anxiously.

I stand up again and yell, "To our spades!"

The crowd pours like a flooded river out of the square and to the large cart full of shovels. Each woman picks one up and breaks into groups to dig trenches outside the city.

Ophira and I dig all day beside Theodon's army, ignoring throbbing, bleeding blisters. When night falls, a woman from our group stands up and shouts, "All soldiers go home! Put down your spades and give them to your mothers. We'll dig so you can rest and give your all for our country tomorrow!"

The women cheer, and the leader of their group bows low to us and takes his troops back inside the city. Theodon breaks formation to turn around and give us a worried nod before another soldier pulls him back by his chest strap. We continue through-out the night with staked torches as our only light.

The sun rises in a vibrant, red haze, and we can see thousands of little shadows assembling on the mountains surrounding Sparta.

Someone shouts, "Mothers find safety within the city!" as trumpets give forlorn warning.

Filthy and stiff from exhaustion, Ophira and I hobble back with them. The women are corralled into the stately assembly building above the square. We arm ourselves with whatever we can gather: shovels, pitchforks, sickles. Some women wear ropes cinched around their necks because they'll rather hang than be taken captive. Our building is three stories tall and set high in the city, giving us a good vantage point. We all huddle at the windows and watch with mouths agape as the enemy assembles into tight, well-disciplined formation. Ophira finds her medal-lion, brings it to her lips, and clutches my hand as she chants something I don't understand. I pray that the Athenians will stay their distance, and every woman jumps back when the sea of men begins to surge forward toward Sparta. Knowing we have nowhere to run, I take Ophira's shaking hand and bring her back to the window. Far off, roaring forward, come the horrid, gigan-tic beasts called elephants leading the charge. They're like noth-ing we've ever seen before. Ophira shuts her eyes tight and brings her hands to her mouth in more whispered prayers.

I'm scared for Theodon and for Sparta. Every time the enemy moves to approach the city, Sparta sends out troops to push them back. Some of their men put down their spears and rush to fill the trenches in segments so that the elephants can cross, all the while under a deluge of spears and arrows from the roofs of the single-story city dwellings walling in the city. As each enemy falls into the trenches, their comrades carelessly shovel dirt on top of them. Once the elephants gain passage, the enemy looms along the perimeter of the city, testing every entrance. Inside the city, our stone streets are filled with soldiers and boys running to their commands. It's amazing that in so much chaos, control is still being kept. Many loyal helots step forward with farm tools in vast numbers to defend the city. We have to buy Sparta time.

An impressive phalanx formation of red-cloaked hoplites, the only regiment left behind to protect the city, marches right outside the square. They look ethereal with their feathered, beak-faced helmets and bronze body armor—like beautiful, deadly birds. Spear and shield expertly positioned, they go out to repel a heavy attack. We can't see the elephants but can hear them, right outside the fortress of our city. They sound like I've always imagined the sea monsters in Nereus's tales, echoing a thundering horn blow. I hope we'll never see one up close, that they will not be let into the city.

Later, we wait, sitting on the floor, listening to the battle in the background, when we hear the men shouting especially loud. We rush to the window to see, to our horror, ten elephants have broken into one of the side streets and are charging down to the square. Ophira clutches on to me in terror.

My imagination can't have created such a creature. It's the height of three men and the weight of ten horses. White horns which the enemy has tipped with iron protrude out of its face, and a long snake-like appendage curls and twists as it charges. On its head are huge, flapping pieces of flesh that move like wings! These elephants trample over any men standing in their way. Spears are thrown at them, yet they bounce off their thick skins. The beasts thrash their horned heads back and forth, throwing men against stone buildings. Worse yet, they grab men with their snakes and throw them against the ground, then squash them with their giant heads.

Half the men go running from them, while the other half courageously stays to either stab the beasts or perish. The elephants start to fall in massive heaps in the streets. One of them goes through a wall, causing a whole building to collapse upon it. Once an elephant falls, the soldiers pounce on the elephant handler in rage. Each remaining elephant is led off in different directions. All goes quiet as they disappear. The women are silent at the horror of what they witnessed. I have a new understanding of how terrified Arcen must have been in battle. I could never have dreamed of these kinds of atrocities and total disregard for life. We hear men running down to the square and see six Citizens' Army men turning around at a familiar voice.

Theodon calls to them, "Stop running! I order you to face this beast together! It's our only chance!"

They gather and steady for the command to throw their spears. The elephant comes into view and speeds right toward the cluster. I spring up, pull away from Ophira's tight hold, and run out the door with Nereus's knife in hand. I stand on the steps of the building as the men release their spears and dash out of the way to every direction. I watch as the furious beast turns around and charges at two of the men, crushing one under its feet and throwing the other with its tusks. I gasp as Theodon catches the elephant's back leg with a rope, stands on it, and sticks his spear into its flank as it turns on him. The beast tries to get away, but Theodon pulls the spear back out, runs around to the other side, and thrusts it in its flank with an earth-shaking death cry. He steps back as the elephant staggers and falls onto the statue of Leonidas, tipping it over and shattering the hero king into meaningless pieces.

My eyes well up with pride as I look upon the baby who was once too weak to cry.

Satisfied he's safe, I start back up the stairs but halt when I hear another trumpeting. I turn to see a different beast coming down the other direction, handlerless and out of control. It has a spear stuck deep in its flank, painting its stone-skin with blood. Theodon has little time to react but manages to raise his shield in front of him as the elephant tosses him against the building. I fly down the steps with Nereus's knife raised, hoping I can get there in time to protect him. Theodon lays motionless as the beast steps back to charge forward with its head down, intent on crushing him. I hit its head at full speed and stab into the spongy flesh of the snake. The elephant reels back trumpeting, shakes its massive head, and throws me. I hit the ground so hard I hear my bones crack on impact. I can't move. I can only watch as Theodon struggles with the beast, spearing it, and hear its thunderous fall.

"Mother!" he screams, rushing to my side. "Are you hurt?"

I try to move but can't, for the pain is unbearable. I lie back down but realize what he said.

"Mother?" I gasp.

"Ophira told me. She came to me weeks ago." He then laughs slightly. "And only a mother would fight an elephant like that."

He tries to lift me up in his arms, but I wince at the pain of the movement.

"Put me down. Leave me here."

He places his shield under me, lays me gently back down, and his voice begins to crack. "I should've come to you, but I was so ashamed—"

I interrupt. "I'm proud of you and who you've become. I only gave you to Ophira to save you."

He nods. Tears escape down his tan cheeks as he kisses my head. "Rest now. Someone will come, and we'll move you back in with the women."

He removes his cloak and bundles it under my head.

But, tasting the blood in my mouth, already I know I don't have much time. I cough weakly, registering sharp pain at doing so.

"You must promise me something, Theodon."

"Anything."

"You must go and bring back Kali before she marries. Bring her back and marry her."

He looks confused. "She's my sister?"

"Yes, but no one else knows. You must marry her once you're granted citizenship so she can own one of my houses. You can both marry others after, but take care of your sister."

He thinks about it for a moment. "I promise."

"Tell Ophira I'm sorry, and tell Kali I love her." I cough more through the pain; it's getting so hard to breathe. "And I love you, Theodon I always have."

I can hear his tears now.

"Don't go," he whispers.

I shut my eyes to rest.

| Beacons | Life 1 Eygpt | Life 2 Sparta |
|---|---|---|
| Mole on left hand--Prophetic dreams | Sokaris | Alcina |
| Scar on forehead--Large, honey-brown eyes--Magic | Bastet | Ophira |
| Space between teeth--Green sparkling eyes | Nun | Theodon |
| Mole by wide-set--Dark eyes | Nebu | Mother |
| Freckles--Brown eyes | Khons | Arcen |
| Birthmark above knee-Amber eyes | Edjo | Kali |
| Two moles on jaw--Black eyes | Apep | Leander |
| Picks teeth--Steel-grey eyes | Vizier | Magistrate |
| Golden eyes--Animal | Sehket-Cat | Proauga-Horse |
| Scar on forearm-- Slate-blue eyes | * | Nereus |
| Big Smile--Grey-blue eyes | * | Demetrius |

* = Not present in that life

# Third Life
# Pirates of the North

# Chapter 1

"What a wonderful wee man, Liam!" my mother says over my shoulder.

"It's me and you and Da," I say, finishing up the last, much larger figure, my tongue half out in concentration.

I scribble away in the dirt on the floor before the hearth where my mother is baking bread for the week. The whole room smells of warm yeast.

"I better not be the giant one," my mother jokes as she cradles her hands around her enormous belly.

My father, walking behind me, stoops to tousle my hair. I swat at him with my stick playfully, but he snatches and breaks it over his leg. He laughs as he throws it in the fire.

"I was making pictures with that!" I cry.

He brings his steel-grey eyes close. "Then you can go pick another fine one when you gather more kindling for your enormous ma there."

She pretends to be offended. "Well, lucky for you both, I won't be getting any bigger. I've been getting sure signs this baby's well on its way."

"Make sure to get to the old midwife, then." He smiles and pats her on her backside as he strides out the door. I run out, trying to help him gather his fishing net. He pushes me aside and says, "Stop that now. You'll get your wee feet tangled." He throws the net behind his back. "Mind your ma and fetch her wood."

I watch him take large steps down to the lough, where the faded wooden fishing boats wait for him. As soon as he is out of sight, I go behind the house and start cracking and bunching sticks.

"Come, Liam, and eat your breakfast!" Ma calls out from the door. I hurry in with my sticks, some falling out along the way, and when I bend over to pick those up, more fall. Once inside, I throw them in the wide basket and look at my plate. The fresh butter is dripping off the steaming bread.

I stuff my mouth as I watch her knead some risen dough, punching it hard with her fists. My gaze drifts out the open, blue-shuttered window to the clear sky, and I hear children playing and screaming. I push my small stool over and cling to the window frame to steady myself. I search for the shouting children but see none. I try to follow the noise and see it is coming from an old woman who lives much farther down the path, closer to the water. She is screaming something I cannot recognize. Then the horns of alarm blow, sending chills up my little back. I feel my mother dash up behind me, and she grabs my shoulders in fright.

"What is she saying, Ma?"

"Oh my lord!" She begins to scream strange little yelps I have never heard her make before. "They've come again!"

I follow where she is looking, and out on the lough where Da fished are ten long ships with massive sails gliding into the harbor. Ma grabs me up, and my legs straddle her hard stomach. I clutch onto her wooden triangle necklace to steady myself and thumb the large blue stone in the center nervously.

She shrieks out the window, "Seamus! Seamus!"

Women go running by our house with their crying children dragging behind. The scariest, most horrifying noise then comes echoing over the water up to us, as all of whatever is coming on that ship roars out. I begin to cry now, and my mother paces the floor, breathing too fast. She opens the door and cries out louder, "Seamus!"

I look down to where he should come. I wish I would see his face appearing up that path, but nothing comes, only an old woman hobbling up the way.

"Get on your way to a safe place, Keelin; it's the Danes!" She keeps limping up toward the hill but screams back, "Run, my girl! Run!"

Ma screams, drops me on the ground, and squats. I clamber on top of her, still crying. She screams again, grabbing her stomach and gritting her teeth. She shrieks out, "Seamus!"

She begins to weep on the ground as I hold onto her. I put my head up and try to call out as loud as I can, "Da! Da!"

When I look at Ma, I know I have to stop crying and help her. I try to rub her shoulder as she pushes off the ground to get back up. She takes me by the hand and begins to waddle up the path in the direction the old woman went scurrying. A booming sound thunders out. I turn to look down to the harbor, where the ships are sailing right up on the sands, like beached whales. Many men bound off the ships with shiny swords and spears raised, making that terrible noise again. My mother pulls me faster so I cannot look back any longer and my little legs can hardly keep up. Ma stops again, drops my hand, and clutches her middle. She bends over and cries. I begin crying again too.

"Hurry, Liam!" she screams, then tries to run again, holding her stomach, but shortly after has to stop.

On her knees with her face drawn up in pain, she looks back to the invaders who are now going into the houses right onshore. We hear desperate screams as the men kick their way inside. Smoke begins to plume up as men with torches light the thatch on fire. My mother looks back up the steep hill to the stone church up top, still much farther than we now are from our home. She turns her head all around her, looking for a place to hide, but there is only some underbrush and a few large stones. "I can't make it, Liam. We have to go back and hide."

I help her back, and as soon as we get home, she rushes to grab the key from above the fireplace and runs to the large, black chest. She unlocks it, takes out Da's sword, and all of the bowls and linens. She yanks a blanket off the bed but leans on the post as she grimaces in pain again. As soon as she can move again, she unfolds the blanket and lays it in the chest. "Get in, Liam."

*I don't understand. Why does she want me to get in the place I wasn't allowed to ever touch?*

She grabs herself again and yells, "Get in now!"

I try to get in on my own but catch my foot on the side and fall in. When I lift my head, her face is much softer. I look into her large, worried, brown eyes and see her many little spots I love so much.

She gives me a white, flashing smile as the tears fall down her cheeks. "Be a good boy, now, Liam, and stay quiet. Bad men are coming, and you'll be safe in here. Don't make a peep." She makes the sign of the cross. "God help us now."

I hear the door crash in on the house next to us. Ma startles at the noise, takes Da's sword in her hand, and holds it up as she brings her slender finger up to her pink lips. I lay my head down, and everything goes black as the lid shuts. I hear her rattle with the lock and shuffle away. Our door crashes in. Ma screams, and I hear things falling about the room. Something heavy slams against the chest. My mother keeps crying, and strange, deep voices fill the air. I almost scream when I feel the chest move but try my hardest to be silent. I crash into the sides as it tilts, rolls, and after a long while, finally hits the ground. I don't know how long I am in the dark; the air is getting harder to breathe. I wait for Ma to come and open the chest. Wait for the jingling of the keys I saw hung over the fireplace and cried so many times to be able to touch. Suddenly the chest is dragged. I listen, trying to quiet my breathing when—SMASH! I jump back against the other side as the whole chest shudders. The lid opens, and my eyes hurt with the sudden light. I hear an eruption of laughter and feel a large hand grab the back of my shirt and pull me up out of the chest like a kitten.

I open my eyes to see the most terrifying men I've ever seen in my life, all gathered aboard a giant ship on the endless sea. Tall men with long yellow or red hair and shaggy beards, covered in sweat, dirt, and blood. They smell like old cheese. I scream and try to run in the air, causing them to laugh louder. The one holding me turns me around to look at him. He is darker than the others with two spots on the side of his face where his beard doesn't grow. He puts me down and grabs both my arms to keep me from running. He brings my arms up for all to see, flaps them up and down like a chicken, and laughter follows again.

The man holding me speaks to me in a language I cannot understand. He tries again, but it only makes the others laugh. He shakes his head, puts me back in the chest, and shuts the lid. Each day he opens the lid once and drops me on the deck to drink beer from a bowl and eat some stale bread. As soon as I finish, he throws me back into the chest. I have no safe place; I can only disappear within me.

After a few days, the chest is moved again and opened. I have to wait until I can see, and once I can, I see a whole village surrounding me. Old people, young people, children of every age all around me, staring at me, saying things I can't understand. One man steps forward with a giant helmet and a long, fur-lined cloak pinned at the shoulder with a large, gold circle. The opening of the cape reveals a massive silver inlayed sword at his hip. He points to me and asks something of the people. No one answers, yet many shake their head disapprovingly at me. The man who took me comes forward and shoves me out of the way. He bends down, grabs the soiled blanket out of the chest, and throws it in a heap on the ground. He closes the lid, carries it on his strong shoulders, and leaves the gathering. The man with the large helmet shouts again, and no one replies. He takes his sword out and points it toward the dark woods behind them.

A fair girl begins to sob. I follow the sound and see a slight girl looking at me with tears in her shining eyes. Another man steps forward wearing the same cloth as our churchman back home. He speaks to the helmeted man and approaches, opening a small purse at his side and handing him coins. The churchman comes to me, smiles, and points to the young girl. She stops crying and walks up at the request of the churchman. The girl puts her slender hand out to me, but instead of taking it, I run back to get the blanket in the road. The girl comes to me and bends down with a sweet smile. My eyes are drawn to the slight space in her front teeth. She folds the blanket, as filthy as it is, and holds it close in her arms. I follow her back to her farm.

# Chapter 2

Her farm is right outside the village with many other farms up the road. Every farm has a fence surrounding each property and outbuildings. We pass a well where she brings some water up for me to drink; it tastes clean and cold. As soon as she reaches a workhouse, she pushes the blanket into a bucket of water and begins scrubbing vigorously. I look out to the cattle grazing beside a long curved-roofed building and turn around to see small horses running in the warm wind. A little dog comes up and jumps on me, knocking me down. The girl shakes the water from her hands and helps me up.

She points to her chest and says, "Thora."

I repeat it to her. She then points to my chest with a small smile and I say, "Liam."

She says it strangely, like it's a heavy word. I try to say it again so she'd say it right. She looks at my dirty shirt, points to the stains, and then lifts it up over my head. She cleans me from head to toe with a cold, wet cloth and I begin to shiver when the wind blows. As soon as she puts the shirt into the tub, she takes a shirt down from the line, and places it over my head, warm from the sun. It touches my ankles and hangs over my hands. She laughs, rolls my sleeves up, and goes back to her scrubbing. They have every kind of animal I've ever seen at market. Every direction I turn something is flapping, chewing, grunting, braying, scratching, running, or jumping. She hangs the blanket and shirt on the line and I watch as the water drips off the corners.

She leads me across the dirt path to the center, where a long wooden house stands, much larger than our houses at home. The roof is twice as high as ours, with a huge open fireplace crackling in the center. There is no chimney, only a gaping hole in the roof. A thin layer of smoke hangs in every room, making me cough. Thora brings me to a back room where a wide oven sits on the ground. She takes a loaf of bread cooling on the stones and pulls off some to give to me. As I stuff the fresh bread in my mouth, she leaves and returns with a rug that she flattens out on the stamped ground. She lays on it, puts her arms up under her head, and closes her eyes. I wonder if she's going to sleep now, but she opens them and points for me to lie down. I do as she did, and she sits crossed-legged beside me and begins talking.

Every day, she talks and talks to me, and slowly I begin to understand her. I follow her everywhere and actually feel like I can't breathe when I wake up and she's already gone off with her mother. Her family sleeps together on a raised bed beside the open hearth. There are other people on the farm, but they live in the half-dugout buildings. They are the workers and take care of most of the hard chores on the farm. These workers are all grownups and never talk to me. Thora always brings me food after her supper and tells me stories as I fall asleep beside the oven, curled in my mother's blanket.

Sometimes I'll wake, screaming for my ma. Thora will rush to me and lie beside me on my rug and tell me stories of strange things that live in this land. She tells me of the dark elves who live underground with corpses and come up only at night to play tricks on humans. They are cunning, quick, and wonderful stone-and-metal carvers. She says they are horribly ugly with unkempt, dark hair all over their blue-pale skin. Then she speaks of the light elves that are the protectors of a house. They live in the sunlight, and you can see them dancing in circles in the early hours of morning or right as the sun is going down. They are beautiful and live forever. Last, she talks about the Loki, evil giants that roam the world's outer realm. She shows me the necklace her father gave her, the large hammer of Thor that she has to wear for protection from these creatures. She pulls out another one for me and places it over my head.

"Two circles?" I ask as I stare at the two connected circles of intertwined reeds hanging on the leather string.

"I made this for you. It's not a symbol of a god, but it came to me in a dream." She drops it over my head. "It will keep you safe wherever you go, even if it is without me." She laughs, since I even follow her to the outhouse and wait outside for her.

As soon as the sun rises, I wait for Thora outside the house, and once she comes, we go running out into the fields to do her light chores or play in the pastures. I help her roll beeswax candles, collect the honey, feed the small animals, and work her loom. Her mother is too busy commanding the other workers around, jingling the keys she hangs on her waist for the outbuildings, and making sure the carts are loaded to bring to market. She has to run the farm alone, since Thora's father is away so much of the time. She hardly notices me at all.

Every once in a while, I'll hear her say when she sees Thora sitting beside me, "Remember his place, Thora."

Which I never understood; this farm *is* my place now.

# Chapter 3

One rainy day, Thora brings me a honey cake to my bed and says, "It was a year ago you came to live with me, and since we don't know your birthday, I will celebrate it today."

The small cake is covered in sticky honey. I put my little finger in it and suck the sweetness off. "How old do you think I am now?"

She thinks about it. "Six years maybe?"

I try to remember if my mother had ever told me my age and can barely remember anything from before coming to Denmark. I look up at her and ask, "And how old are you, then?"

"I will be thirteen next month." But she looks away. "I will be married at a great feast that night."

I glance up. "Does that mean you will leave the farm?"

She looks into my eyes, her light green eyes sparkling. "I will leave the farm but never you." She tousles my hair the same way

Da did and laughs. "You are coming with me whether you want to or not."

There's a great ruckus outside, and Thora springs to her feet to see what it is. I run beside her as a workman comes running out of the barn with a large shovel behind his head. A skinny grey wolf darts out before him with a fat, dead goose dangling from his mouth. The man pitches the shovel at the wolf, narrowly missing him as the wolf shifts to his right and escapes under the fence to freedom.

"Did he get only one?" Thora calls out.

"Got her and her whole brood," the workman replies as he goes back into the barn.

That goose had six fluffy goslings that hatched the other day. I run to the barn with Thora and see five little yellow balls of fluff spilled out on the hay.

"One is missing," I tell Thora.

She nods and looks around. A high-pitched peeping begins, and the three of us move every lump of hay in the barn trying to locate where it's coming from. I turn over a bucket and see the little frantic puff run out and into a clump of hay. I reach in and pull it out as it squirms in my hand, calling for its far-away mother.

"What will we do with it?" I say to Thora as the workman walks away with the shovel full of the rest of its sleeping brood.

She smiles at me. "Now *you* will have something to follow you around everywhere."

I name my new little friend Borga: saved one. After spending half the morning chasing her as she runs away from me squeaking for her mother, she finally stops and begins to stay close to me. I take her to the water bowl to drink and watch as she snaps along the bottom of the bowl with her orange beak, lifts her head up to drink as she watches me with her golden eyes. I hold grain in my hands for her to eat and enjoy how she follows with her tiny yellow wings out when she runs. At night, Borga snuggles in with her head on my neck and makes little peeps that lull me to sleep.

One month later, Borga goes through an odd stage where her plumage is coming in and all her parts seem too big for her. Her peeps are cracking into more of a honking sound. She's becoming braver and braver, leaving my side only to come running back when she realizes I'm away. She'll come flip-flopping back with her head low, honking away in a punishing but reunited tone.

∞∞∞∞∞∞∞∞∞∞∞∞∞∞∞∞∞∞∞∞

It's a crisp spring day when Thora comes out dressed in a lovely white goatskin dress. She shoos Borga away from nipping at her fringe and says, "Time to go, Liam."

"You are getting married today?" I know the answer; I don't know why I asked.

Her mother comes out and commands the workmen to load up the wagon. "Fetch her loom, chests, and featherbed." She takes off one of her keys and, with a wide smile, hands Thora the key on her own silver chain to clasp around her waist. "For your new farm."

Thora thanks her as she wraps it around her waist, and after all of the things are secure in the wagon, I go to sit up on the wagon bench, but her mother points to the back.

Thora nods with a smile. "You will have to keep Borga company."

I bend over and grab the spiky-feathered gosling around her middle, then hold her close to my chest, feeling her downy sponginess. She honks a bit and flaps her giant, orange feet in the air but calms when I settle in between the chests. Thora says good-bye to her mother as a workman drives the wagon nine farms up the common road. It looks identical in size and shape to Thora's old farm, except it's on the right side of the road. There are similar out buildings in slightly different placement. A tall man steps out of the central hall with two other men. I recognize him as one of the warriors who stormed my village and laughed at me hanging at the hand of my abductor. Before even helping Thora down from the wagon, he takes inventory of the contents of her dowry. He grimaces when he sees me holding Borga. One of the men comes to record on dried goatskin exactly what Thora brings with her, and the tall man finally puts a hand up to help her down. He looks at her like food, tasting her with his single-dimpled grin.

A red-haired woman comes out from the house with two children near my age. With her chin up in the air, she leans on the side of the house, watching, as her children lose interest and begin hopping around, playing games on the path, completely disregarding me. The pagan holy man says the prayers for their marriage and all are invited inside for the feast to the fertility god Frey. I put Borga on the ground and attempt to go in for the feast, but Rolf, the groom, sticks his foot out as I step up to go into the house last. "All thralls eat and sleep in the dugouts."

The door shuts and I wonder what "thrall" means. Thora has never taught me that word. I take my small linen sack, filled with my blanket and some clothes Thora made, then walk over to the five dugouts behind the large barn. I notice smoke coming from one. Borga keeps honking in parade behind me, and the noise brings out a young girl. She's a few years older than me, with dark hair, dark skin, and eyes like a stormy grey-blue ocean. She smiles a brilliant white smile when she sees Borga's humorous greeting. I wish I were in the house with Thora but know I must make friends before night falls and the wolves descend in hopes of wayward animals.

"My name is Liam."

The girl scrunches her face up and says, "Liam," like it tastes bad.

I wait, not sure what to say next, and she says, "Una" while pointing at her bony chest. She motions inside the dugout. "Hela has made a soup, and I'm sure we have enough for you too."

I go inside the small, warm space with a fire lit in the center lifting up through a hole in the roof. The space glows orange from the flames and makes the white woman appear magical. I stop at the sight of her, focusing on her elfish-pointed ears as Una makes her way to the mat by her side. The wrinkled woman gives me a warm, though toothless, grin.

Una whispers to her, and Hela turns to me. "Liam, would you like some soup?"

I nod and move to the farthest corner on a straw pile, and Borga quickly waddles in, chiding me for leaving her. The old woman laughs heartily and instantly puts me at ease. The soup, savory and salty, tastes wonderful with the torn pieces of stale bread. I thank them and watch Una tucking herself up in a ball on a mat near the fire to sleep.

I ask Hela, "What does thrall mean?"

She looks down at the fire and takes a moment. "When someone owns your body but not your soul."

"Why did Rolf call me a thrall?"

"Rolf is our master. We have all ended up here by chance, and we must do what we can to survive."

I go to take my sack and goose out to find my own place to sleep when Hela makes a shushing sound and puts her hands down to the straw. "You will sleep with us."

I'm happy to stay here, since it's already dark out. The old, hunched woman helps lay my blanket on the straw and pats my back reassuringly when I settle down with Borga.

# Chapter 4

In the morning, I wait by the house for Thora to appear and make a face instantly when I see she steps out with Rolf heavy around her shoulders, dragging her down awkwardly.

He notices me and yells, "Get to the shovels, boy!"

I take off toward the barn, hearing the flip-flopping of Borga's graceless feet. I shut the door behind me, and Borga goes wild, pecking on the other side of the door frantically.

Thora says behind the door, "Liam, let us in."

I wait and almost laugh at the noise Borga is making. I open the door, and she comes flying in, honking at me with her neck overstretched.

Once she calms down, Thora says, "I'm sorry, Liam. Rolf doesn't allow any workmen in the house."

"You mean thralls."

She looks surprised I know that word but nods. "I don't like being here either. I'm forced to do whatever my parents choose for me. We are both thralls."

I soften a bit and say, "I met the oldest woman I've ever seen. I think she is an elf."

Thora laughs. "Hopefully she is a good elf."

"I think she is. She made me supper and let me sleep with her and Una."

"I'm glad you and Borga found a nice place to stay, then. I worried about you all night." She opens up the door to the barn. "Things will be better for both of us when Rolf leaves for the sea." She pulls her reindeer comb out from her pocket, secures her hair up with the comb, and starts to run. "Come on! Let's explore this place!"

I run after her with my goose flapping behind.

Rolf does go away eventually, and Thora jests about finding his hoards he'd buried all over the farm. We take shovels and dig in all of the places someone would pick to bury a fortune. One day we're shocked to unearth one below a tall fir. We find metal pieces all wrapped in linen: jewelry and coins from countries Thora can barely pronounce. Thora puts on a few of the necklaces as I wrap a gold armband around my skinny arm. I see dark red paint all over the side of Thora's necklaces, and when I point to it, Thora yanks them off. We hurry to put it all back and try to cover it all like it has never been disturbed.

When Rolf comes home and Thora can't spend time with me, I play with Una after her chores are done. She has to feed the animals, collect the eggs, milk the cows and goat, and make the butter and cheese. I help her get through them, and toward the end of the day, we have time to run off into the horse fields. Borga grows so large that she's the fattest goose on the farm. She catches the attention of Rolf one day as he watches her waddle her large rump behind me.

He calls out, "I'm going to butcher that goose before she gets too tough."

I spin around, not knowing what I can say to him. "She's a fine egg layer, Master. This morning, she laid one of the largest eggs we've ever seen."

He shakes his head. "We have got plenty of eggs from the hens. No, I will see to her tonight."

The door opens, and Thora flies out. She must have overheard through the open gables in the roof.

She yells out, "That is *my* goose. She is part of *my* dowry and *I* will say what we do with her. Borga is an egg layer!"

She draws both hands out flat, turns, and goes back inside. Rolf sneers at me and rubs the bottom of his whitening beard but says nothing. I grab Borga's fat body up and run away with her to tell Hela and Una what happened.

Months later, Rolf leaves again, and since his red-haired sister, Inga, goes away to visit her dead husband's family, Thora lets me in to have supper with her and sleep on her featherbed. I'm careful to watch Borga's warning tail-wagging closely, in fear of an accident that will give Rolf reason to butcher her. Even with all the darting outside with Borga throughout the night, it's worth it to be back with Thora. I notice Thora's stomach is getting large when she tucks her body around me, and we fall asleep with my arm across Borga.

∞∞∞∞∞∞∞∞∞∞∞∞∞∞∞∞∞∞∞∞∞∞

When Rolf returns, he carries a dirty sack behind his back and yells for Thora to come out. Inga is home by then, and she comes out wondering why he didn't say her name as well. Rolf bares an oversized grin, opens the sack wide, puts his long arms in, and pulls out the strangest bird I've ever seen. It's a shiny shade of purple-blue, delicate, with a tiny, undersized head. The strangest part is the trailing, thick tail it has, twice its body length. He puts the scared thing on his hand, holds it up like a falcon, and cries, "A gift for the wife of my first child!"

Inga goes back inside as Thora walks unsure, toward the strange creature. She holds her hand out to touch him and laughs. "What am I to do with it?"

"This fine creature will grace our farm with its beauty and provide you with the richest feathers for your decorations."

She thanks him as he lifts the creature in the air; it flaps down to the ground and steps away like a chicken but meows like a cat. Borga immediately dislikes the intruder. She puts her beak flat on the ground, runs as fast as she can after it, sending it flapping off into a paddock.

Rolf turns to me. "If that goose gets that peacock, she'll be turning on my spit."

Thora motions to me to take her away. Borga isn't the only one who doesn't like the peacock. Inga seems to do all she can to drive the bird away. When Rolf isn't around, she throws water and plates at it, and once she tries to catch it in a blanket. I don't blame her; the eerie thing sneaks up and appears like a ghost in a tree beside you.

The baby's born at the end of the winter. Thora lets me come in to see her one morning, and there, lying on her featherbed is a little honey-eyed girl. I smile, and Thora says, "Her name is Erna."

I go to touch the dark fuzz on the top of her head and see a little white mark on her forehead. Thora sees me touch it with my thumb and says, "I think that's a sign that she will be special."

I nod and hope that Thora will still have some time for me. Thora pulls me to her and whispers in my ear, "We are now a family."

# Chapter 5

Rolf is away for harvest time, which means that Thora has to take the goods to market. She asks one of the older thralls to take her into the village. Erna stays with Una and Hela while we venture in. I haven't been to Hedeby since that warrior pulled me by my scruff out of the chest. We take Army Road that leads right into town but have to pay a good sum in order to use the new bridge over the Eider River. I can't remember what the village looked like, and I'm surprised when I see the huge hills surrounding the village in a perfect half-circle.

"Those are the ramparts built to protect the trade center," Thora explains.

I see the break at the end of the road where two narrow towers stand menacingly, protecting a massive, wooden gate. On top of the towers lay two giant shields of iron, horizontal to the sky.

Thora points. "They light those and all of the others on the shore and across the hilltops to warn us of an attack."

When we draw closer, I see the towers are carved with pictures of horses, hawks, and warriors fighting a dragon. Guards stand on the towers with their weapons, inspecting our wagon, and studying us as we pass through. The road changes from gravel to wooden-planked streets, and the noise of the wheels and horseshoes on it sound musical. The village is vast, stretching from the towers all the way to the sea. We pass houses with small fenced yards and trading posts with wide windows to prop up to sell one's goods. I stare at the different-looking people; all sorts of people come here to trade from around the world. We ride by the largest building, the Great Hall, where the chieftain resides, his bodyguard army meets, and the festivals take place. It has the most amazing woodcarvings on all of the posts, every animal you can imagine. Runestones carved with exquisite words and pictures ornament the streets. I wish we could've stopped at each one so that Thora could've told me what they said.

There are people of every class—rich noblemen and women in bright shimmering silks with gold embroidery, and others dressed like Thora, with silver brooches on their pinafores over colorful soft linen shift dresses. Then there are those who look like me, in dreary, coarse wool. We ride down near the shore, where the man driving our wagon stops to unload the goods and Thora has to go negotiate payment. I stand gazing out on the dark blue water to the different-sized ships bobbing at anchor. Past the warships and cargo ships, I see the pilings and stakes sticking up at the end of the long jetties, ever defending us from a water invasion.

High-pitched horns sound, and all eyes go to the longest jetty, where a warship is approaching to unload. Men place long planks of wood across to walk off the ship onto the jetty. About ten men step off, each dragging two huge sacks of loot. The last four are struggling, carrying a man tied at his hands and feet with a sack over his head. I immediately feel sorry for this kidnapped individual. Everyone, except the thralls, cheers for the return of the warriors. Rolf, unfortunately, is one of the first off, and as soon as he sees Thora, he rushes over to pick her up in a suffocating embrace. She looks like it hurts her, and when he puts her down, he opens his sack, showing her all he plundered.

I lose interest in this scene and focus on the four bringing the unhappy person up to Chieftain Toke's house. A crowd gathers, curious to see what they brought back, and someone calls for Toke. He comes out, looking annoyed by this disturbance, and fixes his belt around his embroidered tunic.

He says, "I was in the middle of enjoying my finest mistress."

A woman steps out beside him, closing the front of her silk gown. She has cascading blonde hair down to her ribs and glowing amber eyes.

I whisper to Thora, "His wife looks like a goddess."

"Dalla's no wife and certainly no goddess. Dalla's the town's mistress: a thrall that's saved for man's enjoyment."

"But she wears silk and jewels?" She looks like no thrall I'd seen.

"Men give her gifts for her beauty."

"Chieftain," a warrior with ice blue eyes says, "we've been to Iona and have brought back a gift for you."

They remove the linen sack, and the crowd gasps when they see the tall muscular person is in fact—a woman. She's dressed in loose pants and long tunic that hides her femininity, but her face, with its small features, lack of beard, and long hair, is in fact female.

The chieftain laughs. "And what am I to do with the she-man, Konr?"

"It took six warriors to capture her alive. She fought like a berserker! Held us all off for more than an hour with only her shovel and axe. All we could do was take a large piece of linen, corner her, and wrap her up in it. But she still ripped right through, but not before Orm here tied her legs."

He points to a large and dirty warrior beside him. Orm nods, happy to be mentioned to the chief.

The chieftain quiets and looks at the prisoner. "Well then, Orm shall win her. I have no use for her."

Orm's face brightens as Konr says, "Chief, she's a fighter. No man will tame her."

Orm jumps in. "I can tame this he-woman! Poke her until she gives way to her sex!" The warriors cheer him on as he grunts. "Just need to loosen her leg ropes a bit to get the job done." He begins to untie his belt and lets out a reverberating belch.

The warriors laugh, and the chieftain nods in approval, his slate eyes twinkling at such unexpected entertainment. Orm motions for the men to drop her, then grabs her tunic from behind and drags the strong girl on the ground. Straining with each pull, he tries to look every bit of the man he boasted about. He takes her into a small trading store. Once inside, he gives a snide smile to the warriors, then knocks the stick holding up the window, shutting it with a slam.

The chieftain asks, "Tell me the status of the settlement on Iona?"

Konr begins, "We have secured the—"

A great crashing in the post interrupts the report as Orm runs out, holding his groin and bloody head. He comes out screaming toward the warriors as the she-man charges out after him. Her wrists are still tied, but she has the shop stick in her grasp, swinging it around dangerously. She chases after him, her muscular legs now free from ropes.

Orm shrieks as he runs for cover. "She bucked like a wild mare! She's out to kill me!"

The warriors drop their sacks and raise up their swords. Her indigo eyes blaze with careless fury, and she grunts as she swings at anyone who challenges her. All villagers seek refuge in stores or houses as I find safety with Thora behind the wagon. Warriors stand to hold their positions, yet none brave going against her.

The chieftain brings his hands up in the air and says, "What thrall here is from Iona?"

The thrall who drove Thora's wagon stands up.

The chieftain nods to him. "Translate for me." He looks at the she-man with his jaw clenched and speaks. "I greatly misjudged you, shield-girl. You're not destined to be a thrall. The valkyries, Goddesses of War and Choosers of the Slain, have sent you. You will fight beside me and bring us great victory!"

The thrall translates to her, and she seems surprised to hear her own tongue. She calms slightly and looks around her at the village, then says something back.

The thrall repeats, "Does she have a choice?"

"Everyone has a choice." The chieftain smiles. "There is always death for all of us."

The she-man rests her stick down, takes a deep breath, and the thrall translates. "She will fight, but bed no man."

He laughs. "After nearly castrating Orm, I can promise *no man* will ever try." The whole village laughs and she nods. "Tie her feet, then, and give her my small house in town for her own."

When a few scared men hold up ropes and start to approach her, she yells, "I thought I was no slave!"

Toke replies, "No slave, but you will have to remain tied until you have shown your loyalty in battle. I cannot turn my back on you yet."

She looks angry but allows the nervous men to approach and tie her legs. As she shuffles away to the house, Toke yells, "I will give you the name Gunhilda: shield-girl." He points to his black-smith and says, "Make her the finest armor and weaponry."

Dalla seems upset and turns on Toke. "*She* will get her own house and the finest things and not have to share her bed?"

The chieftain chuckles. "Do not be jealous Dalla; you get to have all the pleasure."

He dives into the space between her neck and shoulders and grunts away as her eyes stare blankly up to the sky. He pulls her back into the house with him and shuts the door.

∞∞∞∞∞∞∞∞∞∞∞∞∞∞∞∞∞∞∞∞∞∞∞

Next week Thora has me take the reins and bring the team into Hedeby. It's Saturday, the day the whole village takes a bath. Thora has Erna on her lap, flapping her chubby little arms in excitement of being on the wagon for the first time. I try not to get distracted by her since I'm trying my best not to hit the side of the road and throw a wheel. Erna gurgles up a storm and makes us both laugh at the troll sounds she's making.

Once in the village, we make our way down the large bathhouse by the shore. The thralls are already busy, coming in and out with steaming buckets of water. The noble class stands in line first, and Thora knows to wait until her class is allowed to line up. By the time Thora can go, I help her in and hold Erna. As she undresses, I stare into the murky water. I turn my eyes while she gets in and look only when her chin is sitting on top of the water.

"*That* is clean water?" I scrunch my nose, happy that thralls are not allowed in.

"At least it's warm. I'm not going to *drink* it." She smiles as she swims her hands through the deep water. The tub is constructed like a giant barrel and looks as if you can fit a whole family in it.

"Hand me Erna." She puts her arms up, and I step on the last ladder rung to hand the naked, fat baby to her.

Erna squeals in delight at being submerged, and I say, "She's going to get sick from being in there." I'm happy with my rag baths in the morning after Hela warms up a pot of water for us. "You will need to wash off after you get home."

I turn away as she stands up and hold the linen cloth out for her with my eyes closed.

"From now on you will take the team in on Saturdays. I don't like the way the other thrall watches me." Thora shivers. "Gives me goose skin just thinking of it."

I help her and Erna up into the wagon as another warship comes in. The warriors get off with great noise. This time Toke's first off the ship. He motions for the four men behind him to carry his things to the bathhouse. As soon as he comes up, he claps and shouts, "Empty the whole bath for your chieftain!"

Thralls go running as a huge whoosh of water comes flooding out of the raised foundation of the bathhouse. I try to think of what they must have done to empty it so quickly, and then I remember seeing that large iron cap at the bottom. The thralls immediately go shuffling about with steaming buckets again.

"Good you were not in there when he came home," I say quietly to Thora.

A great stir comes from the jetty, and again we see four men carry Gunhilda like a roped pig. As soon as they pass Chieftain Toke, he stops them with his hand out, and they lay her on the ground.

She looks up, half-interested, as he says, "You have honored me in battle and out-killed all my other warriors. If you had returned to your chieftain's side and not gone off, slashing your way across the countryside where my men had to hunt you down again, well then, you would not have to come like a slayed stag."

She picks her head up. "Where's my sack of loot?"

He motions the men to take her to her house. "You show me that you're a *Viking,* and I will let you keep your riches."

She begins kicking and squirming, causing the four men to stumble and hit the ground. One man kicks her hard, making her still again, and they carry her out of sight. Toke commands his servants to take his plunder away and begins to disrobe even before reaching the privacy of the bathhouse.

Thora turns to me, laughing slightly, and says, "Let's get home."

We are both happy that Rolf did not return on that ship.

# Chapter 6

Two years pass without much change except for how fast Erna is growing. My days are spent running around after her, keeping her from the dangers of the farm while Thora works. Whenever Erna spins off away from me, Borga notices and brings her back to me by pecking at her gently until she runs back. Erna dances like a little nymph, twirling around in the crop fields. Thora comes to find us after her weaving is done. She holds our hands, as we make our own fairy circles in the wheat. Then we fall back with our arms out and look up at the busy clouds drifting past. On rainy days, we sit inside by the fire and throw peas into a far-away bowl, laughing when they fall out and Borga eats them up happily.

My nights are spent with Una and Hela, which are just as pleasant. Una and I help pluck or debone our supper as Hela tells us stories about her village back in Scotland. It's a terrible day for us when the chieftain sends a servant to come and take

Hela away. The oldest woman in the village has died, and now Hela is the oldest. The oldest woman in the village, freeman or not, is deemed supernatural and given the honorary position of the Angel of Death. She will now be given her own house and her own thralls to assist her in preparing all the dead for burial. Thora tells me that we should be proud of her, but Una and I miss her in our little dugout. We have to fend for ourselves now, and I make sure to stay close to Una. We build one high bed of straw, and I share my blanket with her.

One day, Erna gets away from me while I'm collecting eggs, and she stumbles upon a mother goose's eggs. She runs out with the white goose on her head, darting this way and that with the bird pecking at her hair all the while. I quickly shoo her off, but Una and I roll in laughter all night and whenever we tell the story. Erna gives Borga much more respect after that, and she never eats an egg ever again.

Una and I are cooking a stew over the fire, and as she tastes the stew, the glow of the fire dances all over her perfectly structured face. A pang hits deep in my stomach; Una's not simply a pretty girl like I've known, but now that she's growing so, I notice she's much more. She will soon attract the attention of men—men who are her masters—men who will make her into another Dalla. She'll be sent away to the highest bidder, to sit in her house in silks and wait for her master to come knocking, just as Dalla does. I feel so sick to my stomach, I tell her I have to go to bed without eating. I pull my legs up to my chest, trying to fall asleep before she lies down, wondering if I can ever own anything in this life.

*I hear Borga honking that an intruder is outside. I get out of my blanket and see her glowing purple-white in the darkness; wings flapping and her beak open as rocks are pelted at her.*

*I call out, "Who's there!"*

*I hear only snickering and many feet shuffling off in reply. The moon is three quarters full, bright with a cloudless night, making the barley fields easy to see. Whatever is there dives into the barley, and I watch as the things disappear in the three-foot-tall plants. They leave a trail to follow as the three crisscross and zigzag through the crop.*

*As they begin to come back toward me, I yell, "Get out of here!" and leap into the barley to run after the closest one.*

*They run twice as fast with much grunting and strange panting noises and then completely disappear. I turn in a circle in the sea of barley, waiting for some movement, but none comes.*

*"Liam!" I hear from behind me.*

*I know it's Thora's voice immediately and run toward her. At the edge of the crop in a horse paddock, she lies there holding her round stomach and cries, "Seamus! Seamus!"*

*Then something comes charging out of the woods. A beast, three times the height of the tallest horse and three times as long, rumbles forth with tree trunks for legs and a snake for a nose.*

*Thora screams, "Mother!"*

*The thing stomps at Thora and blows its snake in the air, making a powerful, thundering noise—as I freeze.*

∞∞∞∞∞∞∞∞∞∞∞∞∞∞∞∞∞∞∞∞∞∞∞∞

There's a great feast for the equinox, and everyone gathers for the festival in the village. Una and I are allowed to come, but we have to follow the family behind the wagon for the long way into town. Una has been to a festival before, and she says the walk is worth it, plus there's a bright, full moon tonight. I have to lock Borga up in the dugout, and Una and I laugh when we can still hear her from the fence of the farm. The wagon, even with Inga, her children, Thora, Erna, and Rolf, is still much faster than Una and I can keep up with. After six farms, we let it go on as we walk quickly. All of the warning fires are lit across the hilltops and over the water, with a deep red sky simmering behind, making everything seem so fantastical.

By the time we reach the towers, most of the town is already full. The guards look everyone over as they roll or stride by. I gather they've already started their own celebrations with the great quantity of mead I can smell from all the way down here.

As we are walking by, one of the guards sees Una and yells, "I think I need to personally check that one. Come up here, girl!"

The other one laughs as Una keeps walking through, ignoring them, but the guard pours his bowl of mead down onto both of us. We start to run as we follow the line of torches and regroup by the fire in the center of the Great Hall.

"Now if we rolled around in manure, we would smell just like the guards!" I shout over the noise and laugh, wiping the mead out of my eyes.

She smiles. "Shh! Listen to the music!"

There are a few men playing bone flutes of all different sizes, whistling together in a light, fast melody. When the song ends, everyone in the circle claps while people pass behind us, pushing us into those standing in front of us. It's like swimming in a crashing sea, trying to keep from colliding against the rocks. The door to the Great Hall opens, and out comes Chieftain Toke with his wife and many children. Right before the door can close, Dalla emerges and stands behind his family.

He begins, "Tonight we celebrate the solstice. Now is the time for planting and renewal to begin. Thor has given us a full moon to celebrate, and our seeds will sprout in half the time!" He picks the still, white, he-goat up in the air, as its bloody neck hangs limp down toward the fire. "We must all sacrifice to Thor and thank him for all that we have and all that we wish to have!"

Everyone cheers as he passes the goat off to a thrall who places it along with the other sacrificed animals on the scaffold outside the Great Hall. Toke claps and yells out, "Bring me my valkyrie! The gods and goddess want her here!"

Some laugh as they see her brought, yet again, bound at her legs and arms, but she looks rather comfortable now. She's placed on the ground before Toke and, with the fire behind her, still looks fierce, even bound as she is. Some step back, making it a semicircle now.

Toke looks down into her strange eyes. "The gods are telling me that tonight is the night I should trust you."

Gunhilda smirks.

Toke squints, one eye wider than the other. "You are not going to run this time, or I will kill you myself."

Gunhilda still keeps her smirk but pulls her arms up to cut the bindings. Everyone holds their breath as he pulls out his ornate sword, brings the sword over his head, and chops the rope. Gunhilda barely flinches. She lies back on her freed hands, brings up her bound legs, and holds them so stiff that one slice of the sword cuts the rope. The crowd moves back even more as the giant woman slowly stands.

She strides to the far edge of the circle and snatches a large horn from a small man's grasp. Gunhilda throws the beer back in her gurgling mouth and then begins kicking up her legs in an odd way. Toke laughs immediately, relaxing the crowd, and he starts clapping as the whole circle joins in. The flutes find a rhythm to match, and her legs seem possessed as the top of her body stays straight and stiff. She twirls around in circles, and I see Erna across the way dancing to the beat. Gunhilda comes around to her, and my heart stops when she sweeps her up and spins around the circle with her giggling away, clapping. I can breathe again when she sets her down, but Erna keeps her hands in the air, hoping Gunhilda will come back to dance. The whole village seems to have gathered around to watch her. It's the loudest clapping, whistling and cheering I've ever heard. I have to cover my ears to keep them from hurting, and move closer toward the chieftain's throne, where it is slightly quieter.

Toke calls for Gunhilda and whispers to Dalla, who begrudgingly stands to give up the throne next to him. He pats for Gunhilda to come sit beside him like a favored hunting dog, then passes her a full horn, and they crash horns with a hearty laugh—Gunhilda emptying hers before Toke.

A man steps out of the circle now, and it takes some time for the clapping to die down before anyone can hear what he's shouting. I recognize him as the holy man who saved me that terrible day, long ago. He looks greyer with the years, but since he is wearing the same robe, I remember.

He nods in respect to Toke and speaks with his hands behind his back. "Blessed festival to you and yours, Chieftain Toke."

"It is so good of you to come out and thank our gods on this beautiful night, Ansgar."

He smiles tightly and nervously scratches at his large mole beside his eye with a pasty white hand. "I do not come to praise your gods, Chieftain, but I do respect your festival."

Toke laughs, allowing others to laugh along, then asks, "What will it take for you to love our gods too?"

"What will it take for you to accept only mine?" Ansgar seems to be challenging him.

Toke looks around to all of his people. "If you can prove that your one god is stronger than all of ours, then I will accept your baptism."

A hush comes over the packed crowd.

Ansgar seems to be prepared for this and replies, "My one God and I accept your challenge." He looks around his setting, then puts a single finger up with an idea. "If I were to take that iron poker, red-hot from the fire, and carry it to you in my hand without any sign of damage, will you immediately convert?"

Toke nods confidently. Everyone holds their breath as the holy man bends down to lift the poker out of the fire and holds it up for everyone to see the glowing. He brings it down slowly into his open palm as the crowd stirs uncomfortably, hearing the sizzle. However, the holy man keeps his face straight and strides to Toke, who pinches his thin lips together in a smirk as he lifts the poker out of Ansgar's hands.

The holy man spins around quickly, flinging his arms back and forth, then brings his hands up and proclaims, "A miracle of Christ!"

Toke stands up and orders Ansgar to hold them out for him to examine, front and back. Then he calls to the crowd. "See it for yourselves! No marks whatsoever!"

The crowd makes much noise as Ansgar walks around slowly for the whole crowd to witness.

However, I notice Gunhilda pointing to something on the ground and overhear her say, "He coated his hands in thick beeswax. There the molds lie on the ground."

I look down to the shriveled-up fingers of wax and realize he has tricked the chieftain.

I ready myself for the guards to be set upon him, but Toke shushes Gunhilda. "Do you take me for a fool? Of course I knew what he had planned. But what a fantastic way for mass conversion! This will improve trade greatly."

"But you are willing to be baptized for trade alone?"

He laughs with his head back, tries to cover his outburst with his hand but keeps snickering. "Little does he know this will be the seventh time I have been baptized. To a man with many gods, what is one more?" He keeps laughing. "Plus the Christians always give fine baptism gifts."

Gunhilda takes a swig from a fresh horn, smiles back in admiration as the holy man comes up and says a blessing over the bowl of water he holds in his left hand. Toke suddenly looks stern and respectful as he has Dalla remove his cloak. He strips off his tunic by reaching down his back and pulling it over his head. I see a long scar running up from his wrist past his elbow and wonder what terrible battle he has seen. He bows his round royal head as Ansgar pours the water over. He comes up dripping and thanks him. Ansgar reaches into a sack he has laying at his feet and pulls out a golden chalice.

He holds it up and proclaims, "This is a gift from the pope himself! It was made especially for you Chieftain Toke, to carry your church's holy water."

He brings it up to him, and Toke bows his head gracefully in thanks, but when he rises, Toke points to the holy man's large cross and says, "And that."

Ansgar looks taken aback, and his hand goes immediately to his jeweled cross. "This was a gift *to me* by the pope. I respectfully decline."

"I feel I can't be truly Christian until I have one of those"—he rolls his hand, looking for the word—"things on my heathen chest."

Gunhilda tries to hide her laughter with her hand and looks off to the side. Ansgar stares at Toke flatly, blows out slowly, then begrudgingly removes the thick gold chain from his thin neck and hands it gently into Toke's battle-scarred, padded hands.

He smiles wide, throws it over his head, and proclaims, "I feel the power of Cross now upon me."

"Christ," Ansgar corrects. "The power of Christ."

"Yes, that's what I said." Toke smiles and motions his people to come forward.

Many from the circle line up for Ansgar to bless them, and Toke grows tired of the scene and takes Dalla into the house.

The feast begins without the chieftain, and the Great Hall looks magical, with its long tables set up with chairs, dishes, and many lit candles. The Great Hall is only for the royal and hauld classes, while the peasant class and the thralls have to eat with their hands around campfires in the street. Hela sees us and coaxes us to her with a wave of her withered hand. She's sitting with the freemen and tells us it is fine to sit beside her as her guests. As I eat the tender horsemeat, the fatty juices drip down my chin and arms. Turning my head to lick them off, I notice the sword of the fellow to my right. I recognize it immediately as my da's, the same one my mother brandished the last time I saw her.

I glance up and see the two dark spots on the jaw of the man who dangled me from his arms almost four years ago. The man looks down at me quickly, and I dart my eyes away. I wish I could've pulled that sword from his sheath and stuck it in his greedy, murdering belly. I stop eating and stare into the fire as I think about all the different ways one could kill a man.

He speaks as I'm imagining his guts spilled out all over the wooden planks beneath us. "I'll soon have enough to afford my own thrall."

Most of the circle couldn't care less about what this warrior said, so he has to repeat himself louder.

The man with the ice-blue eyes, who had captured Gunhilda years ago, speaks. "You can't possibly afford a thrall. I'm still working my plot alone with my lazy brother. You can't afford it, Ragnar." He sweeps the hair from his widow's peak back behind his ear.

"You calling me a liar, Konr?" He throws down his plate.

"No, simply wondering if someone found that hoard I'd buried about a month ago near your farm line, is all." He sucks the juice from his fingers, one by one. "Strange thing is, it's empty now."

Ragnar stares back. "Maybe your dimwitted brother here forgot where he buried it."

Orm puts his filthy, greasy hands up. "Calm down, boys. We're friends here." Ragnar picks his plate back up as Orm finishes, "Besides, maybe he found one of them elf hoards!"

He throws his head back and brays like a mule. I can't tell if everyone erupts in laughter from his joke or the way he laughs.

Ragnar says, "Well, elf hoard or not, I've almost got enough, and I know just the thrall I'm going to offer on." He looks directly at Una.

I freeze beside him and watch out of the corner of my eye as he removes a comb from his belt and begins taming his long mustache.

Orm itches low at his crotch with an irritated look. "You're in league with the elves and dwarves and such, being the Angel and all?"

Hela looks up from her plate, and when she sees him referring to her, she nods, like she has done all her years as a thrall.

"Well then, tell me what happens when you pee in an elf circle again?"

His brother nudges him with his elbow. "Why did you go an' piss in a circle for?"

He brings his hands up. "Didn't notice until I was half through, and you know how you can't stop once your start, so..."

Hela clears her old throat and speaks so quietly everyone has to lean in slightly. "It will burn."

Orm says with his nose scrunched, "What will burn?"

Ragnar jumps in happily, "Your piss will burn like you've laid with a sick whore."

"You probably got it from that wife of yours with the beard," Konr jokes.

"She's from the north! They all have beards up there," Orm says.

Hela begins to gather her things like she's trying to get away, but Orm puts his dirty hand up and stays her to ask, "Hold on there, then, what gives you whip worms?"

Hela turns around steadily with her long, white hair cascading and replies, "Eating shite."

The circle erupts in laughter as she walks away, and another warrior starts itching his underarm, saying, "I've been hit with an elfin blow. Rash all the way from my arm to my waist."

We say our good-nights, and Una and I agree we'll follow some of the wagons leaving, since wolves come out in large packs under this moon. As we're nearing the towers, something flashes by us, hooting like a loon. I recognize the strange shape immediately as Gunhilda. She's sprinting twice as fast as any man could run but only half as fast as Toke's horses. We stop and watch as she zigzags in the road with nine warriors in pursuit. She is enjoying every minute, darting and stopping and starting again.

All who are on their way out on the road stops and watches the game as the warriors keep trying to get off their horses at a run and catch her once they come upon her. She runs off the road and leaps over the high fence of a farm. She runs like a wild stag, bounding over the dried winter grasses. More and more warriors are sent out after her as she brings two unfortunate ones down in the grass and keeps running. Halfway out in the pasture, two warriors spread a net between them while riding their horses. They bear down on her as she ducks once, avoiding the net completely, but when she gets back up, another net is thrown on her.

We wait to watch how they drag her back, and she keeps shaking her legs like she's still dancing, kicking them up in the tangled net, humming the tunes of the night.

Una and I continue walking home, replaying the whole crazy night, until we reach our fences, where we can still hear Borga honking.

# Chapter 7

Months pass and Rolf leaves again with the warm weather. Saturday comes and I'm asked to bring Thora and Erna into the village again. We pass by the immense church Ansgar received permission to build, right between the two sacred temples. They've recently finished constructing the bell tower, and I stop the wagon to listen. Boys pull on ropes that send them leaping up into the air, and the massive bells chime so loudly Toke comes bursting out of his hall.

"What is that noise?" he yells as he covers his ears.

Ansgar announces over the cacophony, "Those are the blessed bells that sing Christ's praises!"

Toke looks up, eyes squinted in pain. "Can they praise less excruciatingly?"

Baffled, Ansgar shakes his head, and Toke stomps away across to the bathhouse as he's brought in first. By the time we leave the bathhouse, there's a mob forming. Many are yelling; some go and seek Toke out.

"What is this all about now?" he asks.

Konr raises his fist and shouts, "He murdered my brother this very morning! Ragnar! Struck Orm down before he could even draw his sword!"

Some of the villagers have Ragnar's hands behind his back and push him toward the chieftain.

Toke asks, "Is this true?"

Ragnar nods. "The squab provoked me. Accused me of stealing their hoard for the second time."

Konr shouts as two others hold him back, "He did take our hoard! We found it dug up on our shared property line, and there's no one else on our farm. Orm only went to ask him to show him his trunk to prove he didn't have our property. And he"—his voice breaks—" he pulled out his sword and sliced his neck half through!"

Ragnar fights those who hold him and yells, "No one can demand to check another man's locked chests!"

Toke nods. "True. What lies in a man's locked chest is his own business." His seriousness dissolves immediately into chuckles. "That is, after they have paid their taxes and levies to me, of course."

Just then, the bells ring again, causing Toke and many others to jump. "Damn bells!" He curses up at them, "First they tell us to stop eating horses. Then they tell us how we should marry. How to pray. We can't even abandon our own wretched children in the woods anymore! But now this. These deafening gongs and pings! It'll make a man go crazy."

He grinds his teeth, and I realize this is no time to be deciding such an important matter.

Toke shouts, "Ragnar, you were wrong to take another life without allowing Orm to raise his own sword. Pay him his worth and future worth to his brother, in addition to all surviving dependents, and this matter will be over."

Ragnar shakes his head defiantly. "I will not pay, Chieftain. I feel I was justified, and that would take all my savings."

Toke draws in a frustrated breath as he brings his hands up. "A fight to the death it is, then. Ragnar and Konr, right now in the square."

Ragnar looks pleased, and Konr fills with rage. Both men go to their armor and weapons. Chieftain Toke holds his arms up as Ragnar and Konr stare across with their arms at the ready.

Toke speaks, "No rules except one. Once your blood spills and lands on these stones beneath your feet, the match is done. The wounded has a chance to pay to be released before his life is taken." He waits for each man to nod to him; then he brings his hands down and yells, "Fight!"

Thora turns Erna's eyes away and walks out of the circle away from the fight. I look on as each draws his sword and I'm praying that Da's sword is made poorly and will shatter into shiny pieces. Nevertheless, it is a mighty sword, and Ragnar wields it like it's weightless. Konr catches all of his blows but seems more on the defensive, moving around, trying to keep Ragnar on his good arm. One powerful blow splits Konr's red-and-black shield, forcing him to pitch it. As he tries to turn to grab his axe, Ragnar's sword comes down on his outstretched hand and lops it off in one smooth motion. The hand falls, curled like Ansgar's wax glove, as Konr spills his bright blood onto the stones. Konr screams in agony and grabs the stub.

Toke steps in. "Konr, will you pay to be released, or will you fight to the death?"

Konr doesn't answer but stares blankly at Ragnar in thick rage.

Ansgar speaks from the circle and says in a calm voice, "'The halt can manage a horse, the handless a flock, the deaf be a doughty fighter, to be blind is better than to burn on a pyre: there is nothing the dead can do.'"

Konr hears his words and, with his face drawn in pain, says, "I will pay the murderer."

The medicine woman steps out from the crowd, ties linen around his wound, and escorts him away. One of Konr's relatives hands a bag of silver to the chieftain, and he spits when Ragnar reaches his clenched hand up to take it.

The crowd begins to dissolve as Ragnar holds up the bag and proclaims, "I hadn't the money for a thrall before but I've sure got it now!"

They burn Orm on the pyre in the square that night, and I can see the smoke spiraling up to the heavens from our farm. As soon as Rolf returns, Ragnar appears at our farm. I rush to find Una milking our brown cow.

"He's here!" I huff.

"Who is here?" She glances up, moving the bucket so the cow can't kick it.

"Ragnar! He's speaking with Rolf, and he brought his bag of coins!"

Una looks down into the frothy milk.

"Una, you should hide!" I say, trying to delay the inevitable.

She shakes her head. "No, if he must buy me, I can't change that."

She lifts the two full buckets and walks out trying not to spill them.

Rolf notices her and yells, "Una come here!"

I feel like freezing this moment so it can never happen. But as tight as I shut my eyes and clench my fists, time continues on. Una walks up and rests her buckets down as Ragnar leers at her up and down. He hands Rolf the bag, and Rolf empties it out on the ground to inspect it.

When he sees that every item promised is there, and silver at that, he nods. "Una, you are now Ragnar's property. Go gather your things and leave with him."

I throw up by the side of the barn, and as I wipe my mouth, I watch her run to our dugout. I hurry in after her, and I'm surprised to see her eyes are dry. I push Borga off my blanket with my foot, and she shakes her tail in upset. Folding my blanket, I bring it over to Una.

"That is your mother's blanket," she says, shaking her head.

"I want you to have it." Tears brim, burning to be released. "Thora will always give me a new one, but he looks like he won't give you a thing."

She nods and accepts the blanket. "I will take good care of it and give it back when I make my own."

She bends forward, gives me kiss on the forehead, and wraps her strong arms around me. She turns and pats Borga on her back, sending her running to me.

She tries to laugh. "I'll see you at the festivals."

I see her brave smile as she walks out. I crumple into a ball and cry, causing Borga to get worried and poke my face with her wet beak.

# Chapter 8

That night, as if the blood money Ragnar left behind is cursed, Thora runs into my lonely dugout and cries, "Erna's sick!"

I hurry into the side room, where Thora brought her bed away from the rest of the family. There lies little rosy-cheeked Erna, crying with a deep sweat, her glassy eyes rolling closed in delirium.

Thora picks her up, trying to console her as I ask, "What can we do?"

Thora frets. "I have pressed all the herbs Hela taught me and made it into a liquid, but she won't drink it. Oh, I wish Hela was here!"

She brings her free hand up to her lips in worry.

I take a spoonful of the green liquid and try to put it into the child's mouth, but she keeps turning her head and screams louder. Thora puts her lips to her head and says, "She's burning up!"

Inga enters in her long shift dress with her palm out. "Let me."

Thora, holds the child tighter, but when Inga keeps her arms out, she passes the clinging child over. Inga takes the spoon of liquid from me and holds the child down. Erna clenches her mouth tightly, but Inga pinches her nose and waits until the child is running out of breath. Erna gasps for air as she pours the medicine in quickly. Erna swallows and chokes, then lets out a piercing scream. Thora grabs her up immediately but thanks Inga, who nods and goes back to her bed.

I sit up with Thora, who holds Erna all night. Sometime after she takes the medicine, Erna falls asleep and the flush disappears from her little face. Thora finally relaxes and falls asleep, feeling the worst is over. I see the sun breaking through the terrible night and go out to my dugout when I hear Thora scream, "She's gone! She's gone!"

I spin around to see the pale and limp child in her arms. Thora screams, clutching her to her body, "My little nymph! My little girl!"

Rolf and Inga run in, and Rolf attempts to take the child away from her, but she fights him hard and runs off into the fields we used to dance in. I find her with Erna laid there on the ground as if in deep, sweet slumber. Thora is picking the wildflowers around her and laying them about her beautiful baby. I say nothing to her and help her pick all the flowers in that field, and we conceal her with them. Rolf comes, takes Erna away that night and brings her into the village for Hela to prepare for burial. Thora doesn't come out of her house for months. I try to keep myself busy doing Una's chores, exhausting myself so that I'll fall asleep instantly instead of thinking about the sorrows of my life.

*I walk out of my dark dugout and look out on the low fog surrounding the farm and resting between the surrounding hills. Looking up I see a giant rainbow starting from our farm but ending in the far woods. It has such vibrant colors it hurts my eyes to gaze upon it, compelling me to follow it to see where it leads. I run out, jump the fence like I watched Gunhilda do, and dart to a deer path at the edge of the woods. I let the bushes sting me as I whip past them and have to concentrate on the ground since I'm moving so fast. I trip on a loose stone and go rolling into a large clearing. When I look up from the ground, I see the rainbow glowing all the way from the canopy of the trees to the dried pine needle ground below. All around me, I see different shapes and sizes of mushrooms. But there, sitting on a large red-and-white-dotted mushroom in the very center, is Erna. Erna, wearing a large, coned, red hat, giggling and eating the mushroom she's sitting on.*

*"Erna!" I call out and run to her, but the rainbow vanishes and so does the dream.*

I wake up in the still darkness and almost drift back to sleep, but I see wisps of fog outside the open window. I get up and look toward the skies to see the exact rainbow of my dream. I start running across the farm with the thought that somehow Erna will be waiting there for me to bring her back to Thora; righting everything as it once was. I attempt to jump over the fence but catch my foot and land on my face in the mud. Hopping to my feet, I sprint off, trying to get to the end before it disappears. I follow the path, but when I reach a clearing, I can't see the rainbow anymore, nor Erna in the center. I search around me, see only the trees, and hear faint whispers. The only thing I do see is a red-and-white mushroom growing out of a downed tree trunk in the center of the clearing.

I've heard of mushrooms the warriors eat that make them fight like berserkers, and there are certain mushrooms no one can eat and live to tell about. The one with the red-and-white dots are the latter. I take my shirt off, pick the mushroom with it, and run to Ragnar's farm up the road. I duck between the fence rails, head right to the dugouts, and search the open windows quietly. I know there are no other thralls on the property, so all I have to worry about are the dogs. There, inside the second outbuilding, lies Una, curled up, her hands tucked under her head, and wrapped in my blanket. I check for dogs within and then open the door slowly. I walk hunched over inside the tiny space and tap her on the shoulder. Una leaps from the bed and flies back across the room like I've never seen her do before. She pulls her blanket up to her chest until she sees it's me.

"Liam, what are you doing here?" She clambers to the window to search.

"It's still early. He isn't awake yet."

She turns to stare at my bare chest and asks, "What happened to your shirt?"

I open up the bundle, and she crawls over, curious to see what I brought.

"A mushroom?" She seems equally confused and disappointed.

My eyes light up. "A *poison* mushroom!"

"For *me*?" She looks like she is considering it.

"No! For you to feed to *him*."

Her mouth shuts, she glances in his direction out the window, and then turns back to me. "Do you think he could tell if I cooked it?"

"I was thinking you could cut it up into little pieces and make a stew. Be sure to pretend to eat it yourself, though."

She scoffs. "He never shares his food. I only get the food that is headed over to the pigs."

"So then try it. What is the worst that can happen? Be careful to chop it up real small so he can't see the red."

Hearing the rooster crow and seeing her eyes widen, I shove the shirt in her hands. Running out, I leap over the fence, this time clearing it, and then sprint all the way back to the farm. Over the next few days, I wait for any sign that Una has done what we'd planned. I watch the roads for carts or pyres burning but see nothing. A week later, I see an unfamiliar man appear, bringing Una up the road to our farm. Rolf speaks with him while I watch from behind the dugout. My heart races as the man leaves Una there, wearing my old shirt, and takes a small bag with him. Rolf speaks to Una for a moment and as soon as he turns to go into the house, she runs straight to me and embraces me so hard I fall over.

We both laugh and hurry into the dugout.

Once inside she says out of breath, "I did just what you said! I cut the red mushroom into tiny pieces and made a thick chicken-and-barley soup. I put edible mushrooms in so that if he were to notice a piece, he would think it was some of those. He ate two bowls, belched, and ate another before going to bed. In the middle of the night, I heard a commotion and saw him staggering around outside. He went crashing into everything, mumbled the strangest things, cursed at the cows, and swatted at the air! He stumbled onto the road and took off toward town. His brother came a day later to say he found him dead on the side of the road."

"Why didn't I see smoke, then?"

"His brother took him to the next village where he was from, then came back for the things he inherited. He asked me who owned me before, and since he wanted to dispose of me fast, he sold me back to Rolf! At half the price, from what I could hear."

"I am so glad you're back." I give her another hug.

She smiles and pulls out my blanket from her bag. "It's yours again."

Sleeping next to Una makes everything better. Even though I had to explain what happened to Erna and how Thora hasn't left the house since, our dugout feels happy again.

# Chapter 9

We have one month together before more bad news comes. Rolf returns from the village with Inga on a Saturday. Thora still hasn't left her bed. Rolf goes in to her as soon as he arrives back, and Thora immediately comes out screaming.

Rolf tries uselessly to calm her down. "It will only be for a year or two. Chieftain Toke needs to settle Newry."

*Newry... That name was in my old language and brought back a well-stowed memory.*

"Leave me, then!" she yells, madder than I've ever seen her.

"Inga can stay and she'll manage the farm. You must come with me."

She screams again and runs to the place I knew she'd go. I find her in the spot where we covered Erna in flowers, hunched over in tears. I put my hand on her shoulder, and she cries even louder, reaches over, and pulls me into her. Thora holds me and cries for a few minutes, and when she lets go, I try to dry her tears with my shirtsleeve.

"I will come with you."

She laughs a little through her tears. "What would I do without you, Liam?"

"You won't have to find that out since I'll always be with you."

"Promise?" Her voice breaks as she looks in my eyes.

I glare back, trying to convince her. "Always."

She laughs and hugs me again, and we walk back, holding hands until she sees Rolf. He takes her back inside, looking pleased that she has come to her senses. I go back to the dugout and tell Una that I'll be leaving. Then she starts crying. I try to console her as I have done with Thora, but this time I can't promise that I'll always be beside her. "We'll come back, and Inga will make sure you're safe here. She'll need you more than ever to help run things."

Una sniffles, and her blue-grey eyes blaze with a sparkle of tears. "I'll be alone here, though."

I nod but then remember. "No, you won't." I reach around, pull the honking Borga off my blanket, and say, "I will have to leave her here, and she'll be good company until I come back."

Una smiles. "Will you really come back?"

"If Thora comes back, then I'll come back too." I look toward where Erna died and say, "And she won't ever leave this place for long."

She nods, wipes away her tears, and begins helping me get ready for the journey. We walk back, hands clasped, to the wagon being loaded, and Inga looks on, seemingly pleased that she'll have the farm to herself now. Rolf claps for Thora to come, and I know that means me too. I turn to Una, who's wringing her hands. I feel sick to leave her. The air warms between us as she brings her eyes up to mine, her tanned skin glowing, and something comes over me. I reach out and touch the ends of her dark brown hair as she smiles nervously. Leaning in to smell the lock wound around my hand, it brings memories of sleeping next to her. We draw together for a soft kiss, and when we pull away, we have no words.

I pick up my bag and tell her, "Hold Borga back so she can't follow me into town."

Una forces herself to move and grabs Borga as I close the door. Thora's just leaving the house and gives me a smile to see me there with my bags packed. Rolf awkwardly struts out of the bushes with the flapping peacock at the end of his sword-calloused hand. Thora lets out a laugh to me under her breath, since I know she hates that strange thing too. I sit on the back of the wagon, watch the farm get smaller and smaller, and count the farms until we come to the harbor.

At the end of each of the eight jetties bob great warships lined with warriors' brightly colored shields on their sides. Rolf hands his things to the loading thralls, and I follow behind him as he carries his armor and shield down the jetty. The warship is so much larger than I expected once I near it. Beautiful carvings spread all over the railings, up the mast and length of the oars. Men carry something heavy on, and I can't help but smile when I see it is Gunhilda, again hanging between four straining men. She gives me a wink as they sit her in the bow of the ship where all valkyries belong, under the giant, carved, fire-breathing dragon leading our ship.

The bells ring out again, causing all to jump, and Toke screams from the town, "Cursed bells!"

He launches his spear straight up to the bell tower, wedging it behind one of the bells so that only two bells sound after that.

"One down, two to go!" Toke, now pleased, turns and makes his way up the jetty with his servants behind him.

Rolf points to the cargo ship on the other side of the jetty and says, "Liam take Thora below and make sure she's comfortable."

As soon as we step on the ship I notice most of the warriors didn't bring their wives with them but brought one female thrall instead. Thora notices the same thing, and her cheeks flush with color as she walks down to the small ship's hold with me. The smell of the animals in the hold beside us chokes us. Thora brings out a bag of herbs and crushes some in her hands for us to smell.

Toke's loud voice bellows above us, "Go down under the hold, Kitten."

White kidskin boots appear down the ladder, and upon seeing the silk, I know who is joining us. Thora nods to her in forced respect as Dalla instructs her thrall to arrange her cushions and smooth her silk down to sit without wrinkling. Thora gives me a look. We stay below until I can feel the boat's motion. There is a great rhythmic splashing sound all around us, and when I go up to the top of the ladder, I find it is the thirty-two oars of Rolf's warship beside us hitting the water at the same instant. Each oar has two warriors in its oar port. I search for Rolf and have a newfound respect for him, seeing him there, gritting his teeth and pulling the oar in perfect time.

I look up to the massive white square sail crackling in the wind and above it a large banner flag with the raven on it, the symbol of Odin. The ocean's sparkling this early in the morning, and I wonder if we'll be getting to Ireland before tomorrow's sunset. I go back under, trying to pull out Thora's cushions for her from her things, so she can rest well.

"Thank you, Liam."

Dalla looks taken aback by her politeness to a slave. I get out Ma's blanket, wrap myself in it, and try to shut my eyes with the lulling of the ship in the ocean waves.

At night, they anchor and in the red-sky morning, we all set sail again, following the seabirds toward the jagged Irish coast. The green mountains close in around us, and we head straight into the lough my da once fished. As we draw near the seaside village, the warriors let out a roar of terror that shakes the ship and reverberates over the waves. A shiver runs through me as I remember what that sounds like on shore. I squint and search the houses to see if I can find the one I was born in and hurt to see the women and children running up the hill toward the church.

The warriors thrust the ships up on shore, and I watch in awe how quickly Rolf jumps off with his masked helmet, shield, sword in hand, and other weapons tied behind his back. The fishermen hurry to bring their boats up and run for safety, but many are caught with raised swords.

*Was Da taken this way? Is that why he never came for us?*

Thora, Dalla, the other thralls, and I all watch from the safety of the deck behind the brightly colored shields. The chieftain paces the shore beside his best bodyguards as he watches his warriors pillage and burn the houses closest to the water. All eyes turn to the hilltop, where a great bellow booms over the harbor and lifts over the ships to the ocean, emanating from Irish warriors with raised axes and swords to the air—surprising Chieftain Toke.

He calls to his men, smiling, "Warriors! We have a fair fight here!"

Toke raises his sword as his men drop their plunder and run back to their chief. Toke nods to his men to give out mushrooms to his bear-shirted warriors. Then he walks back to our ship and says to the head warrior standing guard over us, "You and your men take the women to the safety of those caves." He points up shore past jagged rock to a darkness in the face of the cliffs. "We will come to you when we are finished with our game."

I jump off the ship and catch Thora as she leaps.

Dalla frets. "Won't you take us and then you will be safe as well?" She looks up toward the horrifying men charging down the cliffs as she spoke.

He laughs as he helps her out of the ship. "Kitten, 'kings are for honor, not for long life."

He slaps her backside with the flat of his sword and walks off as we start running with the four warriors. The Irishmen thunder closer, and the chieftain shouts out, "FREE GUNHILDA!"

Gunhilda leaps off of the bow of the ship with her shield and sword out like wings. She clears the water completely with her god-like jump, then roars and runs up the hillside, frightening away the men rushing toward her. I'm mesmerized, watching her sweep this way and that, throwing men from her path like playful children.

Thora tugs my arm. "We must go!"

"He said women. I can't go." I notice all of the other thralls remained on the ship.

"You can't leave me now!" she screams over the roar of battle.

Dalla and the guards have started climbing the steep rocks, and I hurry to push Thora up each one.

# Chapter 10

Once we reach the lip of the cave, I'm eager to turn around and watch the battle. The Vikings have made their way to the top of the hill, but there seems to be many lying dead and wounded on the slope. From our distance it's hard to tell if they are Vikings or Irishmen. Pride for the Irishmen wells inside me. My people fight back this time, not allowing what happened to me before, refusing to be vanquished yet again.

Strangely though, I also root for my adopted people. I worry for the chieftain, Gunhilda, and even for Rolf. I worry that if the Vikings are defeated, what will happen to me? Will my people take me back? Can I even speak their language anymore to tell them who I am?

A thought hits me, and I'm surprised I hadn't considered it until this moment, the moment when I'm high up in a jagged cave. I should've run! Run from the beach and up to my people. Would they have accepted me? I look down the teeth-like rocks, wondering if I can still get away before the warriors realize, but I think of Thora. She's sitting cross-legged next to me, holding my hand tight; I hear my promise echo.

There, I sit watching, not sure which side I'm rooting for, when a clamor of many feet echoes from *within* the cave. The warriors lurch to their feet and step in front of us as Dalla screams.

"There must be a tunnel to this cave! Prepare yourselves, men!" the head warrior shouts as I push Thora and Dalla down behind a monstrous rock.

Metal clangs with such force it rings in my ears. Five dark-haired Irishmen, looking identical to the Vikings in both weaponry and armor, collide with our protectors. Immediately, a soldier takes out our leader with an axe to his back as he fights off another with his sword. The other three stand together in a triangle, protecting their backsides, and after some clanging, strike two of their warriors down mortally. Leaving three against three, the Viking splits off to take on each man as Thora clings to my hand, causing all loss of feeling.

I look down the cliffs and decide we should try to retreat to the ship. I nudge Thora, who understands immediately, and we try as quietly as we can to move down the rocks with Dalla in tow. Two Irishmen, finished with our brave protectors, look over the cliff and point to our escape.

"Faster!" I yell out to Dalla and Thora, but the men move agilely down at twice our speed. When our feet hit the sand, we take off as fast as we can, but the men pounce behind us. I hear Dalla shriek as one warrior grabs her.

She bends down; her hand clenches around a large, black rock as he tugs her back up, ripping her silk gown. She twists in his arms, and I hear the rock hit bone as she smashes it into his head. He drops immediately, and Dalla takes up his heavy sword in both hands as the other warrior runs at her. I grab up two rocks of my own and try to reach her. She catches two perfect blows before he turns and slices across her pretty back. I throw both rocks a moment too late, and one stings him in the head long enough for me to pick up a sword. I've never even held a sword before, since it's forbidden.

The man stands there with his sword, smiling at me, slightly out of reach. Blood trickles down his face from my rock wound. I become entranced with the steel-grey eyes looking back. Before I can act, he strikes out at me. I try to dart away every time he slashes at me. However, Thora runs behind him and throws a heavy rock at his back, causing him to spin his sword around, catching her across her stomach.

I scream and stick the steel-eyed warrior straight in his back. The man recoils, stiffens with the skewer, and falls back on the sword, forcing it to go through him as he lands with a gurgle from his blood-filled mouth. I rush to Thora, covered now in crimson, and turn her to see my face and cry when I see her eyes fixed to the ocean.

I cry for Thora, I cry for Erna, and I cry for my mother. I don't know how long I cried there, but nothing matters anymore. This battle, this world, this life—all insignificant now.

Let the warriors come.

∞∞∞∞∞∞∞∞∞∞∞∞∞∞∞∞∞∞∞∞∞

Two powerful arms pull me away from her body. I glance up to see Gunhilda, masked in dried blood, hair blown back from the wet, whipping wind. As I get to my feet, Rolf walks toward her, his arm wrapped in a bloodied bandage. He looks down at Thora and clenches his jaw to hold back the tears.

Rolf turns to the men. "Take the women's bodies up for burial. Dalla will be buried with her Chieftain."

Rolf swings his axe, lops off the steel-eyed man's head, and spits on him. He then bends down, rips the necklace from his severed neck, and comes over to me.

"Liam." He never called me that before. "This is yours."

He places the pendant in my hand, but I care so little of war trophies now. I nod and follow them up the hillside without even opening my hand.

I walk in a far-off state, my legs moving but feeling nothing. Even as I step over the dead and dying, I am numb. We walk right past a small cottage halfway up the hill, and I see my mother and me looking out that same blue-shuttered window. I leave the group and go into the house, and all my young memories come back to me. I see the ground where I traced my last picture, the nail my mother's keys hung from, and the place the chest sat. Suddenly the object in my hand has weight, and I open my palm to see the wonderful wooden triangle with the blue stone I held so many times in her embrace. I run my thumb over it, and the tragedy of it all hits me fast. I fall to the floor, sobbing.

*We could not even recognize each other, life had separated us so!*

The room is filling with smoke; the thatched roof is in flames. I draw a boy, a mother, and father with my finger in the dirt in front of the fireplace. I stand up and let it burn along with the rest of the village. I walk up the hill that my Ma and I never made it to the top of that day and find Rolf laying the bodies out in front of the church we never reached.

Gunhilda lays down Chief Toke beside Dalla and Thora, as other warriors are brought to lie too.

Rolf calls out, "We have no Angel of Death with us, and we can't bring these bodies back to Hedeby in this heat. They will not last. All of us must prepare them as best we can. I order all riches and plunder gathered to be brought here to bury with the chieftain!"

They all nod and go down the hill to bring up what they killed for. Rolf and I start our hole for Thora as Gunhilda and other warriors begin digging the large grave for Toke. No one even stops to rest after the battle.

No one can rest when the dead are waiting.

# Chapter 11

Rolf makes sure there are two chambers in Thora's tomb. We fill the bottom with her finest linens, tapestries, jewels, weaving loom, and bowls. A female thrall washes the blood away and dresses her in the goatskin dress she was married in. We lower her down onto her green cushions and sit her up as if she is awake, supporting her with some of her things. She looks so alive sitting there that it's going to be hard to fill it in. We help Gunhilda lower the chieftain and surround him with all the riches. The other thralls bring up beer, bread, and dried meat they stored for our journey.

Rolf stands at Toke's grave and says, "Bring the chief his thrall! The faithful companion that will follow him in death as she had pleased him in life."

We place her in the chamber next to his, and Rolf chants a prayer to Odin. All the warriors who can still stand give a cheer, and the thralls fill in the tomb.

Rolf then walks over to Thora's grave; he looks toward the men and asks, "Is there a rune carver among us?"

One of the thralls raises his hand, not surprising given that most of the thralls that were brought along are skilled workers.

Rolf nods to his master. "I'll pay your master well to have this large stone at her head to be carved to mark her passing."

The thrall bows to Rolf and goes to get his tools from the ship. Rolf turns to face me, but calls out to all of the thralls. "My wife demands a formal burial with all the things she will need in death." He looks directly in my eyes. "Who will die with her? Who will serve by her side in the afterlife?"

*That's what her second chamber is for.*

I look up to the sky while he's waiting for an answer. I don't want to die, but what do I have now alive? All I have is Una and a goose, and now neither one of them is safe with Thora gone. The sun is setting behind us and makes the colors of the darkening sky seem cool next to the last orange burn of the day. I have no world without Thora. I promised her I would always be with her. I glance down at the small second chamber and know I belong there.

I step forward and say, "I will go with her."

Rolf seems pleased with this. "And so it should be."

He has the thrall pass him her peacock, which gives one last meow before he wrings its little neck. He bends down and places it in her hands. A smile comes over my face at this inappropriate time as I think about how she'd laugh to see that thing buried so close to her.

I bow down beside the hole and lay my forehead on the ground, wondering what the pain will feel like and how long I will feel it for.

Rolf and some of the other warriors laugh, and Rolf says, "You're better off doing this after a few horns of beer. We're not barbarians!"

They laugh again as Gunhilda comes and slaps her arm around me with far too great a force. We sit around on the boulders in front of the simple white church with a large carved cross on the dark walnut door.

One of the warriors hands me a beer, and as I drink, I gaze out on all the gravestones behind us, wondering if my ma is there. With the liquid loosening my tongue, I say, "Never thought I'd be buried in the same place I was taken from. I don't think I could pick a more beautiful place."

One of the warriors says, "It's a great honor to be chosen to be buried in such a way. Most thralls are left out for the wolves. They will have nothing in the afterlife. But now you will have eternity."

I nod respectfully while I think of being eternally a thrall, but then I remember Thora and know it would never be like that. I wonder for a moment if my ma will be there, if they'll share the same heaven. Twilight is creeping in, and the cemetery behind the church begins to look lonely.

Gunhilda hands me another beer, and I ask, "Why aren't you running away now?"

A smirk spreads, flashing gleaming white teeth. "We will just have to see about that, won't we?"

Then she starts slowly hopping from one foot to the other while watching me with a mischievous smile. I laugh, uncomfortable, wondering what she's going to do, but then she picks up the speed into a jig. She begins to clap her hands wildly as she spins around the circle of warriors, now cheering and whistling. She pulls her flute from her thick belt and starts playing to the speed at which her feet are moving. I swallow down my second beer and get up to dance behind her. I attempt to follow the way she moves, but with my second beer, I'm glad to see it's taking hold. As I twirl, it feels like the whole world is spinning, in a strange new way. I hear the cheering and her flute playing and feel like nothing matters, here nor there. Everything is going to be fine. This world is over, and I'm ready to see what the next world holds. I stop turning but brace myself for everything around me to quit turning.

I yell out, "Another beer!" and with a cheer, I'm handed another. I throw it back in four or five gulps, let out a large belch, and say, "Let's get this over with!"

Gunhilda keeps playing a soft jig as we all walk to the tomb. The rune carver has already chiseled the head of a raven at the top of the stone. Everyone waits as I stare down at Thora and I think about what Toke had said before, about how we all have a choice. Death is always a choice, a choice even a thrall and every creature has: the ultimate choice.

I choose this; my soul belongs to no one.

I kneel down as Rolf whispers by my ear, "Repeat these words: I see my mistress sitting in paradise, and it is beautiful and green. She calls to me. Lead me to her."

I repeat it just as he wanted me to, and I hope to see Thora's spirit there but see only an empty graveyard. I hear Rolf remove his sword; I take a deep breath and lay my forehead back to the soil. I clench my mother's triangle in my hand so hard the corner sticks in my flesh. I hear the sword slicing down through the air.

| Beacons | Life 1 Eygpt | Life 2 Sparta | Life 3 Viking |
|---|---|---|---|
| Mole on left hand--Prophetic dreams | Sokaris | Alcina | Liam |
| Scar on forehead--Large, honey- brown eyes--Magic | Bastet | Ophira | Erna |
| Space between teeth--Green sparkling eyes | Nun | Theodon | Thora |
| Mole by wide-set--Dark eyes | Nebu | Mother | Ansgar |
| Freckles--Brown eyes | Khons | Arcen | Keelin-Mother |
| Birthmark above knee-Amber eyes | Edjo | Kali | Dalla |
| Two moles on jaw--Black eyes | Apep | Leander | Ragnar |
| Picks teeth--Steel-grey eyes | Vizier | Magistrate | Seamus-Father |
| Golden eyes--Animal | Sehket-Cat | Proauga-Horse | Borga-Goose |
| Scar on forearm-- Slate-blue eyes | * | Nereus | Chief Toke |
| Big Smile--Grey-blue eyes | * | Demetrius | Una |
| Dimpled cheek--Brown-green eyes | * | * | Rolf |
| Indigo eyes--Musician/dancer | * | * | Gunhilda |
| Orange Hair-- Hazel eyes | * | * | Inga |
| Widow's peak--Ice blue eyes | * | * | Konr |
| Walks like wearing flippers-- Bray laugh | * | * | Orm |
| Pointed ears | * | * | Hela |

*                         = Not present in that life

# Fourth Life
# Ring Around the Rosie

# Chapter 1

Our cart has been stuck in the mayhem of the marketplace for ten minutes without moving. It is exceptionally busy this early, even for Cheapside.

"Move your horse!" a hostile merchant hollers from behind.

"There is no way to go, short of murder!" Hadrian shouts behind him, holding the reins in fisted hands.

Reckless peasants, merchants, and wayward animals dart in front of the carts, creating a constant stream of disruption. I detest the open-air market, the way the streets are lined with shoddy thatched cottages and shambles. Stalls, selling everything from fabrics to spices, are set up all over, and noisy peddlers are advertising their wares. Everyone comes all over London and the countryside to either bring or purchase their goods for the day. The busy and bawdy traffic is the least of the unpleasantness experienced in Cheapside.

At dawn, butchers bring their moaning animals to slaughter at Butcher's Row. There is Pig Lane, Chicken Lane, Cow Lane, and Cock Lane—each lane named for the animal slaughtered there. Butchers tie the doomed lot up and one by one begin slicing them open, spilling their blood, making rivers down the street. They carve them up and discard the inedible body parts on the ground beneath their feet. The sound of dying animals can be heard anywhere you stand in Cheapside, all day long. Blood sits in stagnant pools all over the streets, clotting and thickening as the day progresses, seeping into putrid cesspools. Entrails bake in the sun as rats and flies swarm at opportunistic moments. Every animal has its own smell as it rots on the cobblestones, being crushed and smashed by butchers' heavy boots.

All over London, people let livestock roam the streets, in an effort to clean up the garbage thrown from doorways into the gutters. To my right, three enormous sows rummage through a mixture of bones and decaying debris, snorting away, their fleshy faces covered in filth.

Someone yells from the window above our cart, "Look out below!"

Hadrian looks worried, as he knows he has to try to move quickly.

"Look out below!" they warn again.

He pulls the horse slightly to the left.

"Look out below!"

A full chamber pot is dumped, narrowly missing our cart and splashing up on the wooden sides. The pigs rush over to consume greedily whatever disgusting morsel was thrown down. Whenever I venture through Cheapside, I have to bring a sachet of rosemary to hold to my nose, or else the smell would be nauseating. Hadrian rarely takes me with him to go out. I'm excited to get out of the courtyard and see something different, vile smells or not. Hadrian has new surgical supplies and books coming to him from Paris. We have to go through Cheapside to get to the seaport on the Thames. Finally, we hear the steady creaking of the cart rolling along the muddy road.

The streets open up to a bustling harbor, every bit as smelly and crowded as the market.

"You wait here for me. I cannot get any closer to the dock," Hadrian says without even looking at me.

He motions two dockhands to come with him. I watch his slightly hunched form disappear into the slender vessel at the end of the pier. It is a beautiful, early fall day. The time when the summer heat has faded away and been replaced by a slight cool breeze. The sun glistens off the water, making even the polluted Thames look sparkling and beautiful. Men shouting and running to the farthest dock breaks the solitude of the moment. I turn to what the commotion is and see a large merchant ship coming into the harbor. At first, nothing looks out of the ordinary, but then I notice how slow the boat is moving, like a ghost gliding among headstones.

There are no hands on deck. The boat is coming in unmanned, with only one of its sails still tied, two others flapping in the wind. The eerie sounds of the riggings clanging against the masts echoes over the water. Tenders are launched in an attempt to aid the ship, but are too late as it runs aground on the side of the port. The whole seaport turns its attention to this strange anomaly, and many stand openmouthed.

*Did this ship lose its anchor or pull free from its cleats?*

I watch as men pull their small boats astride and climb up the ropes. They're on the deck for but an instant before they all run screaming off the ship or dive into the water below. The whole seaport knows what that means.

*The Black Death has arrived in London.*

Hadrian comes back with the men carrying a large trunk each. He squints toward the plague ship in annoyed anxiety. "Stay here. I have to see about this."

The cart jolts at the added weight, while the dockhands stand and leer at me.

Hadrian, noticing this, changes his mind. "You better come with me, Elizabeth."

We reach the farthest pier at the same time the men from the launches are landing, white-faced and soaking wet.

Hadrian marches up to them and demands, "What is it you have seen?"

One toothless, shaggy-bearded mariner barks back, "They're all dead, they are! Every last one of them! All strewn across the deck, some burst open, guts all spilling out!"

The others are silent.

"I am a surgeon. I need to know exactly what you saw to diagnose what pestilence they are carrying."

"Guts spilling out is what I'd seen! Jumped off before I could feel for fever!"

His mates start laughing at this. Hadrian gives the man a stern stare.

"Aaagh," the mariner says as he wrings out his cap. "I saw one mate had a giant lump on his neck."

"Any black splotches or blood around the mouth?"

"Look, love to gab with you, but we have to go tell the dock master about this here grounded ghost ship." They walk away.

∞∞∞∞∞∞∞∞∞∞∞∞∞∞∞∞∞∞∞∞∞

Hadrian stops at a fellow surgeon's house on our way back home. We are welcomed in for an early dinner. The table is amply covered with breads, meats, and fruits. The mistress of the house sits at the table, feeding her lapdog pieces of ham under the table.

"The sea urchin said the bodies had been split open. I doubt it was a symptom of the disease, probably the result of bloated bodies in the sun hitting the mast as the decks rolled," Hadrian explains as I wonder how they could talk of such things while stuffing their faces.

Our host asks, "What other symptoms were observed?"

They're talking only to each other; women are not a part of men's conversations.

"The urchin only glanced around the deck and fled. However, he did say he noticed a lump on one of the doomed sailor's necks."

"A bubo." The older doctor strokes his beard at this and concludes, "A strong indicator of the Great Mortality."

Hadrian nods. "Yes, I agree."

"Do you think there are any survivors?" Our host is furiously cutting his steak like he is trying to start a fire, causing the whole table to shake.

Hadrian scoffs. "I doubt they gave much effort in checking, but even if there were, London would not take them in."

"Well, London has been watching for this for a year. They all thought it wouldn't come to us. It has ravaged Italy and France, and now the plague is here."

"You think London has been exposed from these few men boarding the vessel for a moment?" Hadrian drops his fork and knife and suddenly looks concerned.

"That, and I imagine the south wind blowing from the harbor stirring the corrupt vapors from those plague bodies and carrying the Black Death to each and every one of us who breathes." He snaps for a servant, who comes quickly to his side. "Close all the windows facing the south side. From now on, only the pure air from the north is allowed in this house!"

Hadrian gives me a look, and I can tell he is anxious to get home to do the same.

"You do know it is all due to the unfavorable planetary alignment?" A grave look takes hold of our host's face as he says this.

Hadrian nods somberly. "The major conjunction of Mars, Saturn, and Jupiter in Aquarius is an extraordinary event—an ominous event portending pestilence and great death."

"Very ominous indeed!" the doctor exclaims as he tears a huge piece off a drumstick and gobbles it down.

"If in fact the plague has its grips on London, how should we act?" Hadrian asks.

"Depends on how much gold the good Lord or Lady will give you!" He laughs so hard at his own joke, he chokes on the wine he is drinking, causing it to sputter out his thin-lipped mouth.

"You think it unwise to treat lowly classes, then?"

He sputters for some time and, once recovered, wipes his mouth with his sleeve. "It all depends what price you put on your own life. I have heard many of the leading doctors in Paris and Rome have all been killed simply for *talking* with infected patients."

"How can we service the public if we are at risk by being in their very presence?"

"I tell you, Hadrian, if this plague takes hold in London, I will run and run fast. And you and your lovely wife should heed my advice too."

I look up to see the doctor giving me a tight smile with food in his beard.

Hadrian is quiet all the way home, as usual. Dusk has set in, and the church bells are ringing everyone to bed. Peasant children run through the street, chasing each other with barking dogs in tow. I pray the doctor is wrong.

My mother comes to greet us upon entering. "I have had to eat dinner all alone tonight. Did you have plans elsewhere?"

"I am sorry Jacquelyn. There was an unpleasant event I had to discuss with another surgeon."

She pulls her chin up. "That is fine. I was forced to amuse myself at the table." She turns to me and kisses me on both cheeks. "Any news from the market?"

I take her into the sitting room as Hadrian drifts into his library with one of his trunks, barking orders to the servants to close the windows on his way.

"A plague ship came gliding in unmanned, the whole crew dead on deck."

Her amber eyes widen at this news. "It has come at last!" She pulls me down to the bench beside her. "I knew it would come to kill us all just as it has ravaged Paris! We could not hide on this island forever!" She begins biting her fingernails. "We have to leave like we did during the Great Famine."

"We will not have to leave. We will be fine here." I hope I've stopped her before she begins lamenting yet again about the famine that happened thirty years ago.

She shakes her head, and her golden hair spills around her shoulders. "You have never seen the horrors I have witnessed. Men, women, and children were dying by the hundreds! The London streets filled with beggars. Families couldn't keep the water out of their houses. Rain was seeping through everywhere, the roofs, and the walls, under the door—"

My thoughts drift to a seed stuck in my tooth since dinner. I try to dislodge it with my tongue as she rants on until she shakes me to pay attention.

"Fires would not light, bread was molding, and crops were flattened by hail. Eighteen months of pouring rain! Even fine families like mine had trouble finding adequate food, as others were scavenging garbage—eating bird dung, pets, and even people!" She realizes how frantically her voice has risen and sits back in the chair, finishing in a hastened whisper, "It was terrible. I never want to witness such things again."

"That will not happen again." She doesn't even hear me in her tirade.

"My father, very sensible man he was, took us and left. On our way out, we saw families: naked, skin and bones, on their hands and knees, eating grass like beasts! Many fields could not return to production for years, and some were ruined forever. I saw such horrors that I did not come back to London for many years, until your father brought me back." She pulls my chin up for our eyes to meet. "We still have our manor in Windsor. You must speak to Hadrian about leaving at once before this spreads!"

"Let us pray together now that this plague will not hit, and we will not have to go anywhere."

I help her onto her knees, shuffle beside her with our rosaries wrapped around our clasped hands, and we recant our Lady's prayer.

# Chapter 2

The prayers went unanswered. Three days later, Hadrian receives word the mariners who ventured onto the plague ship are extremely ill. Hadrian is called to go look at them. Believing the plague is caused by infected air, he asks me for my sachet of rosemary. He calls two houses down for his apprentice to assist him. He is in such a hurry to leave, he forgets to kiss me before he steps out the door.

"Good-bye!" I call after him, but he doesn't seem to hear me.

Mother and I busy ourselves making smelling apples from black pepper, red and white sandal, roses, camphor, and four parts of bol armeniac. Mother has been advised that holding one of these apples under your nose lends protection from disease. I take my smelling apple and go out to the courtyard behind our stone house. It is quiet and peaceful in the garden. Most of the flowers are past bloom and now giving way to autumn's crisp slumber. I can faintly hear the hustle and bustle of Cheapside. I am not permitted out of the house unless Hadrian gives me permission, so this is my favorite spot to be alone. I sit there looking at my smelling apple, hoping it will keep me safe.

Hadrian comes back looking worried. At supper, he tells us, "It most definitely is the Black Death. It has already spread to the mariner's families, in only three days!"

I can't eat with this news. "Are they going to recover?"

"One man is almost dead, the other two, I do not know."

"You did not touch them, did you?" Mother asks, her thin brows drawn together.

"Of course not! I had my apprentice go in and tell me of their symptoms. I instructed him through an open window, facing north."

We are both relieved at this and feel more at ease in his presence again.

"Is there any treatment?" I ask.

Our servants interrupt us as they bring in our fish dinner.

Hadrian takes one look at it and says, "We will not be having fish anymore. Who knows what water it has come from and what foul air it has inhaled." He pushes the dish back at the servant. "Find something else quickly. Some animal that has breathed only London air, and remember, no spices at all!" He turns back to us. "They could be spices sent from the Genoans' galleys, for God's sake!" I must have shown my confusion, since Hadrian rolls his eyes and spits, "The dirty mongrels we have to thank for spreading this god-awful disease to Europe."

Mother looks embarrassed that I hadn't known this too.

"Is there any treatment?" I ask again.

"Well, if the lesions ripen, one should skillfully rupture it, but who is going to get close to a peasant plague victim?"

"Is there nothing else to be done?" Mother wonders, I'm sure, for her own reasons.

"Well again, if there were anyone foolish enough to attend them, bloodletting would surely draw out the body's heat from fever. There has been some talk in France about certain plague antidotes."

"Antidotes?" Mother perks up at this information. "Where can we obtain them?"

"Lucky for you and Elizabeth, I was so clever to have recently received them from the Parisian apothecary." Mother and I smile at this. "That is what I was picking up at the seaport that day, ironically."

"How much antidote do you have?" I begin eating again at this happy news.

"I have the whole assortment. One mixture of fig, filbert, and rue—all said to be beneficial. A bottle of little white pills of aloe, myrrh and saffron. I also have a few little pots of theriac, mithridate, bol armeniac, and terra sigillata. But the most potent and rare antidote I sent for"—he reaches into his pocket and pulls out a little corked vial—"is this little beauty, ground emerald powder, the most powerful."

Our eyes sparkle as we fix them on the green shiny powder held in the glow of the candlelight.

"How lucky we are, Elizabeth! To have such a wise and wonderful man in our house!"

The dimple on the right side of his face deepens with pleasure at my mother's recognition.

"This is only to be used if nothing else works. Cost me a bloody fortune. Had to sell three horses from Windsor to obtain it, but it will serve us nicely, if need be."

"We made ten smelling apples this morning," I say, trying to contribute.

"Very good. I will need one for my apprentice and me on the morrow. I need to keep abreast of the emerging situation. Even though I have provided us the antidotes—"

Mother interrupts. "But you will only save them for us, right? You are not intending to waste them on your patients, or worse, peasants!" Her voice rises to an uncomfortable pitch.

"Calm down, Jacquelyn." He leans back and stretches his long legs under the table. "Of course I will not waste them on peasants. The emerald powder is exclusively for us, but the other antidotes I will sell at a high price to dying lords and ladies in this city. We will reap a fortune from it."

"So wise, so wise," she says, rubbing her hands together in anticipation.

Clearly relishing her praise Hadrian says, "The question is not what can be done once stricken, but more importantly, what can be done as a preventive measure."

Mother and I lean in, waiting to be blessed with the treasured knowledge.

"Do tell us?" Mother pushes.

"Wine, and white wine is best, should be consumed at least once a day."

Mother nods aggressively in agreement as he continues, "All excessive exercise should be avoided. Also any activity which would open your pores should be avoided, such as bathing and intercourse. They all allow the poison to seep in."

He looks at me as he says this, and I am relieved to be able to avoid the unpleasant act for some time.

"Fine advice. We shall have a glass of wine this very night!" Mother calls the servant, and we toast our goblets in unison.

"To health in the midst of pestilence!"

# Chapter 3

In the morning, I watch Hadrian dress for the day from under the warm covers of goose-down. He pulls on his constrictive hose, which unfortunately clings to every crevice and bulge. He throws his shirt over his woolen breeches that are dingy and loose from the infrequent washing. Lastly, he crawls into his forest-green kirtle, which is made of the finest crushed velvet from France.

He nudges my shoulder. "Elizabeth, please wake for inspection."

I pull down the covers as he takes my pulse and feels for fever. He searches my abdomen, neck, and thighs for buboes: swellings caused by the plague. Finding none, he hands me the chamber pot. Used to this act by now, I casually get up, go behind the painted screen, and squat over the clay basin.

"I have no bowel movement this early," I say minutes later as I hand him my pot.

He looks disappointed. "You should have them regularly. You need to eat more figs. I have mine every morning upon waking. My digestion is remarkable." He points to his full chamber pot by the bed.

Taking my pot under his nose, he inhales deeply and ponders for a moment. "Definitely not with child. Nevertheless, we have only been married three months, so that is nothing to worry about. These are terrible times to bring children into the world anyway." He pulls the urine in for closer inspection. "I see no evidence of contaminants."

He leaves both chamber pots on the floor for the servants to dump out the window later and leaves without saying good-bye. I weave my long, dark brown hair into a thick, shining braid and tie the bottom with a burgundy silk ribbon. I finish dressing with my embroidered burgundy velvet kirtle that mother gave me as a wedding present and go down for breakfast.

Mother is already sitting at the table. "Hadrian gave me excellent praise of my bowels this morning. He said for you to eat more figs." She pushes the figs toward me and then pulls her kirtle up to scratch at a fleabite on her knee, exposing the birthmark that is darkening with age.

"Yes, Mother." I take one and shove it in my mouth.

"You know, I was first wary of your father choosing Hadrian to wed you. He came from a poor peasant family with no title or property. But your father was relentless on the fact that he was a medical prodigy from Oxford and was going to be successful." She scoffs. "Thank God that unruly horse threw that lord off, shattering his leg in so many pieces that only Hadrian could fix it. Had that not happened, poor young Hadrian could not have gone to University, and we would not have our emerald powder, my girl." She pats my knee. "As dreary and boring as he is, it has proved very auspicious indeed for us."

I didn't have much say in the decision but am glad to have served my mother in this way, remembering all the criticisms she made daily about Father's ill choice.

As the weeks progress, Mother and I watch how the city changes from within the confines of our house. The hustle and bustle heard from afar fades, as the church bells ring constantly for funeral services. Men carry coffins on shoulders, with mourners trailing behind, at least twenty times daily down our street. People who venture out do so without stopping or speaking to passersby, holding their herbal remedies close to their noses all the while. Some of our faithful servants stop showing at our house, and no one knows if they fell ill or simply fear to leave their homes.

Hadrian returns increasingly paranoid every night. "We have to ready to leave for Windsor soon," he says at breakfast. "It is getting worse than I expected. Peasants are dropping in the streets off their carts and during their daily rituals. The city put an ordinance out today to force every property owner to make out a will. People are dying so fast they cannot find a notary to bequeath their assets!"

"Have you made out a will?" Mother ventures.

"Of course I have. All my business has been seen to." He speaks with his mouth full of food. "I am worried about the peasants' uprising as the death toll mounts. We need to ready ourselves to leave soon."

Mother wads up her cloth napkin and pushes her chair away from the table. "I can be ready by noon."

"I will wait until I see signs of danger, but we should always be ready." He turns to me. "My apprentice has died."

I am shocked. "I had not even heard the boy was sick."

"Yes, he had been sick for a week. I had hoped he would improve. I left the aloe pills with his mother. I spent the last two years teaching him. What a waste." He drops his fork in frustration.

"The antidotes did not work?" Mother asks with fear. "You still have the emerald powder, though?"

"Yes, I keep it in a safe place." I notice he does not trust us with the whereabouts.

"I need Elizabeth to come with me to my appointment tomorrow," Hadrian says to Mother. "I must attend to a very wealthy lady who is paying triple my normal fees. A highborn woman such as this requires that only a woman can inspect her chaste body."

"There is no servant you can sacrifice?" Mother inquires protectively.

"Only three servants have shown up to work today, and they are all male."

"I will go," I say to Hadrian. "I will bring my smelling apple and be careful."

∞∞∞∞∞∞∞∞∞∞∞∞∞∞∞∞∞∞∞∞∞∞∞

Hadrian helps me up on the cart. It has rained heavily; the manure and human debris stop up the gutters and cause the streets to flood with filth. Rats stream down the side streets, fleeing the water. Rakers kick the rats away as they try to unclog stoppages. As we pull away, I see one raker pull an exceptionally large dead rat out of the gutter by its tail. The streets are so empty I can see all the way down to an enormous bonfire.

Hadrian, noticing the fires, explains, "King Edward ordered purifying bonfires to be lit at every port and street to ward away the plague. Guards are checking everyone entering the city, keeping all foreigners out. A little late for that, Edward," he says in the direction of the palace.

The city is at war but with the invisible enemy within. We get to the nobleman's house in no time due to the small number of carts on the road. Hadrian holds up his smelling apple and grabs his leather supply bag, forgetting to assist me. I jump down but splash foul water up the hem of my kirtle.

Hadrian looks at the hem with disdain. "You should be more careful, Elizabeth."

The servant who opens the door looks ill himself. Sweat beads on his pale forehead. Hadrian pulls me away, noticing the signs of sickness, asks him to lead the way, and keep his distance. The man pulls the tapestry aside that conceals the grand bedroom; only the finest fabrics and tapestries decorate the cavernous room. We can hear labored breathing and moaning emanating behind the drawn bed curtains of the massive, carved canopy bed.

The nobleman is sitting beside the bed. He stands up to shake Hadrian's hand, but Hadrian shakes his head at the request. "Not the time for such things."

The nobleman pulls his hand back and goes to open the bed curtains. He reveals a terrible sight that makes me freeze. There, on silk-tasseled pillows, lays a pale, sweating form with large black-and-blue splotches around her mouth, neck, and legs. Hadrian turns at the half-dressed sight and steps back behind the bed to respect her modesty, though it appears she cares little. Her eyes are glazed and fixed on the ceiling, not even noticing our arrival. Breathing seems to take every bit of her energy, and the lumps under her armpits are so swollen they caused her to keep both arms above her head. I've never seen such a terrible sight. I wish I had the strength to leave.

Hadrian calls out, "Check her neck, underarms, thighs, and groin for buboes and tell me how many she has."

I walk up hesitantly with my smelling apple close to my nose and mouth trying to breath sparingly. Drawing near, I expect her to look at me, but she remains fixed. Even when I pull down her bed coverings to search her thighs and groin, she doesn't flinch.

"I count three buboes, two underarm and one on her thigh."

"Are they seeping?"

"Two are seeping."

"Then we must drain the third."

My heart quickens at this task I never thought I would be asked to perform.

"Come here, Elizabeth." I walk around the bed as Hadrian is pulling out a thin iron rod. "Heat this up in the fire until it is red hot. Puncture the bubo dead center with only enough pressure to break the skin. Do not apply much force or it will erupt all over you." I hesitate, yet he shoves the handle of the poker in my hand and says, "Do as I say."

I heat the iron as he instructed, walk over to the feeble woman, and lean over the large unbroken bubo. As I apply pressure to the purple lump, the flesh sears, and I gag as thick, yellow liquid squirts out. I pull back and hold my apple up but can still smell the rancid smell of pus.

"What else do you need?" I choke out.

"Does it have a smell?"

"Yes, like a cesspool!" I gag again. "Hadrian, I cannot do this," I beg.

"We are almost finished." He says to the man, "Please excuse my wife; women are undoubtedly the weaker sex."

I feel I am failing him, so I go back over to her bedside. "Forgive me, husband. What else do you ask of me?"

"What color is her spittle?"

I lean in yet again and can smell her vile, rotting breath. "I see no color."

"Does she have any other markings?"

I search her body with breath held. "There are black splotches on her chest."

"That is all. Close the curtains, Elizabeth. I would like to speak to the lord."

The tired, forlorn lord stands up to meet him over in the corner of the room.

I overhear him say, "Lord, I do not think she has the extremely deadly pneumonic plague. Victims cough up blood and die within three days."

I hear a sigh of relief from the lord.

"However, that is only good news to us, since it spreads more rapidly than the other form of plague. The lady will surely die."

I hear crying.

"She has what we call 'God's tokens,' those blue or black splotches. Those who present with these are sentenced to die within hours."

"There is no remedy?" he sniffs out.

"Well, there is something that might work, but it is exceptionally expensive."

I can't believe he is trying to profit from this; clearly the woman is at death's door.

"I will pay anything. You must give it to her!"

"Elizabeth, come to my side."

I obey him. The lord looks foolishly hopeful as Hadrian holds out a small vial of golden liquid.

"This is made from theriac, mithridate, bol armeniac, and terra sigillata from the finest apothecary in Paris. Her four humors are out of balance, evidence of the pus that is pooling under her skin in bubo form. This serum is her only hope at correcting it."

Before he gives it to me, he holds his hand out to the lord.

"Three gold coins, my lord."

The lord digs into a satchel tied at his side, brings out five, and places them in Hadrian's outstretched hand. "I want two vials."

Hadrian agrees, gives me one vial, pulls another one out of his bag, and gives it to the lord.

He speaks to me. "Drop the whole contents of the vial into her mouth and make sure she swallows. Hold her mouth closed and stroke her throat if she does not do so willingly."

I reopen the curtains to find her breathing even shallower. I feel terrible pouring the liquid into her panting mouth but do so. She lays there with the fluid pooling under her tongue. I put down my apple, take a deep breath as I close her mouth, and I'm relieved to see her swallow. She then convulses, and I jump back. She goes into a coughing spasm, no doubt the result of forcing the liquid. I break out in tears and run from the room. I don't stop until I'm outside the estate. Hadrian comes out after a few minutes without a glance in my direction.

He hoists himself on the cart, looks down at me, and says, "Get on."

I don't eat dinner that night but choose to sit out in my garden. I see from the walls of my courtyard that the sun is setting red on the horizon. I decide I'm going to try to talk Hadrian into leaving tomorrow. I don't want to become that woman. I don't want to see my mother like that. We must get far away from this rotting city.

∞∞∞∞∞∞∞∞∞∞∞∞∞∞∞∞∞∞∞∞∞

*I'm flying away from the burning city when a powerful gust of wind blows me back to the center of Cheapside. I hit the ground hard and, dazed, get up to see Hadrian digging. I walk over to see hundreds of dead bodies all lined up, heads to the west and feet to the east, side by side. They all stare vacantly at me. Two small children are thrown down, one with purple eyes and another with curly brown hair. Then Hadrian shoves me from behind, and I can't stop falling.*

I awake in a sweat to Hadrian calling for a servant to come and empty his chamber pot. No one comes. He leaves the room and returns minutes later and shouts, "No servant has showed!"

I stand to throw on my clothes.

"Elizabeth, empty my chamber pot." He goes back downstairs.

I walk over to the steaming pot with nose pinched, open the window, and yell, "Look out below!" three times, as required, and pour the contents on the street below.

Upon entering the kitchen, I see an agitated Hadrian pacing. "The fire has gone out, and not a one has come."

"Can we find more servants?"

"Not a one!" he screams as he throws his hands up into the air.

My mother comes to see what the shouting is about.

"I was paying ours twice the going rate, and they still stopped coming!"

Mother senses an opportunity. "Well, we still have most of our staff at Windsor. This only tells us that we must leave today."

He's searching the shelves for something. "I agree. We leave today." Still searching, he fumes, "As soon as we find some bloody breakfast!" He throws down a stone-hard loaf of bread and sounds as if he cracked the slate floor.

"Elizabeth, go into town for your husband and fetch him his breakfast."

I can't believe she would send me out. "I cannot drive the cart myself!"

"There is no need to bring the cart; few people are out. It is safe to walk into Cheapside now." She opens her eyes wide in demand. "Go now and fetch him his breakfast!"

As I throw my coat on, she presses coins into my palm. "Hurry back. I will pack up everything we need."

"Why can't he go?" I say under my breath as she crams my veiled headdress on.

"He is not in a state to go right now. I want to make sure he packs up and leaves before he can change his mind. Godspeed!"

She shoves me out and closes the heavy oak door behind me. I hear her slide the iron bolt so I won't be able to go back inside. I pry my apple out and venture carefully into the muck.

# Chapter 4

If I hadn't been prepared for the desolation, I would've thought I was in the wrong place. Cheapside is empty except for the occasional person covering their mouths and dashing through the streets. Hadrian talked about farmers boycotting the capital because they feared exposure. There is a deep silence. The nearest bakery is closed.

I peer into the store. The shelves are bare, and no one is to be found. Searching all the boarded-up stores, I worry breakfast can't be found. Down the lane, a large cart is being pushed toward me. To my horror, I see two half-naked bodies, strewn like sacks of flour, in the cart. I hold my apple up, suck in my breath, and start running the other way in search of an open shop.

Someone opens a window above and calls, "Sexton! We have a body here!" They wave a black plague flag out the window to signal a plague victim lies within. I run even faster.

Finally, I watch another hunched-over person run straight to a shop around the corner, and I follow. It is an open bakery! I never was so excited to see such a sparse assortment of simple wheat and rye loaves. The person in front of me gets as far away from me as he can and eyes me suspiciously. He snatches his loaf and runs out of the store. I ask for six wheat loaves, and the baker turns his back to wrap up the package quickly. One lane down, I feel the parcel and wonder how there could be six inside, and upon peering in, count that the baker gave me only five. I turn around, reenter the store, and put the parcel on the counter.

"Baker, there has been some mistake. I paid for six loaves but have only received five."

"This parcel's open. How do I know you didn't eat the loaf and come back to cheat me?"

He throws the package on the counter and turns his back. He cheats me and will get away with it. I have to get out of London. Grabbing my inadequate package, I set my mind to hurrying back to the house. A cruck house door slams up ahead on the row. A tall lean young man walks out and starts up the lane. The door reopens, and a boy of about eight runs out after him.

"Father! Where are you going?" he screams frantically.

The man picks up his pace, and the boy grabs on to his arm. He throws him off, sending him into the putrid gutters, and yells, "I can't do this! I'm done! We're all done!"

He keeps walking and turns the corner without looking back. The boy sits in the filth and starts to cry, rubbing the dirt all over his face as he wipes his tears. Uncomfortable with witnessing what occurred, I plan on turning down the lane, trying to avoid the boy. But as I pass the decrepit house the boy ran from, I see a small face peering out.

My feet stop as I see a beautiful little boy with ringlets of brown curls around a perfectly shaped porcelain face. He has large, honey-brown eyes and a faint scar in the middle of his forehead. His face streams with tears, and he searches worriedly to the whereabouts of his father and brother. I'm compelled to look in on this distressed child. I open the squeaky, slight door and catch the little cherub's attention. He seems even more frightened at my invasion, hops off a little stool, and darts to the next room.

I follow, saying, "Are you all alone, little one?"

The air is thick with the smell of excrement and urine. On the floor by the window are two piles of straw with moth-eaten woolen blankets, most likely the children's beds. The adjoining room behind is full of livestock. Chickens perched and clucking, a fat sow grunting, and a small pony eating soiled hay. Through the open back door, a skinny cow groans to be milked. There are gaping holes in the thin walls of the wattle-and-daub house, from which three fat rats are coming in and out. I see one monstrous dead rat under the small table in the front room. Full chamber pots, and items *used* as chamber pots, are strewn about the room. I put up both my apple and a sachet of rosemary to keep from gagging on the horrendous smell.

Turning into a dark, windowless room in the back of the house, I gasp as I see the little child tucked under the arm of a woman lying on the bed.

"Oh! I am very sorry, mistress; I thought the child was alone."

She doesn't move or reply.

"Mistress?"

Stepping forward, I smell the same putrid odor released when I cauterized the bubo at the noblewoman's house. I instantly know she must be very sick. I step back to leave but see the little angel poke his head out to look at me, and I can't go. I go up to see how sick she is and peer over to search her face. I gasp as I see a black-splotched face and pale blue skin, her eyes and mouth open. She must have been dead for days.

Shaking, I try to pull the child away, but he clings on to her tightly. When I walk back to the door, I turn to see he is lovingly smoothing her hair behind her pointed ear. Feeling sick to my stomach, I have to get some air and figure out what to do. I walk out the door and take a deep breath outside. How strange that the cesspool air of Cheapside would ever be refreshing! I notice out of the corner of my eye that the older boy is leaning on the side of the house, staring at me.

"Is this your house?" I ask.

He kicks a pebble with his ragged shoe and doesn't answer. I take a moment to think of something else to say.

"Is your mother sick?"

He looks up. "She's dead, and my father's gone."

I pause, then ask, "Do you think he will come back?"

"No." He looks down again, but continues, "Once he saw that Rowan is sick now too, he told us we were all going to die." He gazes down the street where his father disappeared.

"Do you need some help?"

He nods slightly, seemingly unsure of what I meant.

"Can you help me get Rowan to leave your mother?"

He nods, happy that it's something he can do. He disappears into the house to come back with Rowan awkwardly dangling in his small arms, both children smiling. I bend down and feel Rowan's head; he's hot. His cheeks are flushed, which gives him beautiful contrast to his pale skin. I lift up one of his arms, look down his burlap nightshirt, and see a small bubo forming. The little angel has the plague.

"What is your name?" I ask the older boy.

"Oliver," he answers. Rowan's getting too heavy, and he places him back down.

Rowan must be four or five years old. Oliver runs after him dutifully, trying to keep him out of the street, and herds him back toward the house. Rowan giggles while trying to escape, amazing me how much energy he has, being sick as he is. Something catches my eye at the end of the lane; it's the same gravedigger I ran from before. I can see he's been busy since I last saw him. There must be five more bodies piled up on his cart.

I hurry. "Children, please go inside right now and go play with the animals." Oliver obediently takes Rowan's arm and pulls him begrudgingly back into the house. I don't want them to see the cart full of death.

"Sexton! Sexton, I need your service!"

He looks up in an annoyed manner and doesn't increase his pace in the slightest. He takes what seems like hours to reach where I am standing. I cover my mouth and nose again and try not to look at the grotesque bodies staring out through stiffened limbs.

He pulls the horse to a stop and gets down, wiping his sweaty, dirty head. He's covered in every kind of filth and smells worse than he looks.

"It's going to cost you." His steel-grey eyes look not of this world. I step back, wanting to put as much space as possible between us.

"I only have a single pence."

He sees the wrapped parcel tucked under my arm. "Is that fresh bread there?"

"Yes, four loaves of fresh wheat." I want to save two loaves for the children.

"No forr, I will take your dead for the pence and the bread, but only because you're such a lovely little blossom."

He gives me a leering once-over. I point inside the house, and he thankfully leaves to fetch the poor woman's body. I take out two loaves and tuck them into my underclothes. The sexton comes out backward, dragging the corpse.

"Take keep! Take keep!" he's shouting, trying to dislodge Rowan as he clings to his mother's chest. The sexton drags both of them off to the cart.

"Momma! Momma!" the child's frantically crying.

Oliver is torn between not wanting his mother being taken and understanding she must be taken. He keeps trying to pull his little brother off as tears silently run down his dirty face.

The sexton gives one strong kick to the clinging child. "Away, wenchel!"

Rowan falls off howling, and Oliver tries to pull him up to comfort him.

Oliver spits toward the sexton, "He's a boy!"

The sexton shrugs before hoisting her limp body clumsily, and without sympathy, onto the top of the heap. Oliver shuts his eyes and leans over Rowan so he can't see. The sexton holds his hand out for payment. I tuck the coin into the package and hand the bread over. He greedily takes it and pulls out a loaf with the same hand that just handled days'-old plague corpses. He tears off a huge piece and chews it with his mouth open.

"I usually get peasant rye, but this wheat's a fine treat!"

I walk away from him toward the children while he gets back up on his cart.

"To which cemetery are you taking the children's mother?"

He laughs. "No room left in the churchyard. We have to bury them in Smithfield."

"Smithfield?"

"The king's set aside a whole cemetery for burying the victims of the Great Mortality. Today's a slow day."

Makes me wonder what a busy day would look like.

"You're lucky she won't be thrown into the pits. Get her own box, she will." With that, he whips his horse, and the grim reaper creaks away.

I go back into the house to see if the children have anything they can bring with them, and I see nothing. Everything is crawling with fleas and vermin. I open up the gate for the animals to be released to fend for themselves. I shoo the children back out and then slap off the fleas that are biting my ankles. I take each child's hand but remember the loaves. I pull one out, tear it in half, and the grateful, salivating look on the children's faces tells me that they haven't eaten for days. I start to walk with no destination in mind as they happily chew on their bread.

*Where am I going to take them? Who will take in plague victims?*

I reason the only thing to do is bring them to Windsor with us. We can surely find one of our serfs to take them in once they're cured. No one better to cure them than a surgeon! I see a loaded cart in front of our city house. Mother's on the cart bench, and Hadrian's making sure the items in the cart are tied down tightly. Mother, looking put out at my long absence, grows livid when she sees whom I brought back with me.

She yells, "Hadrian, fetch her at once!"

Hadrian glances up and looks confused at my company. He walks toward me briskly and reproachfully. "Where have you been? We sent you out for breakfast, and it is nearly midday now!" He looks down disdainfully on the children. "Why are these beggars with you? These are plague times, Elizabeth!"

He grabs my arms, shakes the children loose violently, and pulls me to the cart. The children hug each other in fear.

Mother shouts, "Elizabeth! Get on this cart at once! Have you lost your senses?"

I pull back from Hadrian with all my strength and he yanks back with a drawn face. "Get on the cart and do as I say!"

"Can we bring these poor orphans?" I try.

He doesn't even look at them. "Stop this nonsense!" He pulls me again.

"Their father has left them and their mother has died of the Black Death!" I plead.

He freezes at this. "You mean to take in *plague* children! What is the matter with you?" He casts off my arm like it's ridden with plague vapors and pulls his apple out of his pocket to his mouth and nose.

Mother, overhearing this, pounces down from the cart and marches over to me, fuming. "Stop embarrassing me and your husband with your foolishness! Come at once!" She stomps her foot to emphasize the last word.

"I cannot leave these innocent children to die in the streets. We can take them, cure them with our antidotes, and find homes for them among our servants in the country."

"I will not put those filthy children on my cart or in my house," Hadrian says from his distance, as Mother nods in full agreement.

I fold my arms. "Then I will not go with you."

Mother drops her head in total disappointment, and Hadrian smirks. I worry at what I just said. I hold my breath, hoping that he will give in, since I didn't consider how I could possibly take care of myself.

"Oh!" He starts laughing. "So you think you can fend for yourself? With no money or help in a city riddled with *plague*!" He walks to the back of the cart and opens his trunk. Chuckling to himself, he pulls out some of his vials and closes the trunk.

He hands me the vials and says, "God save you." He then goes to ready the cart.

"Elizabeth, get on this cart at once!" My mother rages but I only shake my head. I have never behaved so defiantly, but once I start, I cannot stop. "Elizabeth, what has come over you?" She throws balled fists down on her thick skirts.

Hadrian commands, "Leave her, Jacquelyn! I will not tolerate such disobedience! I will not stand for it!" He sees my mother's hesitation. "She's steeped in plague now. Who knows what filth she's waded in to drag out these miserable creatures? Bringing her with us now could be a death sentence!"

Mother turns back to him. "Should you at least open the house for her?"

Hadrian shakes his head with stern speed. "And leave my estate open for all the scourge in Cheapside to enter? No, she can find shelter with the nuns."

Mother reaches around to hold her veil in front of her face, pulls out the few coins she has, puts them in my hand, careful not to make direct contact. She looks me in the eyes and says, "Foolish child."

Mother walks back to Hadrian's outstretched hand and is lifted up to her seat. They start away, leaving us helplessly in the middle of the empty street. I go up to the house and hit the iron latch to open the door, but it's bolted shut, and I have no key. Hadrian has locked the house up tight. I stare down at the sorry-looking children scratching their heads, which are full of lice, I'm sure. I give them both the last loaf.

At that moment, the abbey bells ring out purely. I grab the boys' hands and walk toward the crumbling stone abbey outside of the city.

# Chapter 5

Oliver and I take turns carrying Rowan, who is exhausted from his high fever.

"How old are you, Oliver?" I ask as he pants, trying to carry Rowan as long as he can to help me.

"My birthday passed a month ago." He heaves the slumped Rowan up higher. "I'm seven."

"I thought you were eight or nine!"

He looks up, and his indigo eyes sparkle proudly. We reach the abbey and walk through the open doors to the chapel.

The pews have been cleared to the side of the vast, high-ceilinged room. Bodies are everywhere, in every state of agony. The smell of the plague lifts into our noses, and Oliver holds tight to my dress as I take Rowan. The sick are everywhere, but there are no nuns to be seen. We stand there, waiting for some-one to come and help us, while people cry out in the delirium that only high fever causes, crying either for water or loved ones, and some simply incoherent.

Right as I am thinking of leaving the horrible place, a nun in full habit comes hustling from outside with two buckets of water hanging off a stick on her shoulders. She puts the buckets down, takes a dipper, and proceeds to fill a wooden goblet repeatedly, while delivering it to each parched mouth. She is so busy and dedicated to the saintly task, she doesn't see us standing there. After she has reached every thirsty soul, she stands up and looks satisfied with the way the sick have settled down. She spins around to grab a pile of cloths and dumps them in one of the buckets. Pulling each one out, she wrings them and places them on every fevered forehead. I know she is never going to stop her chores and notice us, so I step carefully around the bodies lying on rags on the floor and surprise her.

"Sister—"

She jumps and grabs her chest.

"Sister, I am sorry to startle you, but I need your assistance. These children have been orphaned, their mother died, and their father abandoned them."

"We have heard that story before." She doesn't make eye contact, only goes back to her chores.

"The little one is sick with a fever and a bubo under his arm." She now looks sympathetically upon Rowan's sleeping face and holds her hand to his forehead. She traces her finger down the faint scar and smiles.

"I will make a small bed for him." She goes out the back door and returns quickly with a handful of rags. They are torn scraps from discarded clothing but are crisp and clean.

I go to put Rowan down when she stops me. "No, the child needs to be cleaned first."

She beckons me to follow, and Oliver tags behind. She has a wide basin in the back beside an open fire. She fills the basin with hot water from the cauldron and pours cold water in to make it an acceptable temperature. I wake Rowan while pulling his nightshirt over his head, and he cries groggily at the distur-bance. All sorts of vermin go hopping off his body when the shirt is removed. The burlap shirt is stiff and scratchy; the roughness causes Rowan's delicate skin to chafe. Seeing this, the nun takes his shirt as far away from her body as possible and pitches it into the fire.

I put Rowan in the warm bath, and judging by the layers of dirt on the child, I'm sure it is the first bath of his life. Oliver looks on with interest. The nun takes up a rough brush and be-gins scrubbing the filth off; her mouth pinches in hard labor, and the freckles disappear in the red flush of heat to her face. Rowan enjoys it until she pours water over his head and scrubs his scalp. He screams in protest.

Oliver tries to run away at this point, but I tell him to remove his shirt. I wrap Rowan up in a clean woolen shirt the nun has found for him and bring him inside to his bed. The nun orders Oliver to get in the tub in the background. Rowan settles imme-diately into the heap as the curls start to return with the warmth of his fever. As I walk back outside, I can hear Oliver hollering, "Quit it!" as she scrubs the lice off him. I help dry him off and hand him his shirt, knowing he thinks he is old enough to dress himself. I find his heap of rags and a large piece of wool for a blanket, and he looks relaxed for the first time.

After they are both asleep, I go out back to find the nun again, since she seems to be purposely avoiding me.

I walk up and say, "I am not ill but have some experience with caring for plague victims." She still doesn't stop her chores and keeps her back turned. "I was hoping that in return for shel-ter and some food, I could help care for the sick."

Still with her back turned, she says, "You will need to talk to the Mother Superior about such matters."

"Where can I find her?"

She points to a small thatched barn up the hill. I lift my dress off the ground and trudge up the hill. Reaching the fenced-in area behind the barn, I hear a great commotion of clucking and wings flapping. Peering around the large hexagonal chicken coop, I feel instantly intrusive upon spying an older nun with her habit tucked up into her undergarments, lunging wildly around after the scattering hens. After one awkward dive into the corner, she comes up with a flapping, fat hen upside down.

Seeing me, she laughs and says, "God's work is not always pretty!" She walks around the coop to a broad stump, swiftly lifts a short axe, and with a clean chop, the life leaves the golden hen.

She walks up with the hen's feet still kicking and asks, "How can I help you, child?"

"I have brought some plague orphans here for your care and was hoping I could stay to assist you with the stricken."

She glances up to the sky. "Oh! The Lord is miraculous! We are in need of more assistance." She looks back down at me. "God bless you, child, but you know you put yourself at great risk?"

Wishing I could somehow change my mind, I answer, "I have no choice, Mother. My husband deserted me when I tried to care for the children."

She shakes her head. "We cannot all see the grace of God in such perilous times. Only the most devout can see the humanity behind the fear."

Her eyes are small and so dark they reflect all light. She has a mole to the side of her right eye that gives her a painted look, and her smile is comforting.

She thrusts the dead chicken into my hands, tucks her dress farther into her breeches, and says, "Get busy plucking that one for our stew tonight. I have to go chop three more."

The stew is delicious, and the children wake back up in time to have some for supper. I feed Rowan in his bed and make him swallow the contents of one of the vials Hadrian left me. Oliver and I join the two nuns by the fire. They say a prolonged grace and eat in silence.

At the end, Mother Superior calls, "Emeline, why don't you take—I'm sorry child, what is your name?"

"Elizabeth."

"Elizabeth up to our quarters. Poor dear looks tired."

I walk Oliver back to where Rowan sleeps soundly, and he looks nervous that I will be leaving them.

"I will only be upstairs with the nuns. You need to stay here to take care of Rowan. If he needs any help, you come find me."

Being protective makes him understand why he has to stay, and without a word, he kisses his sleeping brother and lies back down on his rags. I follow Emeline up the narrow stairs to a few small rooms with narrow roped beds and hair mattresses.

She points to two of the rooms. "You can take your pick. Normally we have four nuns to a room..." She tries to choose her words carefully, and finding none, she finishes, "...Well, we can all have our own rooms, now."

I take the room closest to me. It makes me nervous to think so many nuns sacrificed themselves to help others, nuns who slept in this very bed. When I lie down on the lumpy mattress and pull up the wool blanket, I wonder how my life has changed so much in one day. I feel alone for the first time in my life, and cry as I realize that I have no idea what I am doing with two small children.

I wake up to someone knocking on the door.

Oliver is there, sniffling, and I whisper, "What it is, Oliver?"

"Rowan is very hot, and he isn't waking up."

I run down the stairs, getting my shoe caught in the hem of my kirtle, and fall at the base of the stairs. I hurry to Rowan's bed and see that he is murmuring restlessly between chattering teeth.

Emeline rushes down behind us. "The child is burning up. We need to get him into cold water."

"My husband is a doctor, and he said the only cure for fever is bloodletting. We need to flush out the impurities."

She sneers at my idea, grabs Rowan up, and carries the child out back. Emeline pours water straight from the well into the basin and places Rowan into the cold water. She reaches for a rag and keeps wringing it over his head. Baths are known to bring on disease and death. Why would she think submerging the child would save him?

I go to Mother Superior and find her leaving her room. "Mother, Sister Emeline is killing Rowan!"

"Calm yourself, dear. Sister Emeline has been taking care of the sick since she first arrived here at fourteen. She may have strange customs, but more people have survived under her care than any other nun. Trust her as I trust her." She calmly walks down the stairs and out to the chapel, where she kneels with her rosary and puts her hand up to bring me on my knees with her . "The best thing you can do is pray to God to allow him to get better."

I kneel with her for some time, and when I open my eyes, I'm surprised to see Oliver by my side in prayer also. I'm not sure if it was the praying or the bathing, but Rowan's high fever breaks that night, and he improves steadily. Rowan begins to get up and run around with Oliver again, and in the midst of great suffering, it's nice to hear the happy chatter of children playing. I do everything Emeline asks from that point, although she does let me show her how to cauterize the buboes and nods in thanks for the helpful instruction. I also get permission to bring the children up into my bed and looked forward to their little arms and legs draping over me every night.

Every few days, the monks come from the municipal almshouse to deliver goods they produced from their acres of wheat, barley, and fresh vegetables. One monk stands out to me. He never makes eye contact with me and gravitates toward assisting the neediest victims. He brings soup to the hungry, cradling their heads in his arms and smiling as they manage to swallow. He sweetly and lovingly caresses fevered heads while giving the sickest their last rites. He performs the most difficult acts, such as washing infected feet, changing soiled sheets, and wrapping seeping pustules, with great compassion.

One day I try to talk to him as he is washing the floors.

"Brother Simon?"

His sparkling green eyes dart up to me. "Yes?"

I grab a rag and get on my hands and knees to help him scrub. He looks like he's uncomfortable seeing me get down in the wetness in my velvet kirtle. I hadn't planned far enough to answer him, so I awkwardly don't say anything. He stares at my left hand on the scrub brush for a moment and seems nervous with me so close.

"You bring such comfort to the dying," I finally say as I keep scrubbing.

"I wish I could do more," he says as he reaches over to pull the veil from my headdress out of the bucket.

I feel childish as I sweep it off my head, releasing my long, four-plaited braid, and wring the veil out swiftly. He puts his hands out to carry it to the table for me. Taking up the brush again, I try to scrub away my embarrassment. He takes his place on the floor again, and after a thick pause, I try to return to our conversation. "I wish I could bring such comfort."

He looks up, catches my eyes, and then fixes his gaze back on the floor. "Mother Superior told me you left your husband to care for orphans."

"They are over there." I point to them right as Rowan jumps on Oliver's back, sending Oliver careening into the ground over in the corner of the chapel. Both of them giggle hysterically.

Simon smiles, and I notice a slight gap in his front teeth. "Looks like you have brought much comfort too."

That one sentence makes me feel more important than anything else in my whole life. I help him finish the entire room.

∞∞∞∞∞∞∞∞∞∞∞∞∞∞∞∞∞∞∞∞∞

Every morning it's a somber job to see which tired soul has expired in the night. Sometimes we're prepared for it, seeing someone in particular distress. Other times we're caught off guard. The occasional patient will look as though he's improving and will be found cold unexpectedly. Malkyn, the Mother Superior, will say a prayer over their lost battle and cover them with a shroud.

The unfortunate job of instructing the sexton is mine. It's the same steel-eyed, vile sexton who buried the children's mother, and they run whenever they see him coming. He shows up this grim morning with a completely loaded cart—shirtless, even though there's an autumn chill in the air.

"Oh, the sun is already shining!" he calls out upon seeing me. "My little burgundy hen waits for me."

With only one kirtle to wear, I'm in burgundy daily.

"Sexton," I holler up, "we have three this morning."

"You, sweet wench, can call me Ulric." He wipes his hands on his hairy chest. "Little ones or fat ones?"

Disgusted by his question, I spit, "What difference does it make?"

"Easy there I simply might not have the room for them, is all. I've had a busy morning," he says as he smiles and pats his full purse.

"I am sure they will fit."

He climbs down from his cart, picking his teeth, then shifts some of the dead bodies to make room. I turn away as I see him unbutton a leather vest, off one of the dead.

"He won't be needing this where he's going." He chuckles.

When I look back at him, he is wearing the vest. Putting both hands on the sides of the vest he says, unashamed, "Don't I look like a nobleman now?"

I guffaw.

"I'm not keeping it. I sell the nicest pieces at a good price, you know." He looks down at my kirtle. "I do have some fine kirtles and can give you one for free if you're nice to me." He leers as I stand, unamused. He shrugs and moves another body. "This plague's making me a very prosperous man, young maiden."

"Matron," I correct.

"Matron? And living in a convent?" He sighs. "And all this time I was worried you were wasting your young maidenhead on God."

I decide I'm not going to talk to him anymore. I point to the shrouded bodies outside by the garden. He yanks off the shrouds, balls them up messily, and tosses the partially rigid bodies over his shoulder. Ulric throws the bodies down like sacks of flour and stashes the shrouds in the front of his cart.

I break my promise. "Those shrouds are for their burial!"

He chuckles as I snatch them back, climb the gruesome pile, and cover those I fed broth to only days before.

"How about a little bas on the cheek for my kindnesses?" he says, pointing to his filthy cheek. "You do know I do this for the sisters out of the goodness of my heart?"

"That and you find out who these people are and collect the death tax for the city for a fair price."

He smirks. "You are a feisty one, aren't you?" he says as he leaps back up on his cart. "No wonder your husband gave you to the nuns." He drives off.

I'm always relieved when he leaves but know all too well he'll be back tomorrow to ferry more to Smithfield's plague pits.

# Chapter 6

That day Malkyn speaks of the recent Papal Bull that has been granted in these extraordinary times of the Great Mortality.

She says to us at breakfast, "His Holiness has purchased new cemeteries and consecrated the grounds to help lessen the need for the plague pits. Due to the great number of priests dying from the plague, the Pope has granted blanket absolution." She turns to me and explains, "Now, anyone can give the last rites. So ladies, I will instruct you. I disagree with the Holy Father's next grant." She shakes her head. "He has waived the autopsy ban so that doctors can learn more about the pestilence. Lastly, there are those in other countries that are blaming the pestilence on the Jews in their midst. The Pope has condemned all attacks on them."

She makes the sign of the cross, and we all continue to care for the ever-increasing sea of sick.

There is barely any room between each rag heap. I give water to a young maiden with a bubo on her neck so large that it contorts her head to the side. She whimpers in pain. I look up to see Simon standing there. He bends down to hold her hand.

"What is your name, maiden?"

"Helena," the redhead answers weakly. "I think I need to be sick."

Simon reaches for the water bucket next to me and holds her up to purge. Vomiting is another torturous side effect of the disease. Sometimes victims will vomit for days. I watch him as he dabs her mouth with a rag and lays her back down gently.

She tries to speak, and Simon puts his finger up to her lips to rest, but she continues, "You can't let those wretched rustics come and throw my body in a pile with no feeling!" Her hazel eyes spin wildly. "Then the pigs come out at night, advancing upon the newly dug graves to feast on our corpses!"

"Calm now, lady, you have nothing to fear. His Holiness himself has purchased consecrated ground to make sure every last one has a dignified burial, free from vandals. Never you think of that anyway; the soul is granted eternal life, and the body returns to ash."

She closes her eyes and begins to breathe easier. I am convinced he is sent directly from God to ease all suffering. I can think of no one else in whose arms I would want to die. Malkyn begins to sing, *Languisco e Moro*, to ease the fears and give a respite of peace from our desperate situation. Oliver and Rowan find me and slip under my arms to listen to her angelic song. There is no other place I'd rather be.

That morning I cringe as I see Ulric coming down the lane. It's a sad morning, since Helena is one of the ten shrouded bodies waiting for transport. I hear him singing something jovially, and I can make out the words as he draws closer.

"Ring-a-ring o'rosies, A pocket full of posies, A-tishoo! A-tishoo! We all fall down!"

My face draws up in scorn as I realize what he's making light of, and he notices. "My sweet blossom doesn't like my little ditty?"

I can't hide my disgust. "You are vile."

"It's a children's song! Little wenchels are singing it all around the streets of London." He laughs. "It really stays in your head." He leaps off. "I have a special treat for you!" He goes behind his cart and pulls out an incredibly sick-looking woman from the death-pale lot. "A bubo-covered Winchester goose!"

He laughs and explains, "Don't you ever get out! That's another name for the loose wagtails—"

I put my hand up to stop him and help her into the abbey, and when I come back out see Helena thrown with her bottom up in the air on top of the heap, her beautiful red hair spilling out over the back of the cart.

"Is there any way you could come here after your first run, when your cart has more room in it?" I ask as I cover her body with her shroud.

"First run! This here's my fourth for the day!" My mouth drops in surprise. "You nuns are working miracles in there, only losing five to ten a day. Elsewhere one out of every two people is dropping. Even on a good day, London loses a small village to the pestilence." He throws another body next to Helena. "If I ever get this thing, I've told my wife to bring me here so my little burgundy hen can nurse me back to health."

I can't imagine him having a wife, poor woman.

Emeline goes to work stripping the Winchester goose, found to be named Gussalen. She holds up Gussalen's discarded burlap kirtle, which is stained with blood from backside leakage, one of the worst symptoms of the plague. Gussalen keels to one side as we're rinsing the dirt off, and we know to get her to a bed at once.

We lay her down as she begins mumbling, "I did everything I was supposed to."

"Yes, you are fine." I pull the wool over her.

"No!" she shouts, violently yanking the blanket back down. "I crouched at the latrines, wafting the stinking vapors over me. They said that I would build resistance to the scourge." She shakes her head deliriously.

I've heard that many people are seeing nuns like Emeline and Malkyn who are surrounded by plague and think that instead of hiding from the pestilence, they would cover themselves in it. I pick up a ladle of water and begin pouring it into her blue-toned mouth, and she spits the water out in my face.

"What is that? Are you trying to kill me? I need ale. Get me an ale!" Her front teeth are missing. I throw the ladle back in the bucket and try to mop the water off my face. "Ale is the thing that keeps the plague away. The more ale and food you consume, the better your health. I need an ale!" Her body goes rigid as she screams this.

I walk away. I thought she was difficult the first night, but when her fever takes hold, she tests the whole chapel's nerves. Her screams and groans rise to such a volume that the other sick beg us to remove her.

Simon comes and carries her out into the small enclosure at the farthest end of the chapel, but we can still hear her screaming, "There is no God! Where is God? Here we are in His house and we all still perish!"

Then she laughs, throwing her head back, braying. When she draws her last breath, all notice because it is finally quiet. The dying all clap.

∞∞∞∞∞∞∞∞∞∞∞∞∞∞∞∞∞∞∞∞∞∞

As Emeline and I are boiling the rags no longer needed by Gussalen, we see that a strange man has tiptoed into the chicken coop. Emeline runs to notify Malkyn, who comes out brandishing a pitchfork. We stand behind her as she jumps out at the man wearing a strange hat and holding three eggs he gathered from our roost. Seeing the armed Mother Superior, he throws down the eggs, puts his arms up, and pleads, "Please, Sisters, I beg you, forgive me!"

"If you are hungry, why not come into our abbey and ask for a meal?" She brings down her fork. He lowers his hands by his side and drops to the ground to try to salvage the shattered eggs. "Forget the spoiled eggs. Follow us to share our supper."

On the way back, Emeline whispers to me, "He is a Jew."

Surprised, I ask, "How do you know?"

"The hat he is wearing is a Judenhut, a Jewish hat."

Supper is served on the stone table beside the garden. Someone long ago had moved a massive rock between two long narrow stones, perfect for dining outdoors. We all say grace while the man hangs his head respectfully in silence during our prayers. When Emeline hands him a large bowl of vegetable soup with rye bread, he bows his head in thanks.

"My name is Daniel. I have fled the persecution in France," he says as if it's a confession.

Malkyn only nods her head slightly.

"I am a Jew," he emphasizes.

Still Malkyn nods. Daniel looks shocked by this casual acceptance.

"How are things in France?" she asks carefully.

He shakes his head. "Terrible."

Malkyn changes the subject. "How do you make your living?"

"Before I was chased out"—he sucks in a belch—"—excuse me, Sisters, I was a barber surgeon."

"How blessed for us!" She looks up again in direct communication with God. "We are struggling to care for the needy and sick, and in these times need every hand we can acquire."

He looks surprised. "You want a *Jew* to assist you in an *abbey*?"

"There is no religious prerequisite for caring for the dying and salvaging life." He looks amazed. "We can give you food and lodging in return."

He looks out past the abbey to the empty unforgiving streets and quickly says, "I would be a fool to turn down that generous offer."

Malkyn shows him to a side barn that would serve as his quarters while he's with us. He bows three times to her as she walks away.

The next morning, I'm slapping away fleas from my ankles and off the patients when Daniel comes up and says, "I know how to purge those vermin."

"How so?" I ask as he takes off his vest and rolls up the large sleeves of his shirt, exposing a large scar stretching from his wrist to his elbow. He leaves and comes back in an hour. He instructs me to make two large circles for him by moving the patients farther to the sides. He carries in stones and builds two high fireplaces into which he throws juniper and ash with sprigs of rosemary from Emeline's herb garden. As soon as he sets them ablaze, the putrid smell disappears and is replaced by a comforting sweet smell. From then on Daniel keeps the fires lit, day and night. He also fumigates over the sick, purging the scourge. That alone improves the spirits of all who enter and languish there. It also cures us of the unrelenting fleas; the heat seems to keep them safely at bay.

# Chapter 7

"—seven... eight... nine... ten—" I hear Oliver counting loudly as I creak the short door to the hayshed open enough to squeeze inside.

I find a seat behind a wall of bales and try to keep from coughing on the hay dust I stirred up in the dark. Light filters in and disappears just as promptly, and I still my breathing to listen for footsteps approaching. Someone much taller than I expect yanks my braid and I turn to see Simon, half in shadow, with his finger to his lips. He sits down right beside me on my bale and fills the air between us with the sweet smell from gathering honey all morning. He points to the outside of the shed, and I deduce Rowan and Oliver are close. We both look down at our hands, in the strange quiet moment we're caught in. Our breaths are the only sound in the dark, but I become increasingly aware of how swift and loud my heart's becoming. *Can he hear it?*

The door swings open, chasing away the shadows, and Simon puts his warm arm around me, ducking us from their view. I'm there under Simon's wing for only a moment before Oliver pounces out and screams, "Ah ha!"

Rowan runs out from behind him, beaming to find Simon there with me.

Oliver yells, "No fair! You can't hide together!"

"How did you know where Elizabeth was hiding?" Rowan asks as Simon pulls me up.

Simon leads the way out and calls back behind him, "I was watching her from up on that hill."

"If you don't play by the rules, then you can't play with us." Oliver crosses his arms.

Simon says in a high voice, "Not even if I brought you both a present?"

Rowan coos immediately, and Oliver quickly forgives him.

"Is it an apple?" Oliver hopes.

"Some figs?" Rowan guesses.

Simon smiles and pulls out a small grey puffball of a kitten with golden eyes from his satchel.

I couldn't believe he had concealed that the whole time in the shed.

They put their hands on him at once, and Rowan says, "His name is Mousie, because he looks just like a mouse."

Oliver laughs. "That's a terrible name for a cat!"

Simon bends down to Rowan. "Mousie is a fine name."

The children take the kitten away to play, and Simon says, "That's to help with the rat problem."

The rats had been getting into the chapel in great numbers. Every morning I would find at least one dead in the corners of the chapel or out in our stock house.

"Thank you, that will most definitely help *and* keep the children occupied."

We walk back together through Emeline's garden. The trace of mint aroma hangs in the air. Simon ducks his height under the bended willow arch covered in lush rose-hipped branches, and opens the small wooden gate. Forsythia grows high all around the small boxwood-edged place, naturally enclosing the garden away from the world. We walk along the narrow graveled path toward the tall stone sundial in the very center. As in a dance, we both part round the dial and come back together as a swarm of birds returns to roost in a massive oak in the foreground, making a ruckus in the quiet peace of the moment. Simon strips a boxwood branch and sprinkles the tiny leaves over my head. I laugh and grab up a handful of dried leaves and throw them over his head as he tries to turn away. I dart out the opposite gated arch as soon as I see him grabbing up an even greater pile and make it into the abbey right before he releases them, catching Malkyn on her way out. Simon immediately apologizes straight-faced, as I hide my laughter behind the door. Malkyn can care less about the leaves and invites Simon to eat with us. I hear him walk off to assist Malkyn with supper.

After our grace, Simon looks up and asks Daniel, "How bad were things in France?"

Daniel looks up with one eye narrow and one eye wide. "You cannot imagine the horrors I have witnessed."

We all sit, quiet. Simon attempts again, "I only ask because I have heard rumors about what occurred in Strasburg."

Daniel dips his bread in the stew, pops it in his large mouth, and states, "They are not rumors. I was there."

We all wait for him to speak again; I wonder if he ever will.

"It was Friday, the thirteenth of February, when they rounded us all up like wandering cattle, hitting us with sticks as they drove us toward the cemetery. I held in my arms my precious Rebecca, who was still asleep upon my shoulder, and my wife by my side. The sky was grey and dull, as the winter sun hid behind thick clouds, and we all cried out when we saw the massive bonfire burning among the graves. They forced us to strip our clothes. I woke up Rebecca, taking off her little dress and stockings, and she cried because she was cold." He pauses with that difficult imagery.

Moments later he continues, "The villagers pounced on our clothes after we threw them in a pile and stuffed their pockets with our savings we carried on us." He turns to Simon with his finger pointing to the sky. "That is the whole reason they brought us there!"

He breathes out, trying to calm himself. "They told us they were going to burn us to keep God from seeking vengeance for our sins and bringing the plague to their city. Jews tried to run in every direction. Many pushed through the mob and out into the streets only to be chased down and beaten with clubs in the sewers. They called out to us, 'Either come and absolve your sins through baptism of water or we will baptize you with fire!'

"I turned to my wife, and she shook her head stubbornly. But I could not think of Rebecca burning in the fire. It was a terrible sight, as devout Jews walked into the flames. I heard their screams of agony and smelled their burnt hair and flesh!" He pauses again, then continues, "I turned to take Rebecca over with me to the water, and Sarah grabbed her from me and leapt"–he begins to sob—"leapt into the flames with her."

We all wait with tears in our eyes as he pulls himself together again and blows his nose in a cloth he carries, in two loud trumpets.

"I knew I disappointed Sarah greatly. She was the daughter of an esteemed rabbi and extremely pious. I was too much of a coward to join them in the flames and took conversion with a thousand other cowards as twice that number of Jews died for what they believed in. Coward. Such a coward." He sits there shaking his head.

Malkyn speaks, "God forgive them for such heinous acts upon humanity."

"All spring they were murdering Jews. Killing them, stuffing their bodies in barrels, and floating them down the Rhine. Even after I converted, they kept threatening me. But when the plague arrived and I treated sick Jews and gentiles alike, a mob came accusing me of murdering gentiles. Poisoning them with the plague! They dragged me down to the well and demanded I tell them what poison I put in. Of course I said, 'I have no poison.'

"They insisted I was on a mission to kill all the Christians to achieve world domination.

"Domination!" He throws his hands in the air but lets them fall like soft snow.

"They stripped me of my clothes, put a crown of thorns on my head, and smashed it into my skin with mailed fists. Then they made ropes of thorns and thrust them up into my genitals. Who wouldn't confess after that?"

Simon winces at this and nods in agreement.

"So," he continues, "I told them I didn't put poison in, but I saw another Jew put poison in. They asked which Jew, and I described a plague victim dying in my care. They wanted to know what he'd done, so I told them he dropped an egg-sized tablet out of a wrapped package into the town well. When they demanded the name of the poison, I thought of belladonna, the only poison I knew. They refused to believe me, said this was a poison never seen before, and threatened to send me to hell.

"They thrust the rope back up with such force, the roping caught in my skin. I told them what they wanted to hear, that the Jew said he made it from the hearts of good Christians and Holy Communion wafers."

Malkyn, Simon, and Emeline all look down at this.

"The mob set on the man I described, and although he was half-dead, the look on his face as they beat him to death still keeps me from sleeping."

Simon rests his hand on Daniel's slumped shoulder. "Though you have been tried and tested, the sins rest on those committing such acts."

Daniel's shoulders still hang low, and judging by the constant circles under his eyes from then on, I would say he slept no better.

∞∞∞∞∞∞∞∞∞∞∞∞∞∞∞∞∞∞∞∞∞∞

*I stand before a wall of fire; the heat makes it hard for me to open my eyes. I feel the weight of two hands. I look down to Rowan's and Oliver's sweet faces.*

*Simon appears next to us and cries, "How strongly do you believe, Elizabeth?" then leaps and disappears into the flames.*

*I pull them back from the fire, but I hear, "Oliver! Rowan!" from behind us.*

*Rowan and Oliver rip themselves from my grip and run into the arms of their father.*

*I cry out, "They are mine now! You left them!"*

*But he smiles and leads them into the fire.*

I wake up and clutch for the warm, floppy bodies beside me, only startling Mousie nestled into the space between the boys and me. He crawls up farther onto Rowan's neck and curls his plumed tail around him out of my reach. Rowan's sweet face shines serenely in the moonlight, and Oliver stretches but quickly settles back into his peaceful dreams. I let their slow and rhythmic breathing lull me back to sleep.

# Chapter 8

Autumn gives way into winter but grants one last sunny crisp day in celebration of harvest's end. The sunset has left a red haze across the sky. I take Oliver and Rowan outside at dusk to run around and they bring their little kitten out with them. The abbey is an island in a sea of wheat, left standing with no one to reap it. You can see the direction of the wind by watching the ebb and flow of the grain tides. Everything is gilded: the grain, the grass, and the trees in the distance. I'm taking in the beauty of the moment, tracing my gaze along the maze of stone walls separating various crops, when I feel the familiar tug on my braid. Simon stands behind me, grinning.

"Your braid is as thick as a mare's tail!"

I run my hands along it, checking its girth as we walk the winding cart's path through the crops.

"I didn't mean that in a bad way," he says with a laugh.

I turn back to watch the children running in circles with long sticks, which the kitten's chasing wildly.

He looks on as well and says, "Amazing how children surrounded with the threat of death ignore it in their quest for life."

He steps into the wheat and lies on his back, gazing up at the sky. I decide to lie down next to him. We seem hidden from the world under the thick tops of grain—our own secret place. He plucks a long stalk and twists it into two joined circles. He holds it out against the blue, then lets it pop out of his hands and fall to the ground next to him.

He brings his hands up under his head, causing his elbow to rest slightly on my shoulder, and sighs. "I, on the other hand, feel like I am waiting for death among the dead."

His heaviness feels palpable as we watch the thin clouds drift by. I turn to study his face as he moves his hands nervously to his flat stomach, then leans over me and looks directly into my eyes for the first time. My stomach twists as I watch him reach out and pick up my braid. He runs his fingers up and down the entwined rope of hair. My heart begins to rise in my throat. He lifts the braid up to his nose and breathes it in. Then, just as quickly, he smiles, drops my braid, and falls back noisily to the ground. My heart slams back down to the pit of my stomach. I stare up at the waving wheat tops in silence, thinking of the strange event that occurred, surprised I was disappointed he didn't try what I'd hoped he was going to. He pulls a shiny red apple from his robe and begins carving it with his folding knife. He offers me the first piece, and I take it, happy for the distraction.

He begins again after a thick silence, "Do you believe in pledging yourself to something of extraordinary importance?"

He slips a slice in his mouth on the blade of his knife.

"Yes, I do." I think of how I feel about Rowan and Oliver.

"Do you believe that no matter what temptation might test you, one must stay true to a promise?" He hands me another slice, which I hold on to for the children. He is back to averting his eyes.

I pause a moment, trying to come up with an honest answer. "I believe everyone has a path and must use their heart as a compass."

He turns to me, smiling. "True, very true, Elizabeth."

He hops up but puts his warm hand down to help me. I call for the children, who come running at once with Mousie pouncing behind them. Simon carves up the rest of the apple while the children drool expectantly before he gives it to them. I decide to eat the last slice I'd been saving. Simon runs after Rowan, screaming in delight, grabs him up in one swift movement, and raises him to his shoulders. As we walk back up to the abbey in purple dusk, I wonder what his heart has told him.

# Chapter 9

The next night, Simon is chopping wood for the fire while the children are collecting kindling.

I hear Oliver scream, "Elizabeth!"

My stomach drops at the sight of Simon vomiting beside the woodpile.

*God, please, not Simon.*

I dab off his face with the hem of my kirtle and walk him back inside. We have some fresh beds ready for incomers, and I lower him onto one. He waves his hand for me to leave him, but I ignore the request. I get him a cool rag for his forehead and place a bucket beside him. He lurches to the bucket a few times and empties his stomach completely.

He's burning up by the end of the hour, and I go to Emeline to see if she thinks we should make a cold bath for him. As Emeline is drawing the bath, Daniel comes and places leeches at all his pulse points. Remembering the two antidotes I have left, I run up to get one. I come back down to Daniel helping Simon out of his robe and turn away to give him privacy as he steps into the bath. He shakes and his teeth chatter in response to the cold, but his fever won't break. His shivering gets so intense that the water sloshes out of the basin. Daniel dries him off and slips back on his robe. Simon looks so feeble walking back to his bed—aged decades within hours.

"E-Elizabeth?" he chatters.

"Yes?"

"E-Elizabeth?"

"Right here."

"S-stay with me."

I lie on his blanket with him and remember my vial. "Before you rest, swallow this, please."

"W-what is it?"

"It is an antidote all the way from France. My husband gave me a few vials of his antidotes as he left and I want you to take it."

"I don't w-want it." He shoves my hand away.

I don't understand. "It can help you."

"If you have s-saved that when others n-needed it, th-then I sh-shouldn't have it either."

I feel ashamed I had selfishly been holding onto these vials in case Oliver or I got sick and watched as others perished. He keeps shivering for hours. I try to keep cold rags on his head, but the fever is so high, they warm up too quickly. Daniel comes to check his buboes and sees he has developed an egg-sized one on his abdomen, above his groin, and a smaller one on his thigh. Daniel became a master at cauterizing without causing the reaction I usually got. But that didn't seem to help Simon either. Every time I give him the water that he begged for, he brings it up minutes later, to only beg for more yet again. His lips crack severely from dehydration, and I see one of God's tokens develop on his chest. I know he doesn't have long. Malkyn comes to sing at her usual time, and I hold on to his shaking hand.

"E-Elizabeth."

"Yes, I haven't gone anywhere."

"W-will you let me have y-your braid?"

I bend down and let him hold it in his hand.

After feeling it for a moment, he says, "C-can I k-keep it with me?"

I realize what he means and say, "Of course."

He reaches in his pocket, gets his knife, and tries to open it but can't manage the skillful movement while his hand is trembling so much. I open it, cut part of the ribbon off, and give it to him. He takes the braid in one hand and cuts into the middle of it. I catch it before it untwines, making the hair above the cut spin out around my shoulders. I tie the piece of ribbon on the top to hold the braid, and he closes his pale hand around it.

He dies around midnight, still clutching my braid.

The Brothers come with their wagon to collect Simon for burial in their monastery's graveyard. They treat his body with such care and place him in an ornately carved coffin. It is nice not to worry about his dignity in death or handing him over to Ulric's apathetic care, but I can't help thinking he would have been embarrassed by all this special treatment.

# Chapter 10

I try to busy myself to keep my mind off Simon being gone, afraid that if I fall into the hole he left, I will never surface again.

A nobleman in the midst of great delirium proves a good distraction.

"I'm filthy! I'm filthy! This whole city's crawling in excrement and disease!"

I wipe his perfectly clean brow. Strangely enough, this man had come in cleaner than we'd ever seen a body.

"You are not filthy at all. Actually it looks like you have scrubbed yourself raw." I look at his extremely chapped and cracked hands.

"I locked the house up and deprived myself of every comfort. Avoided all contact with any living creature. Subsisted in utter deprivation! Look at where it got me."

I remove the last vial I had left, giving them away the way Simon would have wanted. I empty the amber powder into a ladle of water and bring it to his purple lips to swallow. I stand up and throw the glass into the fire. He quickly falls into unconsciousness, but after three days, he improves.

Upon opening his ice-blue eyes, he asks, "Am I dead?"

I reply, "Does this look like heaven?"

I sweep my hand across the sad scene of people coughing on heaps of rags.

"Am I cured, then?" He whisks the hair from his widow's peak back behind his ear.

"I cannot say if you are cured, but your fever broke, and that is a good sign."

"It was all the cleaning I did. I know it weakened the disease."

*Everyone has their own idea of what saved them.*

"Do you know what is happening out there?" He points to the street side of the abbey.

"No, I have not been outside the abbey for months."

I start to spoon-feed him some soup.

"It is terrible. I lost my whole fortune. So many people are dying, and they have no one to leave their property to. Half the houses in London are vacant, falling into ruin and neglect." He takes the spoonful I have waiting and swallows rapidly to continue, "Neighbors are robbing neighbors, and greedy peasants are moving property lines with no one to contest. And that is nowhere near as bad as the problems due to the heriot."

I have never heard someone complain so soon after recovering before.

He continues fuming about the death tax, "Normally one gives the king a horse in payment at a death, but there are so many dying, the horses are all running loose in the streets! It has completely ruined the market! All of my herds are worthless now! I cannot even acquire hay to feed them with the scarcity of labor." He sits up. "Marriage has all but vanished! Society is crumbling. Even the great Edward the III has fled. Animals are dying in the streets and fields because there are no shepherds left to tend to them!" He starts wringing his hands. "I cannot go back! I cannot go back!"

"If you have survived it, we have not seen one person yet that has suffered a relapse."

"It is not the plague I fear but the sounds of the dying and the deplorable state London is in!" He grabs my arm. "Do you know for three nights in a row a man down in Cheapside kept stumbling up and down the streets screaming for his family all night. The lack of sleep I got was probably the very thing that exposed me to the filth. I can still hear it: 'Christiana! Oliver! Rowan!'—"

I freeze and drop the spoon into the bowl. *He is searching for them.*

"Coughing horribly all the while. It was enough to drive us all mad!"

Their father must be sick. I get up while Fendel is still ranting and walk out back. Oliver comes up bringing me a bouquet of juniper berries before he runs up to bed. Can I let their father die alone? However, the thought of losing the only two people I have left scares me more than anything could. Nevertheless, he must be brought here, even if he wants them back.

Emeline tells me she will keep her eye on the children, and I wrap the leather belt Simon wore around me, which holds everything necessary for delivering last rites. I walk down the lanes with lantern lit as a full moon rises. I can't believe how much has changed. Half the houses have doors wide open, with sows sticking their pink faces out at my approach. Black flags wave from every door, pole, and window flapping down the row like the invading enemy has won. Someone opens a window and screams out in agony, startling me into a run.

The children's house looks abandoned, and I almost turn to leave when I hear a rasping cough come from within. The house is in the same condition I left it except that the animals have all gone, turning over the chairs and table in their flight. I walk back to the bedroom where I had found their mother and see a half-dead man in her place. He's struggling to breathe between harsh, hacking sounds and violent spasms of endless coughing. There's a thick red pool of blood on the dingy sheets around his head. The most dreaded form of plague. I'm already in danger simply by sharing the same air as him.

I go to his side.

"Water"—he coughs—"water."

I reach for the bucket by the bed and see stagnant water.

"I will be right back." I take the bucket to the well out back and pull up a fresh bucket. He thanks me after he has a few gulps but soon erupts in more coughing and blood spittle. There is a terrible gangrenous smell coming from inside him.

"Oliver! Rowan! Christiana!" he moans.

"The children are safe."

He stirs. "You have seen them?"

"Yes, and they are free from plague, happy, and being cared for at the abbey."

He relaxes and whispers, "I searched everywhere for them." He coughs again for minutes. "Tell them that I am sorry."

I nod and administer last rites. When I offer him the sacramental bread, he shakes his head, unable to swallow, and convulses again.

He dies before dawn. Covering him with a shroud, I tuck a coin in his hand for burial. I take a black flag from a vacant house to signal Ulric. Instead of returning to the abbey, I walk down to the river to watch the sunrise. A cold breeze blows, and I pull my hands within the fluted sleeves of my cloak. The giant sun breaks the horizon with an ember glow, causing everything around me to burn red. Even the river shimmers crimson. Something catches my eye—objects drifting on the surface, breaking the reflection of the water in flashes. I bring my hand up to shield the glare, and I'm horrified to see dozens of naked, bloated, blue bodies floating down the Thames.

I turn to walk home as someone screams out, shattering the silence of the city, "The Apocalypse is here!"

He might just be right.

# Chapter 11

I have a fever by the time I return to the abbey. Emeline makes sure I am comfortable.

"Keep the children away from me."

She nods. By the middle of the night, the coughing begins. The other sick shush me as I cough uncontrollably. Feeling embarrassed of the terrible hacking, I pull myself up, walk out the back, and cough, hunched over in the entranceway. By morning, I'm coughing up blood. I'm so tired I begin to sleep through my coughing. When I open my eyes again, I'm shocked to see a familiar form kneeling on my makeshift bed.

"Hadrian?"

He reaches into his bag for something. "Lucky for you, I came when I did."

He holds his apple up by his mouth. I laugh weakly, thinking about how silly I must have looked to those dying with that apple up my nose, but end in a coughing fit that shakes my whole body.

"Here, take this." He holds out the green, sparkling vial.

"You are going to waste that on me?"

"Waste it? Do not be foolish, Elizabeth."

Daniel comes burning a bunch of juniper and rosemary over my head, and when Hadrian sees his Jewish hat, he barks, "Get away from her!"

I put my hand up for him to stop as I cough up in my rag. He bends down and pours the vial in my mouth. As I swallow, it feels like I'm gulping down sand.

"Water," I croak.

Emeline is right there to give me some. She looks distrustful of having Hadrian there.

"What is a Jew doing in a house of God?" Hadrian demands.

"Saving lives," Emeline answers. "He is a surgeon."

"A barber surgeon is not the same as a surgeon. They cut hair and pull teeth, for Christ's sake."

Emeline steps forward authoritatively in response to Hadrian's cursing.

"Daniel has been very helpful," I try but cough yet again.

"I see those children survived after all." He settles back down.

I nod thinking, *with no help from you*.

"When you get better, we will take them back with us to Windsor. Your mother is sick with worry. Your place is with us."

I suddenly feel worried that I will survive. I don't want to go anywhere. This is our home now. I ask Hadrian to go and fetch me clean rags and hand him the bloodied ones for cleaning. He holds them far away as he takes them outside.

"Emeline!"

She's at my side. "Yes."

"You must promise me something very important."

"I will see if I can, after you tell me what it is." She smiles a little smile.

"Hadrian cannot take the children if something happens to me."

She agrees immediately. "I can promise that."

Hadrian is back now and hands me the clean rags.

Within hours I'm struggling to breathe. Malkyn gives me my last rites as Hadrian sits next to me. Emeline and Daniel stand in the far background.

"Tell the children that I love them," I cough out. "Make sure they know their father was searching for them."

Malkyn promises.

"He wanted them to know he was sorry."

I hear the cries of Rowan and Oliver coming from the chapel as they run to me, throwing their arms around me and wetting me with their tears. I feel warmth spread all throughout my body from their embrace. I let out one life-long breath and close my eyes.

| Beacons | Life 1 Eygpt | Life 2 Sparta | Life 3 Viking | Life 4 Medieval |
|---|---|---|---|---|
| Mole on left hand-- Prophetic dreams | Sokaris | Alcina | Liam | Elizabeth |
| Scar on forehead--Large, honey- brown eyes-- Magic | Bastet | Ophira | Erna | Rowan |
| Space between teeth-- Green sparkling eyes | Nun | Theodon | Thora | Simon |
| Mole by wide-set--Dark eyes | Nebu | Mother | Ansgar | Mailkyn |
| Freckles--Brown eyes | Khons | Arcen | Keelin-Mother | Emeline |
| Birthmark above knee-Amber eyes | Edjo | Kali | Dalla | Lady Jacquelyn |
| Two moles on jaw--Black eyes | Apep | Leander | Ragnar | Brom Children's Father |
| Picks teeth--Steel-grey eyes | Vizier | Magistrate | Seamus-Father | Ulric |
| Golden eyes--Animal | Sehket-Cat | Proauga-Horse | Borga-Goose | Mousie-kitten |
| Scar on forearm-- Slate-blue eyes | * | Nereus | Chief Toke | Daniel |
| Big Smile--Grey-blue eyes | * | Demetrius | Una | * |
| Dimpled cheek--Brown-green eyes | * | * | Rolf | Hadrian |
| Indigo eyes--Musician/ dancer | * | * | Gunhilda | Oliver |
| Orange Hair-- Hazel eyes | * | * | Inga | Maid  Helena |
| Widow's peak--Ice blue eyes | * | * | Konr | Fendrel |
| Walks like wearing flippers--Bray laugh | * | * | Orm | Gussalen |
| Pointed ears | * | * | Hela | Children's Mother |

* = Not present in that life

# Epilogue

"Come back," Zachariah says out of the foggy distance, bringing me back to the chair on the beach. I look over to see Zachariah still holding my arm, the waves endlessly rolling in.

"Are you okay?" he asks.

I don't say anything for some time.

After some silence, Zachariah tries again. "I'm here to help you make sense of everything."

I finally release the breath I've held inside me since the viewing. "I don't know what to say. This isn't what I expected at all. I don't even know where to start."

I suck in a heavy breath of ocean air, charged with salty ions created from so much forceful motion of water and wind.

"First, we need a little change of scenery," he says with a smile.

Instantly, we're sitting in the front seat of an old blue Chevy truck. The smell of damp beach blankets, salty fishing rods, and warm vinyl engulfs me.

"Isn't this better?" He pushes back on the benchseat next to me, the old leather crackling in protest.

He leans over to check. "Are you sure you're okay?"

"Yes, but it's getting harder to watch with each life." The tears roll down my cheeks and I wipe my nose on my sleeve, only to see him offering a tissue.

"Because you're starting to care about people."

I nod. "Who are they in my life now?"

"I can't tell you that. You will have to see them progress as time goes on. It's important to see each of their journeys as well."

"I think I can guess, though," I say, remembering Ellie's scar and Finn's familiar slight gap in his teeth. I knew they'd been with me since the beginning.

"Maybe this will make you feel better."

I open my eyes to torrential rain hitting the Chevy; a thunder-storm rumbles a safe distance away.

"I love storms, especially when I'm crying."

"I've only known you a few thousand years."

His tight smile warms me. Simply being near him makes me feel better. We are both quiet for a moment while we watch the rain obscure the view out the windshield. I take in the leathery, musty smell of the rusty car and notice the windows begin to fog up around us.

I dab my eyes and clear my throat. "So am I finished? Can I see my family now?"

"Oh, there's more to see yet before you're ready to move on."

"Move on to another life?" I'm afraid of his answer.

"You will—" He put one slender finger in the air to stop him-self, and with a wink, he adds, "Almost got me there." He shifts his weight. "Let's just say move on and leave it at that."

"How many more lives do I have?"

"The quicker we work through all of this, the sooner you'll be reunited." He stops the rain; the clouds begin to part as the sun shines through in thick rays.

"At this point am I supposed to review my lives and talk about what I did wrong?"

*Finn.*

"No need for that. There is no 'wrong.' Everything happens for a reason. Life's not about staying on a path but about surviving the detours. It's the wrongs that sometimes teach you the most."

Zachariah continues, "You're the only one to judge, but if you mistreated someone in a previous life, your soul's evolution will require reconciling it in the next."

*Finn.*

I see Erna's bright little face and then see the image of her lying in Thora's arms.

"Why did Erna die so young?"

"Because that is what Erna planned."

"Well, not why did she die so young, but why do babies and little children die before they even really get to live?"

"It teaches the soul a lesson about dying young, but more importantly, it teaches those around them critical lessons about loss and the miracle of life."

"Does a small child or baby feel the pain?"

"We're careful to take the child gently."

I roll my window down and inhale the thick, sweet memory of rain.

"Will a life always go the way it's planned?"

"Souls may plan a certain goal or situation with their soul group. However, once you actually get in a life and lose your full consciousness, it can be very hard to stay on track."

"What happens when a soul goes off track?"

"Their guides will try to get them back on, if possible, but sometimes it will have to be reviewed and tried again in another life. This can happen many times before a soul can learn an especially hard lesson."

*Did I stay on track? There's no way I stayed on track.*

"Are you saying there's no destiny?"

Zachariah pauses a moment before answering, "I would say it's better understood by saying some things are quite unavoidable."

I hated philosophy classes. The way endless questions made my head spin. "What do you mean?"

"For instance," he says slowly, trying to break it down for me, "if for some reason two soul-group individuals are supposed to meet somewhere but they don't because one party changes their minds and can't hear the push from their spirit guide, then meeting after meeting will be attempted until they connect. It's not necessarily destined they meet at a certain time but destined in that they will meet at some point."

"I understand." Happy it doesn't lead me to more questions. "Is the same true for situations, then? That you might miss the opportunity for a certain lesson, so the spirit guide will make it so the same lesson will be confronted again?"

"Right. The only thing that can get in the way of this is a suicide."

*Suicide.*

He shifts in his seat, causing the worn leather to squeak, and adds quickly, "But we'll talk about that later."

I try to think of something to distract the last thought. "Are all the lives this difficult?"

"Oh, they're all difficult." He laughs at my reactive expression—spirit guides do laugh after all. He continues, "*And* great in their own ways. Every life has necessary value. Simply relax and take it all in."

"I don't know if I want to see any more."

"You need a little break."

He starts up the Chevy, and I fold my arms on the window frame and rest my chin. He slowly drives out onto the wet sand

and speeds up as he veers into the shallow surf, the Chevy chugging loudly in protest. I let the air flow through my hair as I reach my arm out so that my hand coasts like an eagle on the wind. Time dissolves away as the sun dips lower on the horizon, yet the beach never ends. He leaves the steady shore to climb the bumpy sand dunes. Revving over the crest, he stops the car overlooking a quiet bay, where the tangerine sun seems to pause on the horizon, leaving us in an everlasting sunset.

Thinking of the last life I viewed, I break the silence. "I had to die of the plague."

"There were not many good deaths in the medieval ages, you know," Zachariah says with his eyebrows raised.

"What was the lesson I learned in this life?"

"You have to find the answers for yourself."

"Was it to sacrifice for Rowan?"

"That was part of your plan, but can you see it even more broadly?"

"I sacrificed for many people?"

He nods. "Do you see the progression of sacrifices you made?"

"Well, when I was Sokaris I sacrificed others for my own purpose. When I was Alcina, I sacrificed my life in my son's defense. When I was Liam, I sacrificed by choice. And when I was Elizabeth"—I pause now, trying to analyze—"I sacrificed myself for anyone. Even people I didn't know."

"Great observation. That's the first big lesson of incarnating, and to do so in only four lives is exceptional." He turns to congratulate me with his hand on my shoulder. "It takes some twelve lives just to get that far."

"If that was it, then why do I have more lives?"

He drops his arm and puts his other hand out to bring me back to reality. "I said *first* big lesson. There are a few more still."

"If I keep up this rate, I'll be done soon. You must be honored to be my spirit guide." I pat my hand on his shoulder a few times.

"Well, don't get too confident there. Some can get it all in their first life."

"Complete evolution in one life?"

"Jesus, Buddha, Mohammed, Isaiah, Martin Luther, Black Elk, Gandhi, Mother Theresa, and many of the saints; all examples of individuals taking on great hardship and learning the big lessons at an accelerated speed."

"All religions are the same?"

"Most religious figures have the same core beliefs. They are perfect examples to people of their times to illustrate what our main purpose is. It's incredibly unique that these souls remain so close to their paths and endure such hardship without giving into the negative compulsions that usually get in the way of the big lessons. It is extremely difficult to do that in one life and is the reason why these souls are followed and remembered throughout time."

"So there isn't one right religion?"

"There is one God. It's the total absence of negativity, an all-positive energy in the form of pure light; the essence of every living thing; the unseen 'life force.' We incarnate or guide to evolve our life force to a higher state or higher vibration, freeing it from negativity and becoming pure light, a part of God."

"Will I ever get to see this force?"

"You already have."

"When?"

"Many times; when you went through the light; when I touched you to calm you; what you see all around you; and what we are even made up of right now."

I actually like believing this is God. One has only to feel this light to know how amazing it is. It warms you and calms you, taking all fear and anger away. Once it touches you, you have no worries or wants. When you are embraced within it, nothing else matters.

"So a Jew, a Christian, or a Muslim will all become part of the same God?"

"It does not matter *what* someone believes but the *way* someone lives. But yes, once anyone reaches that vibration, they all become part of the same thing."

"You speak of all of the negative things we must experience in order to move on. Looking back on the lives I've seen so far, how else have I progressed?"

"Well..." He pauses a moment. It's refreshing, since he usually has answers so fast. "Your first life, you got sidetracked by lust. The lust you felt for Bastet made all that you believed in and were devoted to disappear. You didn't overcome it; instead you let it take you to a dark place. Then in the next life, you struggled with envy. You couldn't allow Ophira to take credit for the son you gave her. You wanted recognition for him since you felt the son in your care had failed you. As Liam, you couldn't endure and assisted in a murder to fix your circumstance."

"But there were other things that I learned, right? It's not just a focus on one thing?"

"Each life can have a little of everything, but it's the thing you set out to overcome that's most important to that life. The small things that you either succeed or fail at along the way, are of minor importance."

I pull the handle to my seat and it falls back jarringly. I put my hands under my head.

"Speaking of negativity, why is Ulric so horrible in every life? First, he was the vizier who let me sacrifice Nun without giving him a fair trial. Second, he was the ephor who took Kali away. Third, he was that disgusting sexton who robbed the dead and had no compassion."

"Yes, but what's your question?"

"Is he evil?"

"You're forgetting when he was your father. Did you think he was evil then?"

I inhale sharply. I hadn't realized he was the same person. "Well, he might have been worse had I'd known him longer. He did kill women and innocent people and would've killed me had Thora not distracted him. I could still see evil in his eyes."

"Evil? No, there's much worse evil out there." He crosses his legs in front of him. "Sometimes a soul functions to bring negativity to a group; the vessel in which great progress can occur. He may not show signs of much improvement himself, but his soul is learning, nonetheless, from watching how negativity affects people. We call them facilitators up here: those that choose to bring about hardships. They too choose an incarnate group and continue to assist the evolution of the whole group."

"What a minute, a facilitator is supposed to make things easier?"

"You're looking at it backwards. Yes, he makes your *life* harder, but he makes your *advancement* easier."

*I can't stand him.*

"Then he's doing a great job. You're supposed to dislike him."

My mouth drops open. "You can read my thoughts?"

He smiles. "Of course I can. I'm your spirit guide. I know everything about you. Your thoughts, your actions, your dreams; I see it all."

I glance at him. "It's so strange that you know me like that."

"It takes some time to get used to."

I feel self-conscious for a moment, imagining all the things he hears or sees, but then he smiles, and I realize my inner thoughts are pointless.

Putting his hands up in surrender, he says, "I don't think either one of us wants to think about those things."

*Why speak at all? I might as well just talk like this to you.*

"But you're not in *my head,* so I must talk."

"No fair! That doesn't seem right."

"They're not my rules. Plus, if you knew what I knew, you'd be too overwhelmed with all *my advanced knowledge.*"

Scoffing, I put my legs up on the dashboard but decide to bring us back to the subject. "So you were saying... before you started to pick my brain?"

"Oh right, your facilator's incredibly important, though."

"I cringe when I see him, father once or not."

"Then maybe you should focus on some of the good things he does. Such as by condemning Nun, you and Bastet were freed and Aapep got to get his revenge."

"I thought revenge would be a bad thing?"

"It's a vice that Aapep had to work through. You learned you couldn't get away with such lies, and Bastet learned she was not in control."

"I see."

"When he was the ephor he delivered the message to conceive Kali. He came to collect Kali and hesitated long enough for you both to prepare her. When Kali was sent away, it taught her many things."

"I wish I could see others' lives. I'd love to see what happened after my death."

"Later, much later. Let's stick to yours right now." He continues, "When he was your father, he left for work and fled when he saw the Vikings, taking his ship to the farther side of the beach and reaching safety in the same cave you hid in later. He didn't go to help you and your mother, and when he returned to find your mother slain and you gone, he never forgave himself. He devoted his whole life to fighting so he would be ready when the Vikings returned. He lived and breathed revenge, and little did he know he attempted to murder the very son he was avenging. Yet both moments were critical for you to become a slave and choose to die for Thora."

"He left us to find his own safety that day?"

He ignores my question. "And lastly, Ulric performed the important task of clearing away the dead, connecting you to Rowan and Oliver, and even bringing you Gussalen."

"Wow, what a treat that was."

He raises his eyebrows at me. "Not quite Mother Theresa yet, I see." Zachariah unfolds my crossed arms. "He saw the humanity in a lowly prostitute and brought her to you. He is not as *evil* as you want him to be."

"If he's not evil, what is evil, then? Is there a Devil?"

He takes a deep breath. "The other question I have difficulty answering." He brings up one of his legs within his intertwined hands. "As pure positivity and light is what some call God, there equally exists pure negativity and darkness some call the Devil. Heaven exists of pure light, while Hell exists of pure darkness. Just as you will feel great in God's light, you will feel terrible in the Devil's darkness. Earth is a unique place where both can occur. A soul goes there to choose light over darkness, and sometimes badly guided souls are drawn to the darkness. Some become so miserable and set in such sorrow that they can't even see the light. Some are so used to darkness and suffering that when they pass on, they don't go to the light but choose to remain in the darkness."

"Is that what ghosts are?"

He nods. "What we call earthbound spirits. Spirits that have not gone to the light and don't even know they're dead. It can take a very long time to help these unfortunate souls. Ghosts can also be spirit guides one suddenly becomes aware of."

"Can you tell me the next big lesson I have to learn?"

"What do you think?"

"*I have to see it for myself,*" I mimic.

He laughs heartily. "You're finally catching on."

I laugh and say, "I really wish I could read your mind; we could save a lot of time."

"Unfortunately for both of us, it doesn't work that way."

"Why can't any of these lessons sound more inviting? It can't be lessons learned from enjoying life too much? Being too rich? Being too beautiful?"

"Maybe that's all ahead of you? Why don't you go and see?"

"Right." I scoff, thinking about the next big lesson I'm about to throw myself into. "I have one more question before I go on to see the next life."

"You can ask me anything."

"If Simon had lived longer, he would've chosen to be with me, right?"

So familiar were those eyes I'd waited so long to see again—eyes that knew me so well—eyes Ellie promised would soon come.

"Simon *chose* to leave you when he did."

"Why would he have chosen to leave me then?"

"Because if he didn't, he would have failed. He only wanted to test himself so much. He knew he couldn't take more than that."

"Are we going to be together, ever?"

"You must wait and see."

I nod, disappointed.

"But I think you will be very interested with this next life, though." He gives me a wink.

"Well, what are we waiting for?" I laugh as I sit up and put my arm out.

"So that's all I need to do to get you to continue?" His eyes glisten with amusement as he points a finger to his forehead. "I'll have to remember that."

I imagine Simon's shining green eyes as Zachariah takes hold and everything goes black.

# Acknowledgements:

This book could never have existed without the help of the following people:

Patricia, my mother, for my being my first editor, generating plot ideas, and listening to hours and hours of discussing conflict, characters, and basically everything else

Erin, my sister and writing buddy, for going through all of this with me as you were writing your first book. You inspired me to get this story out and for continuing to help me through every part of the process (erinwaters.com)

EJ, my husband, for all your support and encouragement, and for putting up with the many hours I'm off writing

Scott, my son, for all your love and patience

Annabelle, my daughter, for being such a good baby so I could get this book out

Edward, my father, for reading my first drafts—even though you hate how my characters have to die at the end of each life

Jessica, my niece, for being one of my first young adult readers

Bethany Yeager, writer & critique partner extraordinaire, for being so helpful and such a fantastic contributor to the book (beyeager.blogspot.com)

Westport Writer's Workshop with Matt Debenham, for all of your suggestions and comments (westportwritersworkshop.com)

Sylvia, for creating my beautiful updated covers (sfrostcovers.com)

Linda Ingmanson, my thorough and superb editor

Bethany Bears, my wonderful and super quick copy editor (lastdraftediting.com)

Guido Henkel, for formatting both my ebook and print book (guidohenkel.com)

Caro Clarke, for your wonderful, extremely helpful website and personal direction (caroclarke.com)

Absolute Write Forum Members, with special mention to Jim Brown , Lia Brooke (bookewyrme.straydreamers.com), Camilla DelValle, Catherine Miller, Meretseger, Nadia Lee (nadialee.net), and David Gaughran for all your self-publishing advice (davidgaughran.wordpress.com)

Kindle Boards Forum Members

Sneak Peek from the second novel
in the Infinite Series:


# Infinite Devotion

Released 2012

# Fifth Life
# The Pope's Pawn

# Chapter 1

Pulling aside the burgundy velvet curtains, I peer down among the thick crowd surging below. The heavy August air creeps in through the open window providing no relief for us inside. The Vatican square is in all its glory below, despite the heat, and I watch for the procession to come around under our balcony of the Palazzo Santa Maria.

"Lucrezia! Lucrezia! Over here! Your father is coming down this way!"

I fly to Adriana's side and stretch out over the railing to see his tall, massive form standing out among all others with his hooked nose and full mouth beneath the heavy papal crown—his jeweled hand waving to his people.

"All of Italy has come to see your father elected!" Giulia squeals.

"There—the Borgia symbol!" Adriana points at the fountain.

A magnificent fountain, specially made for today, of a giant and powerful bull with one stream from its forehead that flows with red wine. Even though I'm sad to leave our happy place in Spain, I feel great things are going to come of our move to Rome.

The door to our chamber is thrown open, and my older brothers Cesare and Juan run to me.

"Lucrezia! You're here!" Juan shouts as he reaches me first.

Cesare practically pulls him off, trying to give me his hug next. The music starts up behind us, and Adriana opens the balcony doors wide to let the charming melody in. Juan pushes Cesare aside, takes me in his arms, and we giggle as we practice our courtly dances around the expansive tapestry-covered room. Cesare grabs Guilia up and follows us around the room. It's so nice to be together again, since I haven't seen them in months. Juan turns to Cesare, tapping his shoulder to cut in, and even though Juan doesn't want to yield, I let go and take Cesare's hands.

As we dance off, I have a hard time figuring out which brother is more handsome. Both are tall and well built, but Juan has a finer and more delicate face—Juan the poet. Cesare has more powerful facial features, high cheekbones, and a large but perfectly straight nose—Cesare the warrior. Peering into Juan's indigo eyes is like falling into a deep pool, and Cesare's amber eyes are the fire that warms you after. With only one year between them and both on the verge of manhood, it's hard to say whose look is more intriguing.

Out of breath, Juan decides to stop and falls down into a gold brocade chair near the fireplace. "Lucrezia and Giulia, how lovely you both are," Juan says with a sweet smile between catching his breath.

Giulia and I look at each other and blush. Little did they know we'd been standing in front of our dressing mirrors all day primping and trying on all of our dresses for the momentous occasion. I've stayed with the beautiful and good-natured Guilia the last few months, but I have everything I love dearest to me now in one place: Adriana, who is like a mother to me; Guilia the sister I never had; my exciting brothers; and most important of all, my father.

Shortly after the private door that leads directly to St. Peter's opens, my father's procession spills into the room. My father, still wearing the papal crown and gown, holds his arms out to me and embraces me tightly. He also looks to Giulia and gives her an equally warm hug.

He reaches to give Adriana a kiss. "Cousin, so nice to see you've arrived well."

She bows to him instead and says, "His Holiness, Alexander the Sixth, was very generous with our more than adequate quarters."

He smiles proudly at hearing his newly appointed name being said out loud. When she comes up, he still gives her the kiss he intended.

"Come with me to dine tonight. I want Giulia and Lucrezia at my side." He turns and looks us both up and down, hesitating a little longer on Guilia's fine form. "I have two angels dining with me tonight." He guides us both through the door into St. Peter's.

I'm seated in the huge and lavishly decorated dining room, my attention is drawn to the glistening of all the silver and gold pieces strategically placed around the long table. Besides our family all on one side, there are cardinals and noblemen dining with us.

During our first course, Father turns to me. "Lucrezia, given our new circumstances from my election, I feel it would be in our best interest to cancel yet another of your betrothals."

I'm relieved, hoping it will at least delay a few more months.

Cesare explains to me, "Now that we're here, it's more advantageous to choose someone who can be of more use to us in Rome."

"Giovanni Sforza, Lord of Pesaro," Father says more for Cesare to hear than me.

Cesare scoffs loudly. "Sforza? He's a minor prince. I'm sure you can find a greater alliance now from your new position."

"I think he'll be much help to us with his ties to Milan." Father pauses to chew and dabs his mouth with his napkin. "I may be pope, but we've still far to go."

Cesare nods, considering this. "What is the dowry?"

"Thirty-one thousand ducats, I talked Sforza down from fifty thousand." He smiles in delight and stuffs his mouth full. He rests one elbow on the table, and his silk sleeve slides down his arm, exposing a childhood scar running from his wrist to his elbow.

"Lucrezia, he will suit you well. Though he's already a widower, I hear he's quite handsome."

"I care not what he looks like, Father. I could marry a chair if it's most helpful for our family position." They nod happily. "That and the agreement that I'll have a year in Rome before I have to go live with him."

Twelve is a very early age to marry, and Father promised that he'll require me to stay in the Vatican one more year before the marriage is consummated.

"A Borgia through and through, always negotiating just like I taught you." He smiles with his slate-blue eyes squinting.

Pushing away from his empty plate, Father points at me and says, "Lucrezia, get your brothers to dance with you and Giulia. It'll please me to see you all dance, but my Lucrezia dances on air."

After many dances and a rich dessert, Father takes us back through our private door. As he closes the door behind him he pats it. Thick gold rings clank against the hard wood. "I had this put in so I can come and visit my most precious girls anytime, day"—and then he looks at Guilia—"and night."

Knowing my place, I give him another kiss and say, "Goodnight." Walking to my room, I hear Giulia scream in delight as they spin into her abode together and shut the door. I've grown accustomed to my father's lusty behavior and know Giulia is much adored by him. It's the reason he allows Giulia to come live with me, and I'm just as happy to have a good friend. I shut my door and try not to think on it any longer.

# Bibliography

Clark, R.T. Rundle. *Myth and Symbol in Ancient Egypt.* New York: Grove Press, Inc., 1960. Print.

Gottfried, Robert S. *The Black Death: Natural and Human Disaster in Medieval Europe.* New York: The Free Press, 1985. Print.

Kelly, John. *The Great Mortality: An Intimate History of the Black Death, the Most Devastating Plague of All Time.* New York: Harper Perennial, 2006. Print.

Lewis, Naphtali. *The Interpretation of Dreams & Portents in Antiquity.* Illinois: Bolchazy-Carducci Publishers, Inc., 1996. Print.

Jones, Gwyn. *A History of the Vikings.* Oxford & New York: Oxford University Press, 1968. Print.

Pomeroy, Sarah B. *Spartan Women.* Oxford & New York: Oxford University Press, 2002. Print.

Posener, Georges. *A Dictionary of Egyptian Civilization.* London: Methuen and Co.. Ltd., 1962. Print.

Roesdahl, Else. *The Vikings,* revised edition. England: Penguin Books, 1998. Print.

Sauneron, Serge (Author). David Lorton (Translator). *The Priests of Ancient Egypt.* Ithaca & London: Cornell University Press, 2000. Print.

Wilkinson, Sir J. Gardner. *A Popular Account of the Ancient Egyptians. Vol 2.* New York: Harper & Brothers, Publishers, Unknown. Print.

26905928R00179

Made in the USA
Middletown, DE
09 December 2015